Praise for *Everything for Everyone*

"Every socialist needs to read this book. Every abolitionist, every Marxist, every anarchist, every revolutionary needs to read this book. Every person who has ever wondered how the world will function after the final retirement of the market, the commodity form, money, wages, rent, coercive gender roles, prisons, police, class, nation states, borders, profit, and in general the dominating power of any humans over any others. . . . It's a book that will engage seasoned organizers, well-read academics, and street-level agitators. It also could serve quite well as a dazzling introduction for newly politicizing folks who would benefit from a clear end-goal and would want to know what could be accomplished by the movements for human liberation."
　—*Spectre Journal*

"*Everything for Everyone* challenges us to not just write fiction about revolution but to make books that practice the kinds of collaboration necessary to make revolution. . . . This book is an uncompromising, anticolonial, profoundly queer and trans, buoying, addictive, and wholly original creation. . . . *Everything for Everyone* has no patience with docile truisms about how we are supposed to write. Instead, it's a shot across the bow for contemporary fiction, raising the bar on how to crystallize utopian longings in literary form."
　—*BOMB Magazine*

"[I]f you come to *Everything for Everyone* for the politics, stay for the writing. Barring Vladimir Nabokov in *Pale Fire*, I can't think of another author who uses an academic form to achieve a literary result so successfully. Each of the interviewees and interviewers has an entirely unique and authentic voice. The book is utterly plausible as the archival project it claims to be, while also telling gripping stories and slipping in details to delight sci-fi fans (a space elevator in Quito! Sentient algae-based AI! Augmented reality implants for dance parties!)."
　—*TruthOut*

"A love letter to abolitionist possibilities."
—**Lara Sheehi**, coauthor of *Psychoanalysis Under Occupation: Practicing Resistance in Palestine*

"*Everything for Everyone* is the book we all need right now. It lets us imagine what can feel unimaginable in this moment—a total reorganization of social relations toward our mutual survival and the dismantling of the ruling death cult. This is a book we will all be obsessing over, arguing with, and talking about in the coming years as we try to conceive how collective action can get us through these harrowing times. I am grateful to Abdelhadi and O'Brien for making something we need so bad so compelling and readable."
—**Dean Spade**, author of *Mutual Aid*

"Charts dizzying, delightful new futures for science fiction, urban planning, and engaged social practice. I spent fifteen years as a community organizer and never dreamed of seeing something that so bravely, brilliantly combines liberational nonfiction and radical documentary with the exuberance of the best speculative storytelling."
—**Sam J. Miller,** Nebula-Award-winning author of *Blackfish City* and *The Art of Starving*

"Eman Abdelhadi and M. E. O'Brien are changing the game of what the novel is and what the novel can be. Much as James Baldwin, Ta-Nehisi Coates and Imani Perry did with the epistolary form in non-fiction, *Everything for Everyone* uses speculative oral history to expand and explode the limits of what fiction can do. Their imagined oral histories from many parties help us understand the present from many possible points of view in the future looking back, like *Rashômon* meets *House of Leaves*. In *Everything for Everyone*, binaries (of male-versus-female, fiction-versus-non-fiction, past-versus-future) are irrelevant compared to something much more interesting and important that Abdelhadi and O'Brien seek to illustrate: truth, and the way we might find liberation in it."
—**Steven W. Thrasher**, author of *The Viral Underclass*

"Eman Abdelhadi and M. E. O'Brien's tall tales of the future draw on real experiences of the past and present. The book's multiple narratives, equal parts hope and pain, merge into a prayer for collective survival and for the eventual flourishing of our powers of love and invention. Voices from as-yet-unlived lives instill faith that our becoming is not yet done. Abdelhadi and O'Brien have created a vivid image of the possibility that we will one day make a home of the world."

—**Hannah Black**

"The special magic of *Everything for Everyone* is that it combines the genres of the oral history interview with speculative utopian fiction. Every cook, or sex worker, can govern. And this is the life they might build from the ruins of this civilization, such as it is. Such a pleasure to feel one could be making the world over with them."

—**McKenzie Wark**, author of *The Beach Beneath the Street*

"*Everything for Everyone* is a window into a possible future and a powerful antidote to our present moment's ubiquitous moods of anti-utopianism, despair, nostalgia, and capitalist-realism. The interviews collected in these pages chronicle the first stages of the abolition of the family; the history of the ecological restoration projects and interplanetary technologies that might render our planet livable and leisurely; the invention of real democracy; and the armed conflagrations that were necessary along the way."

—**Sophie Lewis**, author of *Abolish the Family: A Manifesto of Care and Liberation*

"I had no idea I was a post-revolution speculative fiction fangirl till I started reading *Everything for Everyone*. . . . Exciting to read something hopeful, intersectional, and an antidote to our dystopian doldrums."

—**Sherry Wolf**, author of *Sexuality and Socialism: History, Politics and Theory of LGBT Liberation*

"Part speculative social science, part abolitionist manifesto, O'Brien and Abdelhadi's genre-bending work of utopian fiction explores the social forms and political possibilities of life after capitalism—the novel ways of organizing life, doing gender, and coping with the psychic costs of transformation that may follow the inevitable crises of capital and climate that lie in our future. Like the best utopian fiction, *Everything for Everyone* gives us the opportunity, as all utopias do, to learn about our own desires and hopes for a way out of our current conjuncture."

—**Katrina Forrester,** author of *In the Shadow of Justice*

"*Everything for Everyone* is a sweeping vision of the type of world and society we imagine can and will provide for us all, abundantly. . . . Here we have a beautiful novel bristling with the necessary changes we must make to survive on this planet. The future has sex in it, and community; it has food and labor and joy. It has trauma and memories of the harm, the nightmare, of capitalist precarity. The future is sure to exist; will it have us in it? *Everything for Everyone* imagines that it will, and, given this remarkable vision, this perpetual possibility, it's now our work to live up to it."

   —**Joseph Osmundson**, author of *Virology*

"*Everything for Everyone* is not a dystopian end of the world, nor even a singularly perfect utopia, but something between. It is a process of making new forms of collective life as the content of revolution, shorn of romance. Indeed, nostalgia is a posture the book pointedly refuses, for the ways that it makes rigid a single version of revolutionary change. A more flexible alternative to left melancholy, though not quite a how-to, *Everything for Everyone* maps out the affinities that draw individual voices into a we, without leveling them out into a single, representative speaker. The oral histories offer a narrative form that can accommodate collectivity, centering the process of turning everything into a resource for everyone. In Miss Kelley's words, they take something that was property and make it life."

   —*Blindfield Journal*

*Everything for Everyone:*
*An Oral History of the New York Commune, 2052–2072*
M. E. O'Brien and Eman Abdelhadi

ISBN: 978-1-94217-358-8 | eBook ISBN: 978-1-94217-366-3
Library of Congress Number: 2022933979

10 9 8 7 6 5 4 3 2

Common Notions
c/o Interference Archive
314 7th St.
Brooklyn, NY 11215

Common Notions
c/o Making Worlds Bookstore
210 S. 45th St.
Philadelphia, PA 19104

www.commonnotions.org
info@commonnotions.org

Discounted bulk quantities of our books are available for organizing, educational, or fundraising purposes. Please contact Common Notions at the address above for more information.

Cover design by Josh MacPhee
Layout design and typesetting by Graciela "Chela" Vasquez / ChelitasDesign

# EVERYTHING FOR EVERYONE

# EVERYTHING FOR EVERYONE

An Oral History of the New York
Commune, 2052–2072

M. E. O'Brien and Eman Abdelhadi

Brooklyn, NY
Philadelphia, PA
commonnotions.org

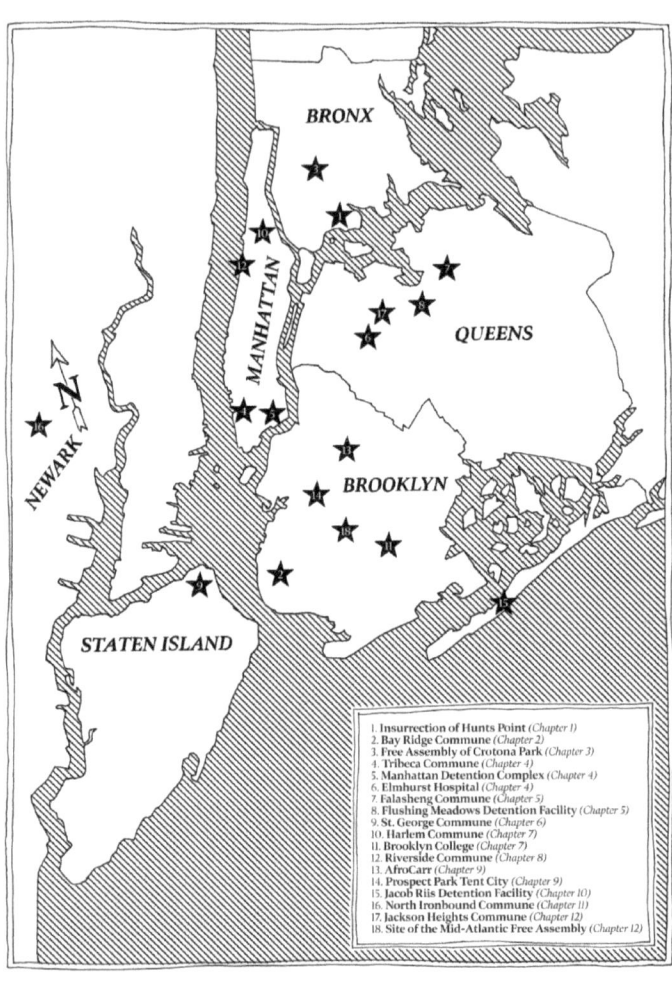

# TABLE OF CONTENTS

# INTRODUCTION: ON INSURRECTION AND HISTORICAL MEMORY

> *It means we take care of each other. It means every-*
> *thing for everyone. It means we communized the shit*
> *out of this place. It means we took something that was*
> *property and made it life.*
> —Miss Kelley of the Hunts Point Commune

In the forties, when Miss Kelley started doing sex work in Hunts Point, she never imagined she would one day act in a pivotal event of the city's history. But on May 6, 2052, she joined with thousands of others to storm the neighborhood's produce market in a riot that would commence a far-reaching transformation of New York. She would go on to coordinate food reappropriation and redistribution for the fledgling commune. By the end of the summer, Miss Kelley and her comrades would be feeding a million-and-a-half New Yorkers across eleven residential communes in the Bronx and Uptown.

The insurrection of Hunts Point, and our interview with Miss Kelley, opens this collection of life histories. Miss Kelley's memories of catapulting burning trash cans and endless meetings began this oral history project, just as those events marked the subsequent twenty years of revolutionary change in New York City. This collection bridges multiple distinct experiences, roles, geographies, and temporalities in this two-decade history. These interviews, we hope, will contribute rich and varied voices of New Yorkers as they experienced the misery and joy of the insurrections, and the growing hope that characterized this recent era. We chose Miss Kelley's words, "Everything for everyone," as a title because they embody not only the ethos of the assemblies, communes, and forums that collectively coordinate fulfilling our human needs, but also a heroic promise made that hot May night in the Bronx, and again and again in the years since.

The transformations of the last three decades are difficult to grasp. Many debate to what extent we should understand these events as a single, unified event—"the revolution," "the insurrection"—or as a heterogeneous set of overlapping processes. Few even agree on a start date. Some mark the definitive rupture with the Andes in 2043, others mark the Global Assembly of 2061. Where any given account draws the line says a great deal about how the authors understand the nature of this period. Is it a toppling of an old order? The founding of a new society? A proliferation of autonomous projects of human flourishing, self-determination, and freedom?

These questions, in various permutations, have long been debated on the streets, in the crowded meetings of free assemblies and virtual planning forums. One could, and many do, define this era through the concrete abstractions that came to an end with these tumultuous events: money, the economy, the family as the basic unit of domestic reproduction, nation-states, borders, prisons, and militaries. Outside of the unfortunate events of the ongoing struggle in Australia, the forces of capital and order have been routed. Others characterize the period through what we have created since the fall of the old order: the world commune, the free assemblies, the planning forums, the local residential communes as a primary reproductive unit, or the production councils. The changes are so vast, so manifold, they elude easy summary.

## About the New York Commune Oral History Project

Our present work will contribute, in a small way, to the ongoing collective efforts to grapple with these questions. The collection offers a selection of the interviews gathered through the New York Commune Oral History Project. The Mid-Atlantic Free Assembly commissioned and facilitated this project as part of a larger retrospective commemorating the twentieth anniversary of the New York Commune.

Our focus is not in offering a definitive account of the recent period. Our scope is geographically and temporally specific. All our narrators share strong ties with New York City and its immediate surroundings, including Newark and the coastal seaboard of what was once New Jersey. The first interview, with Miss Kelley, was conducted in 2067 as part of the fifteenth anniversary commemoration of the

Insurrection of Hunts Point. Subsequently, the Mid-Atlantic Free Assembly commissioned us to conduct a series of oral histories along similar lines over the next five years, in anticipation of the twentieth anniversary commemoration of the New York Commune.[1] We concluded our final interview with historian Alkasi Sanchez in 2072. The interviews themselves focus on the events in between the Insurrection of Hunts Point in 2052 and the Mid-Atlantic Free Assembly in 2072, because it was in this period that the New York Commune emerged. We are excited and honored to be included in the wave of excellent research, memoirs, collections, public events, and celebrations that are marking this anniversary.

New York has always been a global city. Though labor markets and rural dispossession no longer drive global migration, the city continues to welcome climate refugees and those drawn by its rich, dense, heterogeneous communities. The worldwide reach of New Yorkers' life experiences means the accounts here include attention to global events. Connor Stephens discusses his time with the North American Liberation Front (NALF) in the battles of the Rocky Mountains. An Zhou discusses ecological restoration efforts in the Coast Mountains and Great Plains, and Quinn Liu the emergence of communes in what was once China, while Kawkab Hassan recounts the liberation of Palestine and the Levant.

We selected narrators who were involved in key moments in the insurrection. Belquees Chowdhury participated in the reclamation of healthcare systems, the demilitarization of lower Manhattan, and the creation of refuge centers in her commune. Aniyah Reed, in

---

1 In transcribing these interviews, we were forced to weigh in on the ongoing debates on the capitalization of the word "commune." Throughout the text, we capitalize communes when used as a proper name referring to specific residential complexes, such as the North Ironbound Commune or the Harlem Commune. We leave it uncapitalized when describing the abstract social institution. Phrases like the "New York Commune," or the "Andean Commune," and so forth are particularly ambiguous. There is, of course, currently no specific institutional entity called the New York Commune. The phrase refers, at best, to a coalitional network of thousands of planning forums, cooperative production councils, residential communes, and the shared principles and relationships that link them. In the end, we opted to leave some such uses capitalized, recognizing the New York Commune is at least an entity in the thoughts and actions of the city's residents.

turn, was a key player in reclaiming state exploration infrastructure. We have also both been students of gender, sexuality, and the family throughout our lives, and our interest in social reproduction influenced our choice of narrators and our threads of inquiry as well. We were particularly interested in Latif Timbers' work as a gestation consultant, for example. We wanted each interview to reflect the arc of a narrator's life. We did not approach any interview with a specific set of questions, and we tended to follow each person's story as it unfolded before us. Before starting each recording, we let narrators know that they could stop at any point and could refuse any questions they did not want to answer.

We have lightly edited all interviews, including breaking up extended run-on sentences. We tried to balance maintaining some sense of the tone of the narrators' spoken words with our intention to offer a readable text. Occasionally, we add context in brackets; for example, to indicate a narrator is laughing or crying. We decided to only conduct interviews in English because it is the language in which we are most fluent. We hope this effort will inspire many similar works in other languages. We noticed, in editing the transcripts, that some narrators (particularly those from generations close to our own), may have toned down their vernacular forms of speaking—such as AAE—during our interviews. We tried to render those vernaculars faithfully in the transcripts when they appeared in the recordings.

This written version is accompanied by a multimedia presentation, available as holos for those with aug implants or on screens. We also decided to undertake the unusual choice of a small print run of this text on bound paper sheets. Such nostalgic extravagance was hard to justify, and for the printed version we have restricted ourselves to including only twelve interviews. We thank our print publishers, a small Brooklyn-based collective called Common Notions, that has kept alive this anachronistic but aesthetically elegant method through the difficult years of the civil war. Today, they teach paper-based printing and publishing as an art to young people in the Park Slope Commune.

**About the Interviewers**
As the interviewers and coauthors, we met in graduate school in New

York in the tens and have been friends and comrades since. Decades have passed and with them many versions of our lives.

Abdelhadi had a career as a professor, writing various books on the crisis of the self under capitalism. She maintained a life outside academia as a community-builder, artist, and storyteller. O'Brien, drawing on some prior engagement as an oral historian, became a psychoanalyst in the twenties. She wrote over a dozen nonacademic books, including a series that was influential to the transformation of kinship and caretaking relationships within the commune, once known by the phrase "family abolition." Both of us stayed active politically, as we were able, across a range of struggles.

Neither of us were central to the events described. O'Brien, for her part, spent much of the early portion of this period in a military detention camp at Riis Beach. While there, she conducted psychotherapy and taught political theory to her fellow detainees. Abdelhadi spent most of the forties in liberated Palestine, engaging with Arab scholars who were creating new centers for communized knowledge production. In the early fifties, she returned to the Midwest in time to help rioters storm the campus of her former employer.

After the liberation of the Riis Beach Detention Facility in 2053, O'Brien spent two years supporting the struggle in the Mississippi Delta. Then she returned to Flatbush, Brooklyn, where she joined the Ditmas Commune, serving stints coordinating its robust mental health program, later its creative activities program, and finally one term on its leadership council. Her current life is devoted largely to meditation and preparation for death. She hopes the present text will be her final public work.

Abdelhadi also lives in the Ditmas Commune. She finally returned to New York in the mid-fifties after its liberation and is once again O'Brien's neighbor in Flatbush. These days, Abdelhadi's appetite for research has waned, and she spends her time reading fiction, writing poetry, and occasionally performing stand-up comedy.

## Oral History, Trauma, and Collective Agency

Our choice of oral history was deliberate. Oral histories are an opportunity to explore the subject in history; the peculiar and contradictory nature of individual human experience as it occurs during moments of shared collective action. Oral histories are inherently contradictory, unresolved, open, and expansive. Each person brings their own psyche and their own pattern of remembering and forgetting. We came to this project particularly interested in the contradictions of memory.

In part, our interest in memory reflects our own intellectual development. In our varied roles in life, both of us have become historians, committed listeners, and keepers of a belief in the power of people's stories. Both of us have engaged in oral history and interviewing repeatedly and have in turn been changed by listening as an art and as a practice. In our prior lives we were both academics, and we have both been shaped, in part, by the theoretical debates that dominated progressive academia in the tens and twenties.[2] The theoretical writing of that period attempted—and, we would argue, failed—to reconcile the fragmented and chaotic experiences of the subject with the structural determinations of social forces. What was missing was the collective human agency that would only become possible through global insurrection.

With the insurrection, human agency entered history in a radically new way. The commune provided what had previously been missing: a collective actor that could rival the large-scale social forces of impersonal market domination. With it came the material basis for a conceptual reconciliation of the long-standing philosophical debates between agency and structure. Individual experience and shared collective action work in dynamic interrelationship to each other, just as they do within the life of the commune. Like the present work, many new histories reflect this methodological breakthrough: simultaneously fragmented and unified, heterogenous and integrated, open and coherent.

---

2 The anachronism of this introduction's style will be evident to most readers. Even the word "academia" may be foreign, as it refers to a distinct institutional and social life that thankfully no longer exists. Both of us wrote a great deal in the twenties and early thirties, and much less in our current lives. Our style of writing is unfortunately indebted to this earlier period. Present conditions have effectively abolished academia, incorporating knowledge production throughout society. But as a way of thinking, it persists in the minds and words of some members of the older generation. The concluding interview with Alkasi Sanchez articulately touches on some of these issues.

Over the course of our interviews, we identified a parallel unfolding in the emotional and psychic lives of our narrators. Not only did the commune enable new forms of recounting mass history, but also new ways for individuals to relate to their own personal histories. Our older narrators faced the immense trauma of undergoing capitalist crisis, state repression, ecological catastrophe, and violence. This context of mass trauma is a major element to many of these interviews: Stephens struggling with the fallout from the civil war; S. Addams surviving a brutal religious cult built on misogynistic and racist terror; An Zhou witnessing the mass die-offs of North American forests. For a few, that trauma is clearly still with them every day.

We initially imagined the interviewing process itself as grappling with the relationship between trauma and memory. Trauma shaped what and how people remember, and what it is possible to say. Through remembering and speaking, we hoped, these interviews could contribute to narrators working through elements of their trauma. When we felt this happening, it was a powerful experience. Of course, for many narrators, this was not their first effort at processing their traumatic experiences. The narrators' commitment to healing themselves and others were explicit themes in several of the interviews. Kayla Puan talks about recovering from an abusive parent through care networks organized by her commune. Quinn Liu's therapeutic work with refugees in Hangzhou and Flushing is particularly remarkable. These interviews offer evidence that the commune provided a space of emotional growth and reckoning with the past.

But over the course of working with the transcripts, we began to understand a different causal force at work linking the commune to the working through of trauma: the collective agency of the commune, specifically, was essential to this healing. All these narrators participated, to varying degrees, as deliberate and self-conscious actors in a social transformation that was able to challenge and remake global social forces and institutions. The experience of successful collective action, however violent and chaotic, enabled participants to imagine and create new forms of love and solidarity, of being together with each other, and ultimately of healing. The collective agency experienced through the commune offered a powerful anecdote to the collective powerlessness of previous traumatic events.

We are sharing a rich and open story; one we are all making together. As interviewers, we practiced our own agency of selection and control in choosing narrators, in the questions we asked, in this introduction, and in this book's final presentation. Our narrators exercised their own agency in telling their stories, refusing our questions, pursuing their own tangents and thoughts. As in the assembly, the forum, and the commune, we are joined in a shared project of collective emancipation, in tension and in solidarity.

### Pre-history of the Commune: From Catastrophe to Rebellion

The focus of our interviews begins with the citywide insurrection that followed the military withdrawal from the city in 2052 and continues to the present. This introduction is intended to supplement the interviews by outlining some of the prior historical context. This context, particularly the forties, may be opaque to younger readers.

The twenties have recently become an object of mass nostalgia, featured in many dramatic and comedic works. Jumping ahead to the peak years of global insurrection in the fifties, we find the romantic and epic stories of popular struggle, as well as more fact-based historical accounts. But most of the thirties and forties are the subject of neither perverse nostalgia nor heroic dramatization. This period, particularly in areas like in North America where insurrection was not yet generalized, was marked by widespread hopelessness. Climate catastrophe, the spread of fascism, economic crisis, and escalating war were all forms of a mass collective trauma today's popular media seems eager to forget. What stories there are about this period focus on those regions—like the Andes, Xinjiang, or the Levant—where the commune was already in formation.

In addition to the traumatic and less glamorous aspects of this period, it is difficult for contemporary audiences to appreciate the shaping influence of what we once called the "global economy." "Capitalists" are represented primarily as nefarious supervillains in today's popular representations. Though indeed, capitalists and their state agents were often well organized, brutally repressive, and committed to the expansion of human misery, such depictions do little to explain the universal, impersonal domination of the market. As elders, we remember a time when you had to constantly keep track of how much money you had in the bank. This amount determined whether—as one of our narrators put it—"you could afford to get sick," whether you could keep your housing, and sometimes, even whether you could afford food. When you were hungry, you could not just wander down to your commune's pantry and grab a snack. When you were ill, you could not just visit your care clinic and present your ailments. Even clothing and shoes had a cost! You were constantly asked to weigh the costs of your needs against each other. Nowadays, this feels like barbaric dystopia to the youth of our present and a distant, unpleasant memory to our elders.

Unfortunately, explaining the global market before liberation is beyond the scope of this project. We highly recommend *Understanding the Capitalist Market, Understanding the Geopolitics of Imperialist Nation States,* and *Understanding Wage Dependency* as supplemental reading to this section. These pamphlets were published last year by the Andean Commune and are available in nine languages. They can provide an essential aid to understanding the following history.

Throughout the first three decades of the twenty-first century, the global economy had become increasingly reliant on speculative practices increasing both the profits of the ruling class and mass immiseration. Every few years, a bubble would burst, a sector would collapse, and a new crisis would emerge. For example, a housing finance bubble burst in 2008, causing ten years of economic fallout. As the tens and twenties proceeded, these crises became more frequent, with longer-term effects. Global environmental catastrophe caused by extreme weather, warming temperatures, and rising water levels weakened governments across the world, and further slowed economic recoveries.

By the mid-thirties, a perfect storm of economic collapse and climate crisis brought the global economy to a grinding halt. This catastrophe was triggered by the collapse of the value of the US dollar, and its abandonment as an international reserve currency. The effects of this collapse were initially uneven. The poorest nation-states in the Middle East, Northern and Sub-Saharan Africa, Central America, Eastern Europe, and parts of South Asia descended into immediate chaos. States with more complex bureaucracies and higher levels of militarization held on longer. The United States, China, and Russia—the world's most influential global players at the time—were increasingly unwilling to prop up smaller nation-states' regimes with military and financial aid. Ruling elites in many countries made fatal miscalculations in continuing to divest from state capacity through the thirties and forties. Their now-privatized security forces proved much more fragile than the states they replaced. During this protracted global depression, capitalists were unable to set aside their rivalries to coordinate adequately in response to the new insurrections.

Amidst the chaos of economic crisis, geopolitical realignment, climate change and state failure, emerged the conditions to foster rebellion. The prior decades had eroded the legitimacy of the parties of reform. By the beginning of the forties, some form of mass protests, riots, and armed movements had erupted on every continent. Various political factions vied for supremacy amidst the tumult of the period: ethnonationalist, mass fascist, and elite-driven alliances. Pre-insurrection, there were groups who identified as communists and were commonly called the "organized left." These groups and their rhetorical and theoretical framework largely played only a marginal role in the insurrections. Instead, the horror of crisis and the dynamics of struggle propelled mass political development. Increasingly over the course of the decade, these insurrections took on a communist character.

The first communes to rise out of the wreckage were in the Levant (2041) and in the Andes (2043). These insurrections became models for communization as more and more nation-states fell into disarray. The first commune of East and Central Asia emerged in Xinjiang in 2045, and the first commune of South Asia emerged in Chennai in 2047. The fall of China and India, enormous forces in Asian politics and economics, marked the end of nation-state power on the continent.

**Insurrection Reaches the United States**
The US took longer to fall. Without the generalized use of the dollar in international markets, the US government's long-standing practice of deficit spending came to an end. With it, any semblance of

social services or bureaucratic management by the state disappeared. Prolonged and severe economic crisis meant that a significant majority of US residents never again found stable waged employment.[3] Small and medium business owners, effectively wiped out in the crisis, allied with resource extraction firms to become the driving force behind a rise of fascist political movements around the US. Their strongest concentrations were in the Rocky Mountains and Great Plains. Left secessionist movements led by Black and Latinx militants emerged in the American South and centered in Alabama and Mississippi.

Desperate to reignite national fervor and unity as well as restart the economy, the United States began an extended invasion of Iran in 2040. The war lasted for eight years, wreaking a massive and devastating toll on Iranian life. It also destroyed the last of the already fragile legitimacy of the US ruling class. The war, despite massively restructuring the productive economy, was unable to end the nation's economic depression. At the war's onset, US military morale was already weak. As the war continued, morale collapsed completely. With the institution of a draft in 2043, the war became particularly odious to US soldiers and citizens alike. As one indicator of the broad and violent opposition to the war: in 2045, by the estimates of researchers in US military intelligence, more than eight thousand commanding officers in the US Armed Forces were murdered by their subordinates. By the end of the war, the US military was in chaotic disarray and open rebellion.

In the final year of the war, LARS-47 broke out, killing an estimated six hundred million people by 2051. Previously very localized, existing communes across the globe began organizing mutual-aid survival networks to coordinate provisions of water, food, and healthcare. In the United States, where the nation-state persisted, there were increasing confrontations with police, military, and private forces hired by the beleaguered ruling class. People were following the examples set by the

---

3 Readers probably understand the word employment to mean activity, but at the time, employment referred specifically to paid work. For centuries, economic survival depended on selling your labor to the highest bidder in order to meet your needs. The collapse of this form of employment was a significant part of the fall of capital-ism in the thirties. For more information, please see *Understanding Wage Dependency* (Andean Commune).

Andes, the Levant, and others across the world by seizing food supplies, hospitals, and shelter. They reappropriated the means of survival.

Revolutionary forces had much to contend with, including the destruction of private property, the collective seizure of the productive apparatus of society, and the radical restructuring of social reproduction. By and large, however, they no longer had to face a well-organized, centralized military. Just like across the globe, the near complete failure of the nation-state had been essential to securing the success of popular forces in the US. In New York City, this was illustrated at two moments: in 2052, when the US military pulled its forces out of the city to devote attention to the civil war escalating elsewhere; and in 2056, when the US federal government declined military aid to the beleaguered NYPD, leading to the defeat of the police in the following weeks.

## Defining the Insurrections: Communization, Abolition, the Assembly, the Commune

How do we understand the key dimensions of the insurrections that brought us our new world?

Setting aside pockets of counterrevolution, the various enemies of the global commune are no longer serious or immediate threats. Many readers today have never experienced a violent conflict beyond inflammatory accusations in planning forums. The social forms of the present era have enabled the growth and innovation of human knowledge, including an immense and rich proliferation of new approaches to understanding human society. For those who have experienced conflict only through interpersonal domains of commune governance or forum-based deliberation, it can appear mysterious.

We feel that looking back on this period of struggle is a chance to draw out some of the abstract qualities that helped develop its trajectory. Though these concepts have largely fallen out of use, we think remembering them is essential to our collective social development. This global, communist phase of insurrection is charac-terized by four closely related qualities: *communization, abolition, the assembly*, and *the commune*. Each quality emerged repeatedly through our experience of this project.

## Communization

Once an obscure and abstract concept of political theory, by the middle of the forties, *communization* was recognized to accurately describe the new character of insurrection. Hundreds of millions of people were participating in successive international waves of street protest, looting, and mass occupation through the forties and fifties. Amidst the famine of the early forties, and later the pandemic at the end of the decade, looting focused on food, medicines, luxury consumer goods, and small arms. As the insurrections continued, they merged with mass workplace occupations and the formation of what came to be known as the production councils. A key turning point was first recognized in Lima in 2043, as workers occupying a pharmaceutical plant chose to restart production. They sought to directly supply medicines to the urban occupations. Soon occupiers at hundreds of farms and factories across the Andes began production to feed, clothe, and equip the protest movements. The phrase *communization* was used to understand this mode of struggle. The leap to communist relations was a direct insurrectionary act; it occurred without a mediating "transition period."

Communization diverged sharply from many preexisting left models of anticapitalist transition. Self-identified communists and anarchists had varied visions of revolutionary social change: a seizure of state power, the coordinated leadership of a vanguard party, the free market exchange between cooperative firms, the state ownership of wage labor-based enterprises, or a long transition period gradually shifting from capitalist to socialist relations. All such frameworks proved inadequate to understand the direct, antimarket, and antistate character of the insurrection as it unfolded. Communization became the shared framework of the global movement.

## Abolition

*Abolition* has been part of the global lexicon of revolutionary thinking for centuries. Its multiple meanings came into play during these insurrections. It most broadly meant an absolute commitment to destroy the horrors of the old world: to empty the prisons, to burn the police stations to the ground, to eliminate money and coerced work, and to wipe borders, nations, and states from the globe. This commitment, tinged with nihilism and absolute revulsion, no doubt was a central animating force for an insurrection of people who lived through the cruelty of racial capitalism. But abolition also was taken up in a different sense: simultaneously with the prerogative to destroy, emerged the prerogative to preserve, to liberate, and to lift up. To abolish prisons meant also creating new practices for grappling with interpersonal harm and violence. To abolish work meant to unleash the creative capacity for human activity without the coercion of wages. To abolish the family meant to enable people to love, to live, to parent, to care in the rich variety of ways humans are capable of. People form familial relationships of care within the broader structure of the commune—they "family" in the current lexicon—but these relationships are not the basis for material survival. Abolition preserved and transformed authentically loving features of the old society, but in radical and often unrecognizable new forms.

**The Assembly**

The *assembly* provided the main form of decision making in these new insurrections. Assemblies initially referred to nightly or weekly gatherings on street corners during riots and other urban uprisings. As communist relations of production spread through the late forties, these assemblies became sites of production councils coordinating among each other and with insurrectionary forces. New York's history made a particular contribution to what became the global concept of the assembly. The Free Assembly of Crotona Park in 2055 (discussed in our conversation with Tanya John) was a month-long series of conflict mediation sessions between the disparate revolutionary and insurrectionary forces in the greater New York area. Through the Assembly, various insurgent factions integrated enough into a coherent armed fighting force to defeat the remains of the NYPD and other reactionary forces in the city. This convening offered the basic structure of the subsequent assemblies that came to coordinate decisions about production and distribution of goods and services.

The assembly became the shared framework for addressing collective conflicts in the decades since. As the assembly became a basis for mass collective decision-making, it would face new challenges. The insurrections of the fifties came to confront escalating internal divisions in the subsequent decade. Assemblies became the primary conflict mediation spaces to prevent major internal differences from erupting into armed confrontations. Protracted debates focused on topics like First Nations' assertion of land sovereignty, the independence of isolated religious communities, the use of biotechnology in creating new ecosystems, or efforts to reestablish the nuclear family. These debates eventually fostered the particular balance of interdependence and partial autonomy that characterize today's planning forums.

**The Commune**

Finally, the *commune*. The word commune was used to describe multiple new social institutions across multiple levels of scale. It identified the unit of immediate social reproduction, usually involving around a few hundred people who collaborated in coordinating food, housing, personal care, and healthcare. This narrow meaning of the word to describe a unit of domestic life is the most widely used. But the word commune also has more abstract meanings. The word was used to mark the general animating political vision that had come to dominate the insurrection, one of human flourishing in total opposition to the state and to capital, a vision of abolition. The commune also characterizes new forms of collective action, new subjectivities of interdependence, and the concurrence of dependence and freedom possible within this new social form. The word marked when various fighting organizations became strategies of shared survival, in the mode of communization. The same word was also used to describe the regional and global democratic planning networks that emerged to coordinate production and distribution, one of the uses of the assembly. The phrase *commune* links together multiple qualities of this new era of revolutionary society.

There is much to say about the new world that has emerged under the banner of the commune. The project of ecological restoration, climate change mitigation, and biome rediversification has become a massive undertaking, which is discussed in our interview with An Zhou. Though controversial, the establishing of the orbital communes, the lunar settlement, and the building of the space elevator in Quito are tremendously exciting. We are just starting to see the depth of transformations in human relationships to gender, our bodies, our sense of community, our relationship to technology and creative production. We feel profoundly blessed to have lived through the rise of the commune, in New York and across the world. We hope this collection of oral histories offers a small contribution to understanding this extraordinary moment in human life.

—M. E. O'Brien and Eman Abdelhadi
May 20, 2072, Ditmas Commune

# 1: MISS KELLEY ON THE INSURRECTION OF HUNTS POINT

*Recorded on May 4, 2067, in the Bronx.*

M. E. O'Brien: Hello, my name is M. E. O'Brien, and I will be having a conversation with Miss Kelley. It is May 4, 2067, and this is being recorded at the Cecilia Gentili Social Center in Hunts Point, the Bronx. Hello, Miss Kelley.

Miss Kelley: Hello.

O'Brien: Tell me about this space we are in.

Kelley: This is the main social center in NYC for skinners. From here, I help coordinate our quarterly citywide assemblies, the network of support hubs across the region, and our communications channels. I helped found this place about five years ago. There are four of us regulars who help keep the center going. We have events here every couple of days. Some skill shares, a lot of discussions, the occasional talk or game. We talk mostly about sex, about work in skincraft, thinking about sex as care. A lot of people come in and out, both from around the Bronx and from all over the Mid-Atlantic.

O'Brien: Why is it here, in Hunts Point?

Kelley: There used to be a stroll here, ages ago. I worked it for so long. When I moved here, in '41 or thereabouts, it was much different than now. Lots of girls working all up and down the Avenue and all the side streets. This was an industrial area. Auto shops, a big produce market, some rail yards, and a lot of abandoned warehouses. I was having a rough time of things. All strung out. Things were getting tense in Chelsea, and I couldn't hang around there no more. The police was trying to clear us all out, doing sweeps every night. I got arrested a few times, but they told me that if I stuck around they would do somethin' much worse to me.

**O'Brien: What were the police like back then?**

**Kelley:** Well, they was always brutal. Some of my first memories were being a little one and hearing on the news about big uprisings against police murders. But it got worse. The NYPD took over a lot of the drug trade and were starting to try to take control of street sex work. Chelsea had gotten rough. This one cop would harass me for money every night, and made it clear he was running the strip. I will never forget his face. He put these smudges under his eyes, lookin' like a football player? I don't know, it was a thing with the cops he was close to. The cops were basically a gang, just one with a lot of guns. I didn't understand that 'til much later, but the police also changed how they worked with the richies. The police started wanting payment for anything they would protect. Anyone who wanted to do business in the city learned that game. But I think it also showed things were breaking down at every level.

**O'Brien: You left Chelsea and moved to Hunts Point?**

**Kelley:** Yeah, I came up here and been here ever since. I grew up not too far from here, in Soundview. I still talk to my granmom. She had a little place in the Bronx River Houses where I could take showers sometimes. I lived with a few other girls in an old print shop on Cassanova, just a few blocks from here. We did it up nice, like with curtains and a couch and all. We paid rent to a cop who came 'round every month . . . I was not doing so well back then. Strung out all the time on whatever I could get a hold of. I did a lot of coke, but mostly it was tina that had the hold on me.

**O'Brien: Tina?**

**Kelley:** Crystal meth. Spent years tweaking. It got me through the nights. Whenever I went off it, I would sleep for days and I couldn't handle how dead I felt inside. Eventually I stopped altogether, but not until we were in the middle of the insurrection. Where was I?

O'Brien: What life was like in Hunts Point?

Kelley: Even when I was strung out, I still worked hard. Out on the street every night. I wasn't too safe, or safe enough, but I got lucky and made it through. It's much safer now, us running the whole show. Girls got the hubs and the comms, and are always in touch with each other, and no one messes around with us no more. But so many girls died, so many didn't make it through. We did a memorial project here last year, gathered stories from everyone who was working the streets before the commune. Got photos, vids, and holos of who we could, long personal stories from everyone who didn't make it. Kind of like you are doing now, an oral history project, sittin' down with everyone we could. It brought up a lot for me, lots of crying, lots of hugging. It's good for the younger girls to know about because, they don't know. They need to know why we have to defend the commune, no matter what it takes.

O'Brien: [Pause.] This is a memorial for girls who were killed during the insurrection?

Kelley: A few. But mostly it's remembering those who died before. Young skinners coming up now have a very hard time grasping the intensity of violence that was just a part of everyday life. There was a lot of beauty, and love, and care, and goodness too, don't get me wrong. But between all the diseases, and overdose, and so much else. It was just a constant part of life.

O'Brien: Are there any particular stories you would like to share? People you want to have us remember here?

Kelley: Yes, I'd like that. Jamie was my house mother. She took me in and really showed me around the scene. She had so much love, took care of so many girls. She would have these huge group meals. She'd take some abandoned warehouse and have us hang fabric and lights and make it beautiful, and then these platters of food. She was from the islands, and would assign us dishes to cook in her kitchen. She taught me how to fry yucca. Everyone could come, but the house would host. Mostly ballroom, and girls who walked the street. These meals were the most loving thing. I think she had a lot of pain growing up and was making up for it. She went into Lincoln Hospital with something wrong in her gallbladder and they killed her. Like she was healthy, and negative, and had stopped using by then. But they botched the surgery and ended up rupturing some of her organs. Lincoln was a chop shop, and so cruel to the girls.

O'Brien: Thank you for telling us about her. You said you moved here in 2041? How old were you?

Kelley: [Raises eyebrow.] A girl don' discuss her age.

O'Brien: Was it mostly trans women?

Kelley: Sort of. All kinds. A lot of people have notions. Still, after all this time, people come round here asking questions, and they have a lot of ideas about how things worked and who did what, but they don't really want to listen. They have their own ideas, and their own agenda, and want to shove everything into that.

O'Brien: Are you afraid I am one of these people who just wants to use your story?

Kelley: Of course, you want to use my story honey, that's why we've got stories, to use them. The question is what you want to use the story *for*. And I don't really know you.

O'Brien: I understand. Are you up for continuing the interview?

Kelley: [Pause.] I'll try this dance. You got a jaw a bit like mine. You might be okay.

O'Brien: I . . . appreciate your trust. What were you like in the forties?

Kelley: I was so beautiful. I had a lot of work done. I was glorious and so beautiful. I used to walk in the balls, and I always won Face. I was a marvel. I thought very highly of myself back then, even when I was strung out on coke or tina. I think in some ways being full of myself kept me alive, kept me going at all. Like I knew I was better than all of them. I never went out in anything but a dress, no matter what. I always looked great, no matter how bad things got. My dresses were just so much color and life. Miss Reginald, she was a house sister and a designer, she would make them for the balls, and I wore them out on the street when I was working. I took up a lot of space no matter who I was with. I was everything. You could see it in my dresses, in how I moved, in how I talked. People tell me I was so full of myself! But everyone loved me for it. Now I got my feet on the ground a bit more, and not so focused in on myself. But also, things are just a lot easier now, so I don't need the confidence I had back then, no matter what happened. I don't need to front to keep someone from killing me on the street, or get food on the table, or know if someone may be there to take care of me when I need it. Somewhere along the way I learned a bit about how to listen, and how not to need all that to have something to say.

O'Brien: I've heard a lot of people over the years tell me the commune helped them manage their feelings, like made it easier to be able to connect with others.

Kelley: Ccrt. I was always in fight or flight, for like, years. That is part of why I did so much tina. But my fight mode was all about frontin', like really making sure I was always beautiful, always confident, so much so I didn't really see other people as real. First the struggle, and then later the commune, helped me a lot in relaxing that, in being able to actually count on others, to see others, to be able to let other people in.

O'Brien: Tell me about the hunger.

Kelley: Ugh. That's not really something I like to talk about much. I didn't know too much about what was going on in the world back then. I was all messed up in the head. There was the war, I know that, it had been going on forever. The men working the Market got older, because all the young ones got sent off to Iran. Then at some point, I don't know what year it was, everything came tumbling down. Everyone was sick from the cough all that year, and none of the girls could get work because everyone was so scared of the cough. Then everything else started to fall apart. You stopped being able to buy anything. The stores as far as you could walk were empty, the subways and buses shut down. You couldn't buy fec that year, like the bodegas were all cleared out.

**O'Brien:** Fec?

**Kelley:** Like anything? You couldn't buy anything. Shit. Stuff.

**O'Brien: Like feces?**

**Kelley:** Something like that. So, the stores were empty. But the Market was still running! Trucks would roll through all night and day, unloading produce, and then it would get sent down into Manhattan. They had these armed caravans, that were the NYPD, but just hired to guard the trucks. But no food around here, just the shitty brown rice the punks served up under the Bruckner, but you couldn't live on that crap. It was happening all over, from what I knew. Everyone was getting so mad, and in the summer of '50, every night people were out fighting with the cops. I had been in a riot in Chelsea way before, when I first got down there. We burned a police van and beat the pulp out of a few cadets. Now it was like that every night. At first, every time they killed someone we would get up in arms, but at some point it all took on a momentum and we felt like we had to win, somehow, and that there was no way back. Some nights I was too strung out, some nights I was busy working, some nights I was too hungry. But often when I was out, I'd come across some kids and the police going at it. Some nights everyone would be out, like granmom went out one night and said she spit on a cop. For a while, the riots were all throughout the city. Eventually the [US] Army put it down. They started these big kitchens where they gave us crap food, protein paste. God, I hated that protein paste. I was doing a lot of tricks with guys that worked the Market, and I had them pay me in pieces of meat or potatoes. Some days I went without, but I often brought a bit of food to granmom, and to Miss Reginald who I was living with. She was too sick to work so I did my best. Thank god I had stopped using by then, because I wouldn't have made it through the hunger if I also had to hustle drugs. I had been volunteering a bit at this syringe exchange program we set up on the Point, and that helped me get clean. The hunger was so hard. Like it hurt, really hurt. I was dizzy for days, and everyone was getting sick all the time from lack of food. I went through a lot of hard times, but I had never seen anything like the hunger. But we were starting to take care of each other then. All over we started to watch out for each other.

O'Brien: When was the Army takeover in the Bronx?

Kelley: I don't know. I don't remember exactly when that was. It was cold as fuck and they served the protein paste cold, I remember that. God, that was fec. You ever have that stuff?

O'Brien: Yeah, I was in the camp at Riis, before I went south.

Kelley: Did you fight in Alabama?

O'Brien: No, but I helped as I could. I was in the Mississippi Delta mostly, after they destroyed Jackson. Before things got exciting up here. You had something to do with that.

Kelley: Cert, I guess I did. You do flatter a girl.

O'Brien: Can you tell us more about drug use and drug addiction, and your process of recovery leading up to this period?

Kelley: That's a nice question. I could. But I don't think I will. I'll tell you about the Market. Let me tell you about the night we took the Market. That I will never forget. It was the most amazing thing any of us ever saw. I told you the Market stayed busy all through the hunger. We'd see these trucks going in and out. When the riots started, the police set up these huge barricades around the Market, like these metal walls five meters high. They all fortified the Bruckner, sealed it off, and used it just for people from Manhattan or the trucks with all the food to go down into the city. For a while, when we were fighting with the Army, the Market became a focus of the riots, because everyone knew there was food inside. All up and down Hunts Point Avenue we'd fight it out. One night we burned a tank! A lot of folks got shot. A lot of girls got shot.

**O'Brien: The Martyrs.**

**Kelley:** That's what people called them later. I don't know about the term. I get people need heroes. But . . . I don't know how to say it. I think I was really drawn to the image of being a hero, like being a martyr, when I first heard people talking that way. I think a bit like being a diva, it was a way of seeing myself as something grand, something amazing, something that was so big that it could shut out the emptiness I felt. And for me, becoming a part of the struggle, later becoming a part of the commune, meant getting over all that. I mean, I still loved being fabulous, don't get me wrong. But it required actually letting in the pain a bit. Maybe not everyone is like that, but I think that was true for me. So, I could tell you about the girls who were killed—I told you about this memorial thing, so they are really with me. Jakya, Ella, Sydney, Ilaria. I saw Ilaria get shot one night. Like not who did it, just saw her fall in the crowd and when I went over to her, she was passed out and bleeding and didn't make it . . . I may not want to be no hero. But I guess I shouldn't let that get in the way. I should be honoring them. Thinkin' it through talkin' with you. . . .

**O'Brien: You were telling us about the events leading up to the insurrection?**

**Kelley:** That's right. We fought hard, the girls did, with everyone else, as the hunger went on and the Army was treating us bad. Then in '52 the Army mostly cleared out. The taking of the Market happened at the beginning of May that year. I guess the Army had to go down south or out west, because from what I heard the fighting was really kicking off. The police were still out defending the Market, but the street organizations were getting in shootouts with them all over the Bronx so they were all jumpy as fuck. The street orgs weren't that active in the Point; the girls didn't get along with them too well and by then we were pretty well-organized. So, there weren't a lot of police around, not enough, that's for sure. In the fighting people started being able to get along with each other, like everyone wasn't so mean all the time. Some of the street orgs started being more respectful to the girls. I think the commune kind of began there, fighting alongside each other in the streets.

It had gotten hot early that year, sometime in April. It was just brutal, in the nineties at night. The mid-thirties I mean, you know, we used Fahrenheit then. It was hot, there were maybe twenty cadets total guarding the Market, and that night everyone was out. The Army was gone, you couldn't even get their fucking paste. The punks were still out with their brown rice, but people had grown to hate them for it. It was hot, I was in so much sweat, in this slink, this beautiful thing with sequins that caught the streetlights. A lot of people; a few k. We had these big fires in the street. Why was we setting fires when it was already so hot, I don't know, but we had these big bonfires and some kids had set up a catapult and were throwing these burning trash cans over the wall. Then someone got a semi, this huge truck, and drove it into the barricade, and the wall came down. We stormed the fucking Market. We beat the crap out of those pigs and the private troops the Market had hired. We torched their offices. Most people ran off with whatever food they could carry. A lot of people hadn't seen a green vegetable in years, hadn't seen meat, and here it was, stall after stall filled with the best food you could ever imagine.

I got my friend Cindy to bring Miss Reggie some shrimp, because I know how much my Reggie love her some shrimp. So, all these people were all over the Market. And we stayed. We held that market. Some police came in the morning, and we used that catapult and hurled these burning trash cans at their cars. We took the

Bruckner then, shut the whole thing down. It was maybe a hundred people in the morning, and then a few hundred more came in the coming week as we argued about what to do. When I remember the night, I see the trash cans on fire flying through the air and everyone cheering and running over the wall when it came down.

**O'Brien: Sounds incredible.**

Kelley: Oh girl, it was. It was so beautiful.

**O'Brien: That was a turning point in it all.**

Kelley: Yeah, I've been told. The birth of the New York Commune. The night it all broke open. The Battle of Hunts Point.

**O'Brien: We are coming up on the fifteen-year anniversary.**

Kelley: Yeah, I'll be speaking. They are doing a to-do. I have my slink picked out.

**O'Brien: What happened after you all took the Market?**

Kelley: Well, we mostly had meetings. A lot of meetings. We called them assemblies. People talking for hours. I had never done a meeting before. Well, I had done NA [Narcotics Anonymous], but this was different. People kept coming and going, taking food. At the end of the second day, we decided to start doing distribution systematically. People went door to door all across the South Bronx, and then we started connecting with people in Harlem and slowly across the city. They started trying to figure out who needed food most, how much food people needed, how they were currently getting it. They cleared out the food in thousands of boxes, one per building if we could get a good contact. Then they started sending trucks out to the farms.

**O'Brien: Farms?**

**Kelley:** Mostly agriculture within driving distance. I went to visit some of the farms in the Hudson Valley and a big one around Lancaster. Global shipping was breaking down by then. By the time we re-established shipping lines, years later, no one wanted to be shipping food halfway round the world again. Unless it was *really* special food. So regional agriculture. But at this point, in the couple of years before the insurrection, the farms had mostly been under military jurisdiction. Then the military cleared out, and many of them hadn't gotten paid and didn't have any supplies and were pretty freaked out. Some of them had been taken over by farm workers. They worked out these deals with the farms. No money, and not exactly any exchange. But people went out to help staff the farms, others found, or stole, or built the equipment they needed, and they started to build out these networks for getting food into the city that didn't involve money. Hunts Point became the distribution center for half the city. It was lucky the Army and police were too busy elsewhere, or more and more, were fighting it out with each other.

**O'Brien: You say they did all this? Who is "they"?**

**Kelley:** Oh, I guess it was me too. I argued a lot, and I had a lot to say, but it was hard for me to see it as something I was doing too. I had never done anything like that. I guess no one ever had. I have all this political language to understand the insurrection at this point, talking about communizing and all. I guess I learned that lingo once the insurrection started really poppin' off everywhere, after taking the Market. I had to start seeing what we were doing at the Market as part of something bigger. But in the weeks after taking the Market I focused on what I was best at: taking care of people. About five hundred people came to live in the Market and work on food distribution. I made sure every one of them got taken care of when they were sick, had friends or a sweetie or decent sex, had a safe place to sleep, had ways to learn something new and help out. Me and the girls took charge of caring for everyone. We set up a drug detox, and a kitchen, and a clinic, and a school. Eventually that got shared around, but for the first few years we decided it would be our job to make sure everyone who came our way would get what they needed. It was an inspiration for a lot of people in trying to rethink how to live. I found my role here at the beginning, and I focused on that so I wouldn't find the rest of it too overwhelming. My role was to make sure everyone was taken care of who came to work here or came to live here.

**O'Brien: It must have been a lot of work.**

Kelley: I don't know about that. I guess in a way, but I have rested more in the last fifteen years than I ever did in my decades before. Life before all that was work, the awful impossible work. Compared to all that, this is my retirement . . . I can't believe it's still here. Fifteen years later. I've been living here ever since. It's a big one, our commune, spread out over the whole neighborhood. Our main role is keeping the Market going, in getting food into the city and out to where it's needed. We also make some farm equipment in the warehouses here and do all these rural/city collaboratives. We think of Hunts Point as the connector between the rest of the area and the Bronx and Manhattan. A million people have gone out from the city to work on the farms for a season or so over the years, and most of that we coordinated. Lots of farmers have come into the city to meet kids in the canteens, to see how people depend on them, or to help with the agricultural science research unit we set up at Hostos. I ran food distribution for three years, but it was too much for me. Too much responsibility and conflict. It kind of makes you the president of Hunts Point, when you are running the food. I keep thinking it should be a group, but people really like to have someone to blame. But I'm still a part of the commune, still here. Now I run the Center here, I guess. A lot of us from those first days are still around.

**O'Brien: What does the commune mean to you?**

Kelley: It means we take care of each other. It means everything for everyone. It means we communized the shit out of this place. It means we took something that was property and made it life.

**O'Brien: There's the commune where you live, but also the commune of the whole region.**

**Kelley:** Yeah, I started to see that as we took over making sure everyone got fed. That it was all in layers. That me and the girls could help take care of those hauling the food in and out, that they could take care of the borough, the borough could take care of the city, the city could take care of the whole region. And the region could take care of us. It's all the commune. It's all for everyone. It took a lot of fighting, and a lot of dying, and every day it seemed impossible, but we made it through. Somehow, we made it through. I may not be as pretty as I was, but that's okay. I'm proud, not proud in the same way I used to be, but proud of us.

**O'Brien: How did you all end up deciding to distribute the food?**

**Kelley:** We fed the revolution; you can know that for cert. They—I guess I mean we—figured out pretty quick that the best way of handing out food wasn't exactly through families or grocery stores, but through big, coordinated living projects of whole buildings, blocks, or neighborhoods. As people pushed back the army and the police forces, fighting it out neighborhood by neighborhood, more and more people took to living like we did here at Hunts Point. People still had families, I guess, people they would live with in apartments, or raise a kid with, or sleep with. But everything was taken care of for the whole block together, with assemblies to try to sort out the tricky bits. So, if you couldn't get along easy with someone you could just move into another apartment in the building and it was no big deal, you were taken care of. We would distribute food through these communes, or through neighborhood canteens, and it ended up being a huge support for people breaking into new ways of living. And with a decent place to sleep and eat, people got a lot bolder fighting it out in the streets. For some years, across Queens, Manhattan, the Bronx, a chunk of Jersey around Fort Lee and Cliffside Park and Edgewater, and a bit of Mount Vernon and New Rochelle—everyone who was really in the struggle ate from a canteen supplied through the Hunts Point Market.

**O'Brien: Was everyone taken care of? What about landlords? Ex-cops? Asshole business owners?**

**Kelley:** Cert we weren't afraid to starve someone out or take some messier and bloodier steps. So no, no bosses, no pigs, none of them could come around while sticking to their old ways. But if they gave up whatever they had, quit their old jobs, and came to us without property or power—that was a phrase I learned then, I remember people used it, "without property or power"—then sure, we would be happy to feed them just like everybody else. We'd keep an eye on them, though, to make sure they didn't try anything too sneaky. It was usually the neighborhoods that took care of that. We took care of it for the Bronx, and we made sure that we weren't shippin' no food to no owners.

**O'Brien: How did sex work change with the commune?**

**Kelley:** Oh, it completely changed. You know, there were years of fights about if we were even allowed to keep doing it. People had all sorts of ideas about what was proper and who should fuck who and how after the Revolution. I never had any time for that. I guess because those of us in skincraft were running things up here right from the go, and we were one of the first communes in the whole city, we managed to shout those people down. But it was like the world turned inside out. No one was using money, or exchange, we decided that early on. And the girls were in charge—like we figured out housing, and food, and healthcare for everyone who came to work the Market—so there wasn't anyone who could boss us around. Of course, lots of girls stopped fucking and never looked back, or settled down or became agricultural engineers, and that's all fine and good.

But a lot stayed in the work. I did, I kind of liked being a skinner, as a break from the stress of arguing about food distro. At first, we thought of it like physical therapy for disabled people. Like if we knew someone couldn't get a good fuck because of how their body looked, a girl would volunteer to work with them. But what people found to be sexy has changed a lot over the years. Now disability isn't the big deal for sex that it used to be. For a while, we focused on putting on sex parties that were fun and safe and could help people open up to try things they hadn't. We had some really great ones, and lots of people in the network still organize stuff like that. A lot of girls got trained as therapists, helping people talk through sex. We found sex is really at the center of so, so much. So many emotional problems get tied up with how people relate to sex. Sometimes talking helps sort through all that, sometimes fucking. I have always said the most important thing about a person is what makes them come. A lot of people who got into mental health in the communes kept forgetting that, so we had to be there to keep bringing it up. Some skinners focus on working with people after major changes in their lives, like when they change genders, or go through menopause, or get in an accident that changes how they fuck.

O'Brien: It sounds like sex work—I mean skinwork—became like a holistic therapeutic practice, integrating all these different kinds of care work.

Kelley: Yes honey, that sounds about right. It was so different from what sex work had been in a lot of ways, but the experiences and skills of walking the stroll actually helped out a lot. The biggest difference was that we made sure the skinner always runs the show, and gets lots of support, and is in touch with a network of other people doing work like they are. The girls have to be in charge.

I still call them girls sometime, but I know I shouldn't do that. These days, most in skincraft are a lot more flexible about gender than I ever was. Everyone feels better when they have a way of contributing. Speaking as someone who is open to having a lot of really different kinds of sex with a lot of really different kinds of people, we find a way to make it into something helpful, and kind, and good for people. That's where our social center comes in, to be a space for skinners to talk through what it means to do whatever it is we do year by year in a world where work has changed so much.

O'Brien: Anything else you want to share?

Kelley: Somewhere inside I'm still the girl I was when I first came back home from Chelsea. I want everyone to love me, everyone to see how beautiful I am. I don't admit it too much these days, but I don't want to be forgotten. So many girls have died, and only a few of us remember them. I want people to remember me. It's silly to say, hearing myself now, but it's still how I feel. I try to do all the history projects I can, vids, and holos, and talking to whoever comes my way. I tell myself it's so everyone knows the history, and knows how hard we fought, and how hard we have to defend it. And that's true, maybe. It's true. That history does matter. But I also do it because I know I'm going to die too before too long, one of these days, and I want my voice to stay with people. I want people to remember my face. I guess I'm still trying to take up space after all this.

**O'Brien: You enjoy the nostalgia, and you enjoy imagining yourself in that heroic history.**

Kelley: Yeah, I guess I do! The battles were so glamorous, like they turned us all into heroes in one way or another. And I had always kind of thought of myself as a queen, like I maintained an inner sense of my beauty even when things were hard . . . I imagine you must get this a lot doing oral histories. I have gotten to know how I tick over the years, and I see what I get out of it—I like nostalgia, you are right. I like the sense that I understood what was happening when I was young, fierce, and beautiful. Things are amazing and exciting now, but they are very confusing—I have thought a lot over the years about what I get out of thinking of myself as a hero, or as a queen, or whatever the story I'm telling myself is. History is so much actually just people telling the story of themselves they want others to remember.

**O'Brien: I think people are going to remember you, Miss Kelley.**

Kelley: Thanks love. You are a sweetheart. Thanks for recording this.

**O'Brien: Thank you, Miss Kelley.**

# 2: KAWKAB HASSAN ON LIBERATING THE LEVANT

*Recorded on September 20, 2067, in Brooklyn.*

Eman Abdelhadi: Hello. My name is Eman, and I am interviewing Kawkab Hasssan for the New York Commune Oral History Project. We are recording at a cafeteria of the Bay Ridge Commune on 76th Street and Third Avenue in Brooklyn. Kawkab, are you ready?

Kawkab Hassan: Sure.

Abdelhadi: I'm going to start with some basic, demographic questions.

Hassan: Shoot.

Abdelhadi: How old were you on your last birthday?

Hassan: Forty-seven.

Abdelhadi: Where do you live?

Hassan: About half the year, I am here in Bay Ridge—around the corner, on 77th between Fourth and Fifth. The other half, I'm in Palestine, in the UCL.

Abdelhadi: For those who may not know, what does UCL stand for?

Hassan: United Communes of the Levant.

**Abdelhadi: Great, thanks. And here in Bay Ridge, what size unit are you in?**

Hassan: Well, the block is full of townhouses, so the unit is the whole block. The Commons are on the corner, and when the weather is nice, we just shut the street down and do meetings over barbecue.

**Abdelhadi: Nice. Any partners at the moment?**

Hassan: Ugh. People of your generation always say partners like it automatically means romance. We're all partners! Everyone in the unit is a partner! But if you mean romance, a couple here and there. No live-ins. I don't like that shit. Too messy.

**Abdelhadi: [Laughs.] Fair enough. Okay. I want to get a sense of the places you've lived throughout your life. You were born in 2020—**

Hassan: Uh-huh.

**Abdelhadi: Where were you born?**

Hassan: Here, in Brooklyn. I grew up a few blocks from here. I actually applied to get into the unit on my old block, but they were filled up. I'm in the next one over, so that's pretty damn close. The buildings are really similar, so yeah, *hamdellah*.

**Abdelhadi: Hamdellah. But you haven't been in Bay Ridge your whole life?**

Hassan: Nah. I moved to Palestine when I was sixteen actually, when the Gaza Rebellion started, and I was there—well in that region— until the Fall. I first came back in '63, after the borders were liberated. I couldn't risk trying to come back before then, because I was on all the feds' lists.

**Abdelhadi: Shit.**

**Hassan:** Yeah. I didn't set foot on this continent for twenty-seven years.

**Abdelhadi: Wow. That's crazy.**

**Hassan:** Yeah.

**Abdelhadi: We'll get back to that story for sure. For now, let's talk about your childhood. Tell me more about your family.**

**Hassan:** Kinda typical Bay Ridge family for the time. My parents are both second-generation Palestinians, both sets of grandparents were living here in the neighborhood.

**Abdelhadi: Where in Palestine were your grandparents from?**

**Hassan:** Gaza.

**Abdelhadi: I see, so your parents met here?**

**Hassan:** Yeah, they met here. They met at a bodega that belonged to my grandfather, my dad was working the front desk all the time, and my mom would come in to buy snacks.

**Abdelhadi: Awww!**

**Hassan:** You're still nostalgic for that couple fec, huh?

**Abdelhadi: I just like snacks. [Hassan laughs.] Was your dad still working at the corner store while you were growing up?**

**Hassan:** Yeah, he took over after my *jiddo*. *Baba* was always talking about expanding and renovating and all that, but he never seemed to have the money. Or maybe he couldn't get his shit together. Maybe both. Good guy, but like he wasn't organized. Also, the rent was really fucking high in the city. So, he couldn't really keep up. We were always barely hanging on.

Abdelhadi: What about your mom?

Hassan: She worked odd jobs. There was a *Knafeh* shop on Fifth Avenue—Jerusalem Sweets or something. . . .

Abdelhadi: Nablus Sweets.

Hassan: Right, right. Wasn't sure. . . .

Abdelhadi: "Jerusalem" is always a good guess. [Laughs.]

Hassan: Exactly. Anyway—she would work there or as a cashier at this pharmacy chain—I think it was called CBS or CVS, some acronym—things like that, on and off.

Abdelhadi: Did the two of them get along?

Hassan: Oh hell no. [Laughs.] No way. They hated the fuck out of each other. Neither of them could muster the guts to leave though. They just kind of stayed and got on each other's nerves. It was annoying.

Abdelhadi: Why do you think they hated each other?

Hassan: Well. I don't know. They just weren't happy. Shit was always falling apart.

Abdelhadi: Like what?

Hassan: You know, just . . . there was always some crisis. The car broke down. We were behind on rent. Someone forgot to pay for the Internet, and it got shut off. One of us would get hurt, and the bills would dry up all the money. Endless fires to put out, ya know?

Abdelhadi: Yeah. It's how a lot of people lived those days.

**Hassan:** Yeah. But there was this feeling of being alone. Like everyone else had their shit together and we didn't. And there was this feeling of it being their fault. [Long pause.] I think they both would wake up every once in a while, look at their lives and think, "Fuck! How did I get here?" They took turns blaming each other. Mama blamed Baba for the business failing. She thought he wasn't creative enough. She would see these new stores with the fancy yogurt and the Organic Whatever the Fuck and come home and get on his case for not renovating, for not expanding, for not changing the products, blah blah blah. He, of course, kept saying how he didn't have the money for any of that. It was the same fight.

**Abdelhadi: And what did he blame her for?**

**Hassan:** Oh. Um. Our existence. [Laughs.] He basically thought they got married too young. She got pregnant right away, with my brother Karam. I think he hated her for that, and hated Karam a bit too, probably. All of us really. We ruined his life.

**Abdelhadi: Did he say that?**

**Hassan:** No. But he made sure we knew.

**Abdelhadi: How so?**

**Hassan:** He just did. . . . Can we move on?

**Abdelhadi: Sure. Was Karam your only sibling?**

**Hassan:** No, we were three total—two older brothers and me. Karam, Kamal, and me. They thought they were being cute with having the kids' names start with the same letter. Then they realized it stood for KKK, and it wasn't so cute anymore. [Laughs.]

**Abdelhadi: Ouch! [Laughs.] What was their approach in terms of parenting?**

**Hassan:** There was this whole idea at the time, that you just needed to work hard and get good grades and "make it." Like, go to college, get a good degree, and all that fec. But like they were kinda distracted, and none of us were that good at school. One of my brothers, Karam, got decent grades. But me and Kamal were terrible at school. And my parents couldn't really do anything about it. Sometimes it felt like my mom would remember that we existed and that we had to get good grades, and she'd make some effort. She'd like try to set down "family homework time," and that would last like two days. Then she'd just lecture us. And she'd always be like, "I didn't go to college and look at me! You don't want to work these shit jobs!" As if going to college guaranteed you a good job. But we all knew college cost money that we didn't have. There was like the one kid in class who was like a genius and would get the scholarship or whatever. But the rest of us weren't going to make it. And our *kharra* schools with their kharra teachers knew that. We all knew. But we were supposed to pretend we believed we'd make it, we were supposed to act like it was possible and going to happen for us. But it was bullshit and we all knew that. So, we were just waiting for the play to end, so we could hang up our costumes and go back to leading our kharra lives.

**Abdelhadi:** Damn.

**Hassan:** I mean, it's easier to know that in retrospect.

**Abdelhadi: What did you think at the time?**

**Hassan:** Well. I don't know if I really thought about it. I was going with the flow, zoned out. I always had something I was obsessing about. Like in middle school, it was anime—remember, the Japanese cartoons?

**Abdelhadi: Yup, yup.**

**Hassan:** So yeah, I was into those, then I was really into sci-fi in high school. I was kind of a loner, honestly. Obviously, I wasn't going to fit in with the white kids, and there was only a few of them in our high school anyway. And there were enough Arab kids that the other people of color didn't really take you in, you know? It was like, "Dude go hang with your own people." But the Arab kids weren't into me either, my parents weren't that social, so I had no idea what was going on in the little Arab world of the neighborhood. We only knew the people in our building and my grandparents.

**Abdelhadi: Did you not have aunts, uncles, or cousins nearby? Both your grandparents were from the neighborhood, right?**

**Hassan:** They were, but they weren't around like that. My mom had three older sisters, but they had all moved away before she got married. One of them was in Westchester, one had moved to Michigan, and the other lived in the UAE. We didn't really have the money to go visit and as their families got bigger, they stopped visiting too. It was pretty distant. On my dad's side, I had another aunt. She never married. I think she was a dyke. No one ever talked about it, of course. [Laughs.] So, we'd visit my grandparents, who were nearby. But honestly, both parents worked so much, they didn't have time for much else. And especially with my mom, her sisters were all bougie. Like they all went to college and married up, so there was always this like … tension. We were the black sheep, the ones who didn't make it.

**Abdelhadi: That sounds like it was hard.**

**Hassan:** Whatever. It was what it was.

**Abdelhadi: How'd you end up moving to Palestine?**

**Hassan:** I'd grown up hearing about Palestine through my grandparents and my parents, and it was in the air in Bay Ridge. Honestly, I'd been dreaming of Palestine my whole life. Sometimes I'd have to remind myself that I'd never actually been there, because it was just so present. It was always there.

They wanted us to forget, you know? That was the whole plan. The Zionists. They thought, "The old will die, and the young will forget." We made it our business never to forget. Every house in this area was like Little Palestine. We took it with us any-where we went, used any chance to remind ourselves and everyone else that we were an exiled people, that our land had been stolen. I can't believe they thought we'd do anything else. . . . Anyway, where were we?

**Abdelhadi: I'd asked how you ended up in Palestine.**

**Hassan:** Oh yeah. When the uprising first began, I wanted to go. Gaza had been under siege for like thirty years or something—since way before I was born. No one in or out. People had water for a few hours a day, electricity at random times, it was a big fucking prison, with two-and-a-half million people crammed in. And they'd bomb it every few years, brutal shit, just relentless. And people from Gaza would just have to rebuild over and over and over. When I was four, I remember they bombed, those were some of my first memories—watching those buildings fall on stream, people sifting through the debris of their homes, and all that.

Anyway, when I was sixteen, and Thawrat Gaza started, I was ready. You didn't have to tell me twice. I had been working odd jobs around the neighborhood, mostly under the table, since I was four-teen. Had a little money saved up, just enough for a ticket.

**Abdelhadi: They let you in?**

**Hassan:** Who? The Zios? Hah! Of course not. We flew into Egypt, hitched a ride to the Sinai and crossed the border—

**Abdelhadi: Who is we?**

**Hassan:** My friend Talal was in a similar boat as me. One of my only friends growing up, also an Arab burnout. We just decided we'd go, and we did. He spoke better Arabic than me at the time, mine got better eventually of course. But at the time, he could get by.

**Abdelhadi: So, you got to Egypt, and got to the Sinai—I thought those borders were closed at the time?**

**Hassan:** Well, Egypt was falling apart. They had had an uprising in 2010, or 2011, or something—2012? Can't remember, but they had overthrown the government, then the military took over a couple of years later. The military reign lasted decades. But it was like everywhere else where when the economy started collapsing in the thirties, they couldn't keep up. There were massive famines, because so much of the Nile had dried up, and Egypt couldn't grow food anymore. Plus, the heatwaves were killing more and more people every year. When the markets crashed, they were truly, truly fucked. By the time I went—well, this was 2036—there were riots all the time, mostly over bread and grains. It started in Port Said, because they have always had big unions there. So yeah, the Egyptian Army was kinda distracted with all that.

**Abdelhadi: Gotcha. And that was also happening all over the Arab world, right?**

**Hassan:** Oh, hell yeah. Syria was still in tatters after the civil war in the twenty-tens and twenty-twenties. Iraq had never recovered from a US invasion in the early two thousands. Jordan was barely hanging in there. It was all a fucking mess and people were over it. The Levant was where the first governments fell, you know. Everyone was realizing they had nothing left to lose, and it was time to fuck shit up.

**Abdelhadi: Good reason for an uprising.**

**Hassan:** Yeah, exactly. I mean think about it: why would you care if you're getting arrested for protesting when you can't feed yourself or your family anymore? For so long, these fuckwads had everyone convinced that if they just put their heads down, they could get by on whatever meager shit there was. But eventually that was obviously not the case anymore. It didn't matter how quiet or obedient you were, there was nothing to fucking eat. The whole region imploded.

**Abdelhadi: Yeah.**

**Hassan:** So anyway. Uprisings everywhere. Egyptian Army really could barely keep that border to Gaza closed even when they weren't busy quashing uprisings. By then, it was an open secret that if you could make it to the Sinai, you could get through.

**Abdelhadi: How'd you make it to the Sinai?**

**Hassan:** Dollars. The dollar hadn't fallen yet, and we bribed our way through. The Egyptian pound was in the toilet by then, it was like a hundred pounds to a dollar or something, I'm telling you—people were starving. So yeah, even as teenagers, whatever American money we had got us through. Plus, Egyptians had never been down with Israel. Their government was, but they weren't. Egyptians always thought that was some fuck shit. So, when we said we were Palestinian, when we said we were from Gaza and we were just going home, people were down with that.

**Abdelhadi: That's beautiful.**

**Hassan:** It was. It really was.

**Abdelhadi: But why wasn't the Israeli army guarding the border?**

**Hassan:** Oh, they would have. But the Final Intifada was already underway, there were riots and strikes all the time, and they were really distracted.

**Abdelhadi: Tell us more about the Final Intifada.**

**Hassan:** It was a mass insurrection that started in the early thirties and ended with the liberation of Palestine in '38. People were rising up all over Palestine, in FortyEight, and in the West Bank.

**Abdelhadi: Wait, I just want to make sure it's clear for readers and listeners. By FortyEight you mean within the borders of what was then Israel?**

**Hassan:** Yeah, Palestinians were split up. There were the people who'd gotten Israeli citizenship and lived within Israel. There were the people in the West Bank, the people in Gaza, then the people in these, sort of, no-man's lands that had been taken over by settlements.

**Abdelhadi: What do you think made the Final Intifada different from the first three?**

**Hassan:** Two things. First, there was a lot more pressure from FortyEight. It wasn't just the West Bank rising. That had started to happen in the twenties, that you saw more agitation in FortyEight. The second and more important thing was pressure on the Israeli state. In the twenties, you had massive boycotts of Israel by individuals, companies, universities, and industries all over the world. Those got stronger and stronger, until the main holdout was really only the US government. But by 2030 in the US, shoring up Israel had become unpopular. By the mid-thirties, it had become financially impossible. No more money for surveillance, for the military, for all the fancy weapons that came from the US. That, plus the market crashes, spelled the end for the *dawla*.

**Abdelhadi: How were the market crashes affecting things?**

**Hassan:** Horribly. Similar to everywhere. The state couldn't afford to keep up the luxuries they gave to working-class and middle-class Jews, because the global economy was faltering. So no more free healthcare or free housing for new settlers. None of that. That really brought down buy-in for the whole Zionist project, and of course it upped the insurrectionary pressure from Palestinians—who were literally starving.

**Abdelhadi: Okay, so what happened when you crossed the border?**

**Hassan:** When we got into Gaza? I reached out to a distant cousin who lived there, Ahmad. Ahmad was amazing. He had been living with his *katiba*—that was a small resistance militia or brigade. They were living in an old UN school that had been shelled and hollowed out. Only the outside wall survived, and they built a little tent city inside. When we got there, they welcomed us in. People really familied their *kata'eb*, because so many families were broken from the shelling.

**Abdelhadi: Who were some of the other folks there besides Ahmad?**

**Hassan:** Well, the most important person to me was Ahmad's wife May. She had such a crazy story. Her family got a notice to evacuate in 2007 when she was a baby. They did what a lot of families in Gaza do, they divided the children between relatives' houses. So that if the houses got bombed, someone from the family would survive. Her older brother carried her in a blanket and fled to one aunt's house. Her other brother took their two sisters—they were five kids total— to another aunt's house. Her parents stayed back to gather valuables and documents from the house. They were there when the rockets struck. It had been sixty-three minutes since the notice to evacuate was dropped on their house. By 2014, one of her older brothers had managed to reunite the siblings. He'd worked like a dog to rent a one-bedroom apartment in this old building. But once again, when the bombings started, an evacuation notice came. "You have thirty minutes to leave." This time they were ready. They had a bag packed with everything and they fled. But one of her brothers and one of her sisters were at work, their building was bombed, and they were killed. It kept happening again and again, every few years, a new round of bombings. Families breaking up and trying to re-form. So yeah, we already knew how to make families out of survivors. The katiba was just another version of all that. We'd cook and do housework together, and we'd read about struggle and plot.

**Abdelhadi: What were you plotting?**

**Hassan:** Resistance.

**Abdelhadi: Like?**

**Hassan:** You know, guerilla ops. Mostly targeting the border to Gaza. There was a sense that if we could break the geographic hold, they wouldn't have a chance to control us. Our strength was always in numbers, and that's why they had separated us into different groups. We were opening the prison gates—the border to Gaza. We knew we couldn't form a big army. Too much surveillance for that, too easy to bomb the shit out of wherever we were gathering. It always had to happen in small groups. I think that model really influenced the communes later, how everything had to be local first. You had to know who you were dealing with, there had to be trust, you were accountable not to some big, anonymous dawla but to like your actual neighbors and housemates.

**Abdelhadi:** Mm, definitely.

**Hassan:** It took a year of intense planning and coordinating with resistance fighters across Palestine, but eventually the border between Gaza and the rest of Palestine fell. The IDF couldn't hold out, between the mass defections, the international condemnations, the weapons and supplies drying up.

**Abdelhadi: Tell me about the day the border fell.**

**Hassan:** [Long pause.] It was the most beautiful day of my life. There had been marches, so many marches. There was a sense that as a movement, we had tried guerilla warfare on its own, and it hadn't worked. So there had to be both a military presence and just mass uprising. People in kata'eb would work on bombing the borders, blowing up military outposts and all that.

But most people were just organizers, and they'd work on the marches. The marches were like big fucking parties. It's where everyone let out steam from the stress. The stress of the random bombings, the stress of the raids, all of it. We cried, and we sang, and we danced. The *dabka* lines were bigger than you'd ever seen.

There was a big march that day. It was supposed to be the biggest one, but people were worried. Worried that everyone was getting tired of being out and about all the time, we worried no one would show up. But then the Israelis—they attacked a school bus that morning. They straight up shot up this bus, killed all the kids on their way to school. This photo went up on Ours of the bus in tatters, bits of flesh everywhere. It was horrifying. . . . And everyone came the fuck out. Like seriously all of Gaza marched that day. At least a million people marched to the border.

We stood there and the army started shooting at us. And we started shouting: "More will come, more will come, more will come." Because it was true. More would come. It was literally do or die. The soldiers were overwhelmed and kind of backing up. They had no real strategy. Ours was to do what we had always done as Palestinians, refuse to stop existing. Refuse to disappear.

Those of us that were armed started shooting at them, some people made Molotov cocktails. And of course, they shot at us, but when our *shuhada* would fall, more would come. They couldn't stop us. They started to see that.

This woman got on the mic. A comrade. I forget her name. She was killed a few days later. She grabbed this megaphone and started shouting, in English, "Drop the gun and run." It became a chant, and everyone picked it up. Hundreds of thousands chanting at these soldiers, "Drop the gun and run." And eventually they did. They dropped their guns and they ran. And to tell you the truth, we didn't run after them. Because it wasn't about them. It was about us, how big and beautiful we were in that moment. How unstoppable. We knew that we had done what our parents and grandparents had dreamt of doing—we knew that nothing would ever be the same again. They were what Darwish had called them, *aaberoon*—passersby. Us. Palestine. That was forever.

**Abdelhadi: Incredible.**

**Hassan:** Everything fell into place after that. We marched and the rest of Palestine marched. And everywhere the chant was the same, "Drop the gun and run." The IDF fell in a few weeks. We liberated huge swaths of land in those months of marching. The "mixed" cities first and Khalil and al-Quds. Basically, everyone in the Israeli government defected, anyone who had the money or the means to get out did.

**Abdelhadi: What happened to those who stayed?**

**Hassan:** With every flare up in the uprising, more and more people had been leaving. Over the course of the years leading up to 2035, hundreds of thousands went back to Europe and America. Whole cities emptying out. They mostly already had dual citizenships in Europe, in America. Most of the Ashkenazis left. The people who remained were the poor people. The Eastern Europeans, the Arab Jews. A lot of them came around to insurrection, because the state wasn't meeting their needs anymore anyway.

**Abdelhadi: What about the settlements?**

**Hassan:** We knew most of them had their own militias. So, the elders' council, which coordinated across kata'eb, would assign different settlements to different kata'eb based on their size and our sense of how much weaponry they had. People were encouraged to join the katiba that was liberating their or their parents' or grandparents' villages, whenever that was possible. We had already had extensive debate within the liberation movement about what to do with the settlements. We knew they would be the last holdouts because they had always been so isolated and militant. They were taught they were vulnerable and could never live with Indigenous people. They were also the most heavily armed.

**Abdelhadi: Can you tell me more about those debates?**

**Hassan:** Some people wanted to just blow them the fuck up. They said that even if they surrendered, they didn't want these settlements on the land. They didn't want the reminder of what had happened: the genocide, the expulsions, almost a hundred years of apartheid and occupation. But that view lost out. Water was very scarce. And there was all this infrastructure built for these settlements, and we didn't want to waste it. I remember one meeting, May said, "They have their names on it, but we built it." Even if not literally, every piece of infra-structure had been the result of shit taken from Palestinians. So why throw that away? It could be put to good use.

**Abdelhadi: Did your katiba get sent to any settlements?**

**Hassan:** Yeah, a few. The hardest was called "Sderot." It's where Najaf is now, or where it is again. It had been Najaf before they killed or expelled everyone in '48. Yeah, so Sderot was tough. Gaza had just been liberated, and they were terrified. And they didn't realize yet that surrendering was inevitable. Plus, they had more guns than people; they'd been stockpiling guns for fifty years.

**Abdelhadi: What did you do?**

**Hassan:** What we generally did in settlements. We showed up and surrounded the town. We had megaphones, and we communicated that we were there to negotiate their surrender. That they wouldn't be harmed if they laid down their arms and did not harm any of the infrastructure. We gave them three days to surrender before we cut electricity. Another three days before we cut water. Of course, no resources were allowed in or out.

**Abdelhadi: How long did that last?**

**Hassan:** Three weeks! They had a lot of supplies, bunkers, stockpiled food and water, etc. They had a lot of protocols. It was just a matter of time though, because they no longer had a state backing them. How long can you hold out a settlement in a liberated Palestine? One of the days, a group of men came out, hands in the air, to negotiate with us.

**Abdelhadi: What did you end up negotiating?**

**Hassan:** The elders' council had sketched out a process where every settlement would have to submit to a collective process of redistri-bution in tandem with the natives of the locale. Some elders whose parents had fled from Najaf into Gaza participated in that process. I didn't stay for that, I wanted to see the rest of Palestine, and keep marching on. You can go visit Najaf though and look through the village archives for some of those accords; you can probably interview former settlers and some of the folks at the negotiations. Most are probably still living there, that's what usually happened.

**Abdelhadi: Did all the settlements surrender this way?**

**Hassan:** I wish. A handful refused to surrender, and things got bloody. Big shootouts until the settlers ran out of ammunition, or food, or energy, or hope. It was always inevitably a losing battle, because kata'eb could always get reinforcements when they needed them, but the settlers didn't have anyone to turn to after the IDF fell. As soon as the shooting stopped, reconciliation committees would be set up to figure out next steps.

**Abdelhadi: So, what was next for you?**

**Hassan:** I went to fight in Lebanon. After we liberated Palestine, the rest of the Levant followed suit. Palestine was the model. We were occupied by Israel. Others were occupied by their ruling classes. People were done with occupation—no matter who was doing it. So yeah, I spent a decade fighting in kata'eb. First in Palestine, then in Lebanon. Then I wanted to settle down a bit, and I worked on commune councils. It was a good life. But I missed my family here in America. I always wanted to see my brother again, my cousins, and just New York. This damn city sticks to you, you know.

**Abdelhadi: Hah, tell me about it.**

**Hassan:** So yeah, that's why I came back. Now I go back and forth every six months or so. It's a long trip though.

**Abdelhadi: You take a clipper?**

**Hassan:** Yeah, I usually do a high-speed train from Gaza to Cairo, then catch another one from Cairo to Rabat or Casablanca. From there, a clipper to New York. The whole thing takes a week or so.

**Abdelhadi:** Yeah, the train systems aren't as good here as they are in the SWANA region. I heard that they're working on solar planes in Cairo?

**Hassan:** Yup, there was a test launch yesterday. We may be flying again soon!

**Abdelhadi:** That would really be something. I haven't flown since 2045!

**Hassan:** We've lived long lives; you never know what will happen next.

**Abdelhadi:** Yes, when I first visited Palestine in 2016, I sat around a cafe in Jerusalem, and my friends and I dreamt of the day we could drive from Beirut to Jerusalem on a day trip. You helped make that a reality. It's been an honor talking to you.

**Hassan:** The train ride is even better than the car ride would have been! Thanks for this, it's been fun to reminisce.

# 3: TANYA JOHN ON THE FREE ASSEMBLY OF CROTONA PARK

*Recorded on December 1, 2067, in the Bronx.*

**M. E. O'Brien:** Hello, my name is M. I will be having a conversation with Tanya John for the New York Commune Oral History Project. It is the first day of December 2067, and this is being recorded at Tanya's apartment in the Crotona Commune. Hello Tanya.

**Tanya John:** Hello M.

**O'Brien:** Could you introduce yourself, however you'd like?

**John:** Sure. I'm a coor of the Crotona Commune and serve as a rep in the Mid-Atlantic Free Assembly. Hold on, I'm getting a call. [Long pause.] Okay, sorry about that. I shouldn't have to take any more calls.

**O'Brien:** You have an implanted phone?

**John:** Yeah, of-c. Where was I? You don't have a phone?

**O'Brien:** No, I guess I just use my watch. What's a coor?

**John:** A coor is a sysadmin. A ranner? The word comes from "coordinator," I think. Basically, I make sure fec doesn't get in the way of other fec.

**O'Brien:** Like you administer the commune?

**John:** Right.

**O'Brien:** You were introducing yourself.

**John:** Yeah, I work a lot. I am an auntie to tons of kids. I play music. I like parties. I'm good at managing things. I love my commune. I've been around. My new hobby is making drugs.

**O'Brien: Drugs?**

**John:** Synthetic hallucinogens. I'm taking a class in neuropsych.

**O'Brien: You play music?**

**John:** Yeah, I DJ. I've run parties here in the Bronx for twenty years. My big gigs though are on the Jakarta Circuit.

**O'Brien: Jakarta, the city?**

**John:** I guess? The Jakarta Circuit is clubs, a dance party scene. It's big all along the rim of the Indian Ocean. The music is a wild mix, evolved from these dance barges that would run back and forth along the coast from Karachi, running through Colombo, Chennai, Kolkata, and then turn around in Bangkok. This scene was made by the kids that would take the barges back and forth, and then crash in the shanties and communes along the circuit. Then the dancing went online, and it got popular. It's very catchy, very exhilarating. These days the servers are offshore near Jakarta. I play a show once a month or so. They are big.

**O'Brien: Big?**

**John:** Maybe twenty thousand kids come out on average?

**O'Brien: I am confused. These were in person and now they aren't?**

**John:** Yeah. Ugh. I'll try to explain again: they came out of the dance barges of the forties, but later became full sensory. In some cases, the same boats. Like now some of the old shipping freighters that had become international dance clubs now just house the server systems for immersion parties today.

**O'Brien:** Like online virtual clubs?

**John:** Right. . . . You should look this up. . . . You wanted to talk about the Free Assembly? The first one—of Crotona Park?

**O'Brien: Yes! I'm sorry I am still a bit confused about the clubs. Let's loop back around to that at some point. Maybe let's start with your growing up.**

**John:** Sure. I'm from the Bronx. I grew up in the Bronx River Projects. My dad was from Karachi. My mom was from the DR. My mom was a teacher, taught music in high school. My dad used to do food delivery and then he got sucked into running for one of the orgs.

**O'Brien: Orgs?**

**John:** Street organizations. The gangs. My dad worked for one of the old gangs, MS-13, doing pickups.

**O'Brien: What were you like as a kid?**

**John:** I got into music and parties early. I had a lot of friends, I got along with everybody really well. As a teenager I was into sex. Dated a lot. Enjoyed the drama. Always had something going on. I had fun.

**O'Brien: How did you get involved politically?**

**John:** I wasn't really that political. Like I wasn't in any political groups. I mostly liked to dance. I got really into organizing parties. I ran these monthly parties that would move around. They were totally wild. We were one of the first that started syncing between implants and externals. Like full sensory immersion, aug sense, but onsite. We had all these DJs coming in from all over. The music scene was blowing up in Nigeria around then, and we got in that just as it got really popular here. It was so fucking fun. That's kind of how I spent my late teen years and early twenties. Made plenty of money from it. Calling them parties may not give the right sense. They would go on for a weekend. Everyone would live together in big empty buildings, and we would cook and eat together, and then people would dance or sleep based on their drug cycle. But also like we'd do like these workshops, and discussion groups, and fec.

**O'Brien: Did it ever get messy, like serious conflict?**

**John:** We took fights onsite really seriously. We put a lot of work into negotiating between the orgs to not get into it at the parties and had these resolution forums for people to work it out. The NYPD was no-go across a lot of the South Bronx at that point, so everyone needed support to address problems that came up, and we did that through the party organizing.

**O'Brien: What was your party called?**

**John:** Oh, we changed the name around a lot. Initially I called it Thalassa, but we changed the name a half a dozen times and people knew it was the same party. Despina, Galatea, Proteus.

**O'Brien: Those are . . . moons?**

**John:** That was the joke. Moons of Neptune. Some of our first aug sets were underwater. So, a roundabout joke, I guess. It made sense when we were tweaking.

**O'Brien: Underwater dance parties. That is amazing. Could you explain, for people who don't use implants or augmented environments, how tech worked at the parties?**

**John:** Sure. By the time I got into the dance scene, this was maybe when I was thirteen or fourteen, in '44 and '45, wet tech had become a huge part of music. This meant kids had these head implants. We would have surgery rooms at the parties, for kids to get new augs. There were a few veteran medics from the war in Iran, where auggie implants were big on the US side of things. The medics knew a lot about how to do simple, quick neural implants. And lots of soldiers stateside were stealing and selling anything they could get their hands on, so we had a steady source of auggie supplies of all sorts. The tech was actually pretty sturdy, and infections and complications pretty minimal, because it was all designed for field combat conditions. Well, sometimes kids died but a lot of people were dying, things were a mess during that time, and the tech was a lot of fun, so we dealt with the death. These medic vets taught a lot of people how to work with the tech, and kids were mad scholastic about it.

**O'Brien: What were the augment implants like?**

**John:** Usually bugs in your ears, another for your eyes, and then one on the back of your neck. They added additional sounds and visual elements to what you heard and saw, like added to your reality. Many people know about this now from phones, but then it wasn't much in civilian life besides the dance scene. So, when we'd have dance parties there would be the music in the external environment from speakers, and light shows from drones flying around, but then there would be this whole other level to the show in transmitting to people's implants that would reshape what we saw and heard, so it would make all these levels of experience that the DJs could play with. And kids could talk to each other, add to the environment with glove controllers, so what everyone saw could be mutually shaped by each other. You could select what your implants took in, so like only seeing stuff your friends made, or a narrow bandwidth from the DJ, or whatever.

**O'Brien: That sounds really interactive.**

**John:** It was genius. All the circuits these days do this, but my parties were some of the first that did it in North America. The first of the really genius DJs were coming out of Lagos, but because of the heavy use of auggies by the US Army in Iran, all these vets in the Bronx had it already, so we became one of the first of the big dance scenes to take all this up.

**O'Brien: That is all fascinating. Were you paying any attention to what was happening nationally and internationally at the time?**

John: Yeah. I didn't think of myself as focused on that sort of thing at the time. But I got really into talking with dance kids and DJs, and at the time this was heavily a scene based on traveling circuits. A lot was going down, like kids' squats getting raided and people getting locked up, and I remember trying to get a handle on the bigger context. I think one turning point for me in thinking about the international context was in 2051. The US military decided to tank the whole Internet, like everywhere. They burned most of the satellites, crashing them into the atmosphere, had a virus that wiped out most of the servers, they just tried to fry the whole thing.

**O'Brien: Yes, I wanted to ask you about that. I thought with the discussion of aug tech you may know something about it.**

John: They were desperate. This was during their occupation of NYC. The civil war was going poorly, they were losing ground all over, and everyone hated them everywhere. I don't know their thinking. But they crashed the Internet, and the cell networks, and basically any way we could talk to each other. It was really terrible for our parties, because it became so much harder to get DJs in from Africa. Two things started to emerge to replace the old Internet at that point, but they were both just starting, and it would be years before they really worked. Both replacements, strangely, were kind of connected to the dance scene.

So, one replacement was aug meshes. All these veterans had full shielded comm systems built into their heads, and they could have these encrypted, unblockable channels with each other to talk and share data. There were a lot of vets around, particularly in a place like the Bronx, and a lot of them came to our parties because our parties were very cool. We figured out how the vets could link to people's digits and phones, and suddenly we had this mesh network that traveled through all their auggies and couldn't be shut down. It only worked locally, but piece by piece we started linking it up to cover the borough, and later the city.

**O'Brien: You said there were two replacements for the Internet?**

**John:** Right. The other innovation was the dance barges. I don't honestly know how they pulled it off. But I knew a lot of kids coming in who had spent months on the barges in West Africa, the Southern and Eastern Mediterranean, the Jakarta Circuit I described before, and another along the coast of China. It was this whole global world, and our scene in the Bronx was very tied up with it. So, when the Internet went down they built these huge servers on the barges and set up these hacked satellite uplinks and transmitters to all the port cities. It was patchwork and broke all the time, but it managed to reestablish international communications. The dance kids would show up in new cities with link protocols on their auggie chips and get a city partially back online.

Years later, I think in 2055, the NYPD tried again to shut down the Internet in the city. This time everyone got hooked up to the meshes, and it became the beginning of the nets we all use now. But originally it was dance kids and vets who made it happen.

**O'Brien: That is an incredible story.**

**John:** I know, right! I used to say dancers were the neural links of the new world.

**O'Brien: Switching gears a bit—how did you get involved with the street gangs?**

**John:** I started dating this guy when I was nineteen, so in 2049. Lawrence Sands. Sex was great. He sold military hardware to the orgs. Through that I got to know a lot of them, got pretty tied up with the scene. At this point things were starting to shift in their fights with police. For a long time, the politics were hard to parse. Like when I was a teenager it felt like the fighting was over drug turf and who would collect the taxes, and the gangs were fighting each other as much as the police.

**O'Brien: But that was starting to change?**

**John:** Yeah. By the time I really started to know the orgs—around 2050—it was mad political, and all about abolition and "we care for our own," and all that fec and spittle. At this point Lawrence and I were really into negotiating these truces between the orgs, and they started ranning together to take out police stations. All through the winter of 2050 the police were losing it, like I think the orgs destroyed five police stations that year. Then the US army came in, and rounded up everyone in camps, and for a few weeks the fighting was reduced to drones sniping at each other. But the Army couldn't stay, things were getting too hot down south. For the next two years or so the orgs were in a constant shooting war with police. Like for days at a time, whole neighborhoods would be under lockdown because the orgs and the police were doing this block-by-block thing, and no one could go outside. It was a mess. Older people were really freaked out by it all. People were already mostly caring for each at the neighborhood-level during all that, and the communes were springing up.

**O'Brien: Were you involved in the communes?**

**John:** Not really. Not initially. The parties became a bit of a hub around healthcare and people finding housing and stuff. We'd always invite reps from the communes to talk with the kids who'd come to dance. On the blocks around the main stage, they'd set up tables and do all sorts of stuff. Crotona was the big commune in the Bronx. I think Hunts Point started in '52 after they took the Market. I was also getting to know a lot of the leadership in the orgs and introduced them to a few of the politicos from the Crotona Commune. There were a lot of conversations happening all the time about what was coming. After Hunts Point started distributing the food, it felt like we were right on the cusp of something. I would like to think our parties played a role bridging everybody, or at least everybody who liked to dance.

**O'Brien: How did the planning for the Free Assembly start?**

**John:** The NYPD was a bit on the run. They started abandoning the Bronx. This was 2053 or so. The orgs were kind of running things, but they were also getting all political.

**O'Brien: Could you explain what you mean by "political"? We were both using it earlier, but what exactly are you describing?**

**John:** Well, Crotona Commune had these old heads, like nationalists and commies, who were always showing up everywhere and always talking about how we should all work together. They had these, I don't know, agendas? Platforms? Ideas of how things should work in the future? The dance scene I was in initially had none of that. We just took care of each other and believed in that. The street orgs might occasionally name-drop the Panthers, but they were mostly about making money for a long time. But what we started to see was a convergence between these different currents.

Ultimately the Free Assembly was where it all came together, but it was slowly percolating for years before then. By 2050 you would start hearing like young thugs and tweakers repeating something they had heard commie from the Crotona Commune say, like they were really thinking about it. I was kind of one of those kids too. Like I was always coor of the parties, but I started thinking about our work using some of the concepts the olds from Crotona were spouting. But I'd also argue with them.

**O'Brien: What were those arguments like?**

**John:** I remember this one chap, Cassandra, was an old commie. We would fight about her opinions about our parties and how we needed discipline and whatever. But slowly she started actually paying attention to what was happening in the orgs, and at the parties, like actually thinking about what things could look like on the ground. And she kind of had to shift gears, from thinking about there being this future party that would run everything—party like a political org, not party like a dance party—to seeing what was beginning to emerge. It was—it was really direct. Like care for each other, off the pigs, abolish the prisons, whatever it was, to do it directly and all at once. That's what

I mean when I say political, this convergence around what was slowly becoming a shared vision of direct revolution, direct communism.

**O'Brien: How did these convergences happen concretely? Like where did people talk to each other?**

**John:** Honestly? For a while it was literally inviting people to our parties, and these arguments people would have, sitting around plastic furniture we would set up in the streets around the party. I tell you: dancers were the neurons of the new mind. Eventually that evolved into assemblies and all.

**O'Brien: Do you know what made this politicization possible?**

**John:** Probably a lot of factors. I'm not cert. It started in the forties, and then I was pretty exclusively in the dance scene before I met Larry and started connecting to the orgs. One big turning point I remember clearly was Hunts Point in 2052 or so. It was really inspiring to everyone, really gave a sense that anything was possible. The Hunts Point militants were like wild cards, a bit out of nowhere—like, not just old political heads like the Crotona Commune and not just drug dealers with artillery like the orgs. They had all this energy and really believed anything was possible. I think it was people from Hunts Point that first proposed the idea of a Free Assembly. A lot of them are still around, you should talk with them. Hunts Point had been doing something like it [assemblies] every week, but the idea was a really big one, like bringing everyone together. The dance kids got into it. I think our experience of taking care of each other at the parties had a big impact in beginning to shift our thinking about what was possible.

So, everyone was getting into the idea of the assembly, and trying to bring in others, trying to make it citywide. Like we'd send out these little teams to pitch the vision of an assembly. So we'd have these cars full of like one enthusiastic tweaked-out dance kid, someone from one of the communes, and some jacked street fighter from an org. I guess it was kind of the vision the Crotona Commune had been pitching, but shaped through what was happening in Hunts

Point, with a heavy dose of dance solidarity. It was like they were pitching the new world, and it would start with the Assembly—the Free Assembly of Crotona Park. I loved those conversations, like they were turning my mind upside down. These delegations went to the other communes—in Harlem, Newark, Brownsville, Jackson Heights—like we'd go every week trying to negotiate to get them to come. And then students at BMCC [Borough of Manhattan Community College] were doing this long occupation, so we invited them. And then all the orgs and paramilitaries. We even sent a car down to Alabama to invite some of them to come up.

**O'Brien: What was happening in the other boroughs?**

**John:** Because of the dance scene, I actually knew a lot about what was happening around the city. Like, at that point the subways weren't really working, and no one had jobs, so a lot of people just stayed in their neighborhood and a lot of struggles had this whole hyperlocal thing going on. A few of the orgs had strong international connections, but there had kind of been a breakdown in citywide org coordination so a lot of them were actually very isolated in the Bronx. But because of our parties, actually tons of kids rolled in from Harlem, Queens, Brooklyn. I heard a lot about what was happening.

Queens got all divided up in these little fiefdoms. Like, the kids had to snake their way through these endless checkpoints, since every little neighborhood got under the control of some different cult, or political group, or gang, or church, or these sort of protocommunes. A lot of struggles over access to water and sewage and such. I think Jackson Heights was the only really true commune, like where they weren't a cult in disguise and had full-on pop assemblies and could actually reliably take care of each other. I think the Jackson Heights Commune was like, most of the neighborhood.

Brooklyn had all these alternative land projects happening, like they tore up their streets to make farms and had tons of co-ops. But it was still all money-based, and from what I gather everything was heavily infiltrated by the NYPD, and no one could turn their sustainable living projects into fighting organizations. I mean, the tech they pulled together was helpful for the communes, but they were utterly useless when it came to politics. The Brownsville Commune just executed all their suspected informants and undercovers. I think that got too ugly, honestly, but they emerged as the only force that could actually effectively fight the cops in Brooklyn. And Staten Island was just a nightmare. I think only here in the Bronx were the lines super sharp. Initially that was about the orgs and the cops fighting over drug turf, but it became more and more political as time went on. The hard part here was getting everyone else on board, like the olds.

**O'Brien: That is all super interesting. You have a really good overview and understanding of how all these rapidly changing pieces fit together. I can see why you would make an excellent organizer and coordinator. What was your role in planning the Free Assembly of Crotona Park?**

John: I was in my twenties at this point, and really good at running the parties. I knew how to get people working together. So, I pretty much took on and ran all the logistics for the Free Assembly. We didn't know how many people would end up coming. I think in the end we guessed there were nearly seventeen hundred people who passed through and participated in one way or another, and over four hundred who stayed for the whole month. Most of those people were representing other collectives, residential communes, worker councils, orgs, schools, whatever it was. If you were only representing yourself or a few friends you could watch but not talk so much. It was really a space for all of the networks to sort it out together. Mostly our operations were centered in the park.

**O'Brien: People stayed in Crotona Park?**

John: Not quite. All our meetings were in the park, but mostly people were sleeping in the surrounding neighborhood. The NYPD had been completely cleared out of Crotona and were scared to come back. It was the summer of 2055 and the weather was perfect. We set up this big tent city in Crotona Park for the meetings, and all the apartment buildings nearby hosted people. Everyone came from all over, like what later became the Mid-Atlantic Free Assembly. But

Crotona was the first one, the first major gathering like this. I hear it became a template for other efforts around the world. Which . . . is not something you can say about very much from the US side of the insurrection.

In most ways we were way behind. Like, the revolution was already a decade old in Lima or Xinjiang, and the US was very deeply divided and had some really hard things to sort out about whiteness and all. But in this one way—the assembly as a social form—I think we did offer a model to everyone else. I ran childcare, security, training facilitators, food, everything. Well, my team ran it all. I enlisted all the dance kids. Like, we were an army of tweakers just working that whole year to pull it together.

**O'Brien: What was the planning like?**

**John:** We had a dozen working groups, and they started meeting weekly, and later daily, each morning. No one was working at all by that point, and the communes were taking care of everybody's basics. They got food from Hunts Point and served it in cafeterias, had nurses setting up clinics in some old storefronts on the block, had big assemblies in the biggest room in the neighborhood to figure out how to keep the power on or the toilets flushing. Who was in the commune was usually pretty loose, like all the buildings walking distance from an old elementary school, or something like that, and to be in a commune, you ate most of your meals at the canteen. Slowly they became more integrated, more formal, but they still have this surrounding area of people that depend on the commune for their basic needs but aren't fully in it. Remember, this was at a moment when the stores and supply chains and everything had basically broken down completely, so the commune infrastructure was literally the main means of survival.

**O'Brien: You were starting to talk about the planning for the Free Assembly?**

**John:** Oh, yeah. We had core ranners in each group, who would generally have no real decision-making power but would put in the hours. We worked really hard to get a lot of older people involved. We knew a lot of the olds around Crotona were just terrified of everything, and we thought this could be a good way to tie people in. One team finding housing for people, one team dealing with food, one team with water and sewage, one with childcare, that sort of thing. A truce council ran security. I was really into resolution tables at this point, like strategies for addressing conflict. The first phase of the Assembly was all about working through all the old fec and spittle that had built up between people. We had this format to raise and hold conflict and it mostly helped. At least to get people to tolerate each other. Also, facilitation. Our core facilitation team was at least forty people.

I can tell you about my aunt, she kind of stands out for me as a neighborhood person who was changed by this process. My aunt was an old, like she was in her sixties when the Crotona Assembly happened. So maybe she was born in the nineties? Eighties? I'm not sure. She was too scared to leave her home. It had been so bad for her for a long time. She was scared of diseases, and getting shot in crossfire, and a lot of other things. I think she probably had schizophrenia, but you could carry on a conversation with her easily, and actually, all her fears were very well founded. Like they were things that happened to people all the time. She had this little apartment she had been in for forty years at Murphy Houses on Crotona Avenue. I know my mom would scrounge for groceries for her through the forties, and then after Hunts Point, I would bring her building food from there once a week.

**O'Brien: It sounds like she was very isolated.**

**John:** Definitely. I got it into my head to get her roped into the Assembly planning. She started leaving her house for planning meetings. My aunt was really into sewing. She had trained as a tailor when she was younger, and an old boyfriend of hers had this industrial sewing machine. So, she got a group of old women to sew our meeting tents. Like, initially that was just joining tarps to make bigger tarps, but then they started making them more and more elaborate. Like, these huge patterns of stars and street maps and everything cut out of tarps and trash fabric and even leaves from trees. Then she ended up working with some Latin Kings, one of the OG street orgs she had always been terrified of. The Kings took on getting the metal poles and erecting the tents. It was wild watching her control her panic attacks and then go into these meetings with kids a third of her age and tell them how the tents were designed.

**O'Brien:** That sounds really moving.

**John:** It gets better! I remember when the tents went up and we all stood under them and looked up at these beautiful patterns above us, like an old cathedral. Her face just lit up, and it was like the new world belonged to her too, it wouldn't leave her behind. She made something so magical. People coming to the Assembly commented on how beautiful they were. The Crotona Commune still sets them up in the park for special occasions. Through connecting to the Crotona around that process, my aunt started getting better mental health care, started eating with other people, and lived the last part of her life connected to other people.

**O'Brien:** That's a great story. What is her name?

**John:** Abigail John. She passed away last year.

**O'Brien:** I'm sorry.

**John:** It's okay. I'm really proud of her.

**O'Brien:** What happened at the Assembly?

**John:** Basically, the Free Assembly was a month of intense meetings between every major armed tendency in the Mid-Atlantic. The meetings happened in the tents in the park, usually thirty to fifty people in a tent there to talk about some specific topic, with smaller breakout groups.

**O'Brien:** What sort of topics?

**John:** Everything you could imagine. How to distribute food, how to keep water running, how to defend against the pigs, what to do about the holdouts, who should have guns, military strategy, everything. Like we were discussing how to do everything necessary that had once been done by the stores, the jobs, the entire government, and putting everything they did on the agenda to actually sort it out, what we were fighting for and how we were going to get there. Like, I facilitated a six-hour meeting about how to deal with child abuse allegations in the communes. At this point there were communes of some sort in every borough, and it had completely broken open people's ideas of family. And no one liked the old child protective services system, they had done so much harm. So, we were arguing about what could be done, what should be done, if someone thought a kid was being abused. All of life was up for debate in a way.

So, we would meet all day. Then every night there'd be one general assembly where all the various groups would report on their decisions, and it would get argued about. After that everyone would go back to their factions and try to convince their comrades to go along with whatever they had hashed out. The first week was just trying to get people not to shoot each other. It was resolution tables around the clock. After that, things started to settle down. We made all the participants do shifts with cooking, cleaning, childcare, and I think that helped. All these old politicos and jacked gangsters doing dishes together, I think it helped settle people, helped make people listen to each other a bit more. The facilitation team were fucking heroes, I'm telling you.

**O'Brien: What did you all decide?**

**John:** Kind of the beginning of everything! A lot came out of that month. People say it was a major turning point; when the rev really came together. The communes agreed to a mutual cooperation and defense pack. We hammered out a platform, some mix of communization and oppressed nationality self-determination fec. I didn't really like the platform, honestly. But it won over the org leadership, and they more or less dissolved themselves into training the People's Army of the Free Assembly. I think it also helped that basically everyone was fighting the NYPD at this point, so we had a deep sense of camaraderie through that experience.

**O'Brien: "The People's Army"?**

**John:** That's what we called the armed defense efforts of the communes, but it wasn't like the North American Liberation Front or formal armies. It wasn't really an army at all. Basically, we decided the only way to defend the New York Commune was to arm and train nearly everybody who had given up property and power—that was the criteria—in how to use a gun. The orgs did the training, but in the third week of the Assembly we decided to form this "council of grandmothers" as we called it, like literally, really old women. Well, elder feminized people. But mostly women. They made the military decisions and decided when someone had to be disarmed. The army was just literally everyone who the grandmothers hadn't decided to disarm.

**O'Brien: Were any of the meetings virtual or augmented?**

**John:** No, not really. For someone who has spent a lot of my life online in augmented environments, we decided that people really needed to be present and really, really face-to-face. People would report back to their communes or their orgs at night, and a lot of that happened over phones and such, but the meetings themselves were overwhelmingly face-to-face. The Mid-Atlantic Free Assembly, that I work with now, is generally online. But when anything gets tense, or really serious, we set up some extended face-to-face assembly for a few days or a couple of weeks. The Free Assembly of Crotona Park was an early reflection of that intuition that people needed to live and work together in one place to sort things out. I think my sense of that came out of doing our resolution tables at the parties, and seeing how people who were living together, even just for a weekend, could work things out.

Talking about all this, I have to say. It was so fucking exhausting. Like, so many meetings. They went on. For weeks. I loved it, but I also hated it. I feel exhausted thinking about it. I can't believe I did it. Never want to sit through that many meetings again. And every time I thought they'd be over someone would bring up some fec and we'd be right back at it, and I was this close to losing my mind. I was so fucking tired when that was all over.

**O'Brien: What in your mind is the legacy of the Free Assembly of Crotona Park?**

**John:** It was definitely the most exhilarating and life-changing thing I was ever a part of. I think that was true for everyone. Like, up to this point in New York, at least, there were all these struggles breaking out everywhere, and a lot of sense that the old world was falling away and couldn't last. But it wasn't until the Free Assembly that we started really having this direct sense that we could actually build a new one, like make a world that could carry us through all this. And I say "we," and I'm talking about the organizers and the communes and the street orgs, but I'm also kind of talking about everybody. Like, there were at least a million people in networks that were represented in the discussions of the Free Assembly. That's a substantial portion of the population of the Mid-Atlantic. And coming out of the Free Assembly, all those people felt like they were  part of something that linked us all together. Though the political platform we hashed out there had a lot of problems—I personally think it was steeped in a kind of subtle racial essentialism that was a part of the political underdevelopment of the orgs—it was solidly a commitment to do away with money, property, and police, and the state and all that. That was crystal clear, and I can say through the month of discussions everyone slowly came to understand what that meant, what could be possible through that, and that this new world was worth fighting for, and it was worth dying for, and above all it was worth living for.

**O'Brien: That's beautiful. It gives me goosebumps hearing you.**

**John:** I told you about my aunt before. I could tell you about another person who comes to mind, when I think about how the Assembly changed things. I had a much younger sister, fourteen years younger. Her name is Monique. So, I was born in 2030, she was born in 2043. When she was coming up, it was like everything was hell. The cough hit hard when she was four or five, the hunger came after. She had all these awful health problems from what a disaster the hospitals were and not getting enough food and everything. My parents were always hustling to try to figure out how to keep her alive. She grew up reading fantasy novels, watching old stream shows; my parents were worried about her getting hurt in the streets and kept her in. She had cognitive disabilities, developmental disabilities. She tried to come out as a girl to our parents when she was five or so, and it didn't go well. It was a hard childhood.

**O'Brien: Your family dealt with a lot of suffering.**

**John:** No more than usual. So yeah, then they all came to the Free Assembly. So, she was twelve at the time? And she totally dived into the youth workshops at the Assembly. Like, she loved it so, so much. Her youth group put on this play about the history of revolution in the Caribbean. They prepared the play all month, and then performed it in the last days of the Assembly. She played this psychiatrist from Martinique who went to Algeria. Like, she gave a whole speech in the play to hundreds of people. It was so wild! I have never seen her speak to a group before. Our parents moved into the Crotona Commune later that year, and my sister's health improved steadily through her teen years. She transitioned to be a girl her first year in the commune.

She still has chronic fatigue but she's doing really well. She is, what, twenty-four now? She works in this big garden or little farm they have in Crotona Park. She spends a lot of time just sitting out there, enjoying the view, carrying on conversations with whoever comes by. On days the weather is bad she goes and plays games with younger kids or reads them books. She is exploring what other kind of three-hour she could do to help contribute to our commune and is getting help in sorting that out. But she has a good life now, a life made possible by the Assembly, by the commune, and I feel like I did something good in my time by contributing to making that possible for her.

**O'Brien: That's lovely.**

**John:** I know! Oh, she also sings. She sings at the music events I organize for our commune. It reminds me of when she gave that speech. That was the first time she talked to a group, but now she does it all the time.

**O'Brien: How did the dance scene change since the Free Assembly of Crotona Park?**

**John:** It got way more international. Like, there are still dance barges doing circuits or going back and forth on the ocean, but way more of it is online now. Music genres are much more likely to take shape spanning continents, with kids in tight friend groups that include people a thousand miles away they may not meet until someone takes a dance barge across the ocean for their sojourn. Plus, there is this whole other side of it, around the communes, like the events my sister sings at. Most of the communes have clubs or dance parties every weekend. But the scenes are really different. The dance barges and the giant virtual online parties have their own special vibes, in the types of music, in the age bracket of their main audience, and in the tech you need to join.

In contrast, the commune dance parties are really meant to include everyone. So, they rarely have much in the way of drugs or alcohol, you don't need implants, and they weave together all this music from across multiple generations. But it's usually the same DJs, the same people, doing both kinds of parties. I DJ these huge parties on the Jakarta Circuit, but I also bottom line these Sunday night dances here at Crotona Park where olds, like, salsa together or get down to classic house. Music and dancing have always been important to community and struggle, but it's really so appreciated and precious in the life of the communes. A lot of people really into music bridge these two very different sides to our work, our art.

**O'Brien: That is lovely to hear about.**

**John:** Yeah, I'm kind of proud of it. Crotona Park was one of the first communes that really welcomed in dance kids and saw the possibility of bridging this whole specialized world of dance with the question of intergenerational community building. That started happening after the first Free Assembly. I like to think I played some role in making that all possible.

**O'Brien: Let's stop there.**

**John:** Sounds good. You should swing by on Sunday night for a salsa-reggaeton night. It's a great scene.

**O'Brien: I'd like that.**

# 4: BELQUEES CHOWDHURY ON STUDENT AND WORKER OCCUPATIONS

*Recorded on January 22, 2068, in Tribeca, Manhattan.*

Eman Abdelhadi: This is a recording of an interview conducted by Eman Abdelhadi. It is January 22, 2068. We are in the Tribeca Commune in Manhattan, in the home of Belquees' family. Hi Belquees!

Belquees Chowdhury: Hi Eman!

Abdelhadi: Oh hello! And what's your name? [**Long pause.**]

Chowdhury: That's Hala! They're being shy right now.

Abdelhadi: Aww, hi, Hala! How old are you?

Chowdhury: Come on! You know the answer to that! [Long pause.]

Chowdhury: They're about three.

Abdelhadi: Adorable! Are you and Hala the only ones living in this apartment?

Chowdhury: No, I have another nibling, they're six, my father, and my two sisters. My father comes and goes. Ever since *Amma* died, he likes to stay on the move.

Abdelhadi: I've heard you do a lot of hosting here in the Tribeca Commune.

**Chowdhury:** Yes. TC includes forty-one buildings in this neighborhood, organized around a large canteen and meeting hall two blocks west of here. We go there for our meals. This building that we're in is mostly used to host travelers who come through the region. It has eleven flexible housing apartments. Our apartment is one of three in this building with permanent residents.

**Abdelhadi: Forty-one buildings is huge! It's gotta be the biggest commune in the city!**

**Chowdhury:** One of them, yeah! We have thirty-five hundred residents. But our footprint is even bigger, because we have a lot of flexible space. All the communes can welcome travelers, refugees, kids on sojourn, visitors, and all that. But we kind of specialize in hosting. When city or borough assemblies aren't virtual, we like to host people here. That's why we spent a lot of time building meeting spaces. We have like twenty large halls, a canteen that can easily feed three times our resident population, and lots of flexible space.

**Abdelhadi: How does the flexible space work?**

**Chowdhury:** Every building has a few permanent residents, and they serve as hosts and caretakers who facilitate visitors' use of the rest of the building. The apartments around us are full of Mi'kmaq who have a lot to say about Asiatic bittersweet. I'm not involved, to be clear. I am sure they would love to tell you all about it.

**Abdelhadi: Full of what talking about what? I didn't follow that last bit at all.**

**Chowdhury:** Sorry. Mi'kmaq are a First Nation up in the North. Asiatic bittersweet is an invasive vine they farm. Or are trying to destroy. I'm actually not really clear on which. Right now, there is an assembly happening over how to deal with invasive vines in North America. They tried to figure it out on the forums but there was way too much conflict. Someone finally called an IRL. But this building is filled with visitng Mi'kmaq botonists who have very strong feelings about this particular plant.

**Abdelhadi: You light up when you talk about the commune. Have you been here for a while?**

Chowdhury: Yeah! I helped set this all up! It's been my heart and soul for the better part of the last decade.

**Abdelhadi: Are you from this area?**

Chowdhury: No, I'm from Queens. I grew up in Woodside. I first came to this area twelve or thirteen years ago to study at a school that was here—BMCC. It stood for the Borough of Manhattan Community College. You ate lunch at the canteen, right? That was that building, that's where the school was.

**Abdelhadi: Oh yeah! Hard to believe that was a school building.**

Chowdhury: Yeah, it's gone through a lot of renovation and repurposing. I was part of the student occupation here, and then when we liberated the detention center, I helped set up the Tribeca Commune. It's a long story.

**Abdelhadi: I'd love to get into it, but let's start with Woodside first. I want to know more about where you grew up. What year were you born by the way?**

Chowdhury: End of 2030 or beginning of 2031. I'm not totally sure. My parents are from Bangladesh, they moved here together in the mid-twenties. *Abba* drove taxis and my mom worked as a nursing assistant. We loved each other, but there wasn't really time for anything but surviving. That was when prices were crazy, and we just kept working more and more to get less and less. I started working when I was twelve. Abba would take the taxi to a discount store upstate and fill it with canned and bottled drinks—those were still a thing back then. And I would put them in coolers of ice and sell them on street corners and the park in the summer. Sometimes I would babysit, other times I'd pick up shifts in some of the restaurants on our block. Anything I could find. Eventually, when I was seventeen, I started cleaning at Elmhurst Hospital where my mom worked.

**Abdelhadi: Seventeen? Uh oh, so you started working at a hospital when LARS-47 hit?**

**Chowdhury:** [Laughs.] Yup! What can I say? I'm drawn to crisis! No, but for real, I learned a lot there about organizing and about collective action. I'm grateful for that time. My mom had already been teaching me about organizing, because she was involved in worker and patient strikes that happened throughout the forties as they were closing public hospitals. Before Elmhurst, she worked at Queens Hospital. I grew up with all these meetings happening in our apartment, dozens of people crammed in, talking about their next action.

**Abdelhadi: Tell me more about that!**

**Chowdhury:** So, the workers kept going on strike over pay and patient care. The hospital was turning away patients who couldn't pay or provide insurance. That was pretty much everyone at this point, because the depression was so bad. People could hardly afford food, let alone these insane fucking hospital bills! And we never had huge public investment in hospitals—the system relied on the idea that people or their employers could pay. And when gradually everyone was pretty much out of work, the system had nothing to sustain itself. So yeah, it was definitely an incubator for struggle.

One of my favorite direct actions was when workers started sabotaging the billing. [Laughs.] Bills would mysteriously disappear from people's accounts. But of course, that didn't last long. The workers weren't being paid consistently and supplies were running low. The first couple of strikes helped a bit, but then they started closing hospitals. When they went on strike in '45, the hospital just shut down. It was fucked up. They started just shutting down the hospitals, because nobody was funding any of it and the government couldn't keep up with running anything at that point. My mom and a lot of her coworkers ended up moving over to Elmhurst Hospital. But the City was in the middle of abandoning that hospital too. They wanted to close it and were reducing resources to it every day. The writing was on the wall—this hospital would close too. Until LARS-47 hit.

**Abdelhadi: What happened then?**

**Chowdhury:** LARS was nuts, because it made people hallucinate. And people were already stretched so thin, taking care of their loved ones and neighbors while they were in full-blown psychosis was really impossible. So, everyone rallied around the hospital once the pandemic started—workers, patients, everyone in the neighborhood. The City and the feds were useless, of course. What do you do with mass support but a city government that doesn't care? At that point, "city government" was basically just the police and skeletons of previous infrastructure that had been gutted by budget crisis. Everyone was demanding more, and finally, in early '48 I think, the City announced they were officially closing the hospital. The response was huge. The nurses started a full occupation of the building. About five hundred people from the area joined in. They had these huge assemblies every day, and they made the decision to keep the hospital open. The [US] Army was everywhere at this point, they had tanks and gunboats lined up at LaGuardia. The political situation in Queens was a mess. Extremely fragmented, very chaotic. Every neighborhood had a totally different thing going on, and it was all rumors and confusion.

**Abdelhadi: How did they keep the hospital running in the middle of all that?**

**Chowdhury:** The nurses, well, the Assembly they ran, but the nurses were the heart of it, decided they would keep Elmhurst open, and not charge any money for anything. It was still a totally wild idea. I gather people were trying something like this in other uprisings years before, but we didn't know anything about that. It felt like we were just making it up as we went along. Hundreds of people would turn out to the

Hospital Assembly every night to try to figure out how to keep the hospital running. Maybe a million people came to Elmhurst during the occupation for care. The Jackson Heights Commune had just started, and they initially kept everyone fed. Then the problem was how to get drugs. There was this big drug plant in the liberated zone in the Mississippi Delta, just outside the Jackson Fallout Zone—this was Jackson, Mississippi, not Jackson Heights. It was modeled after liberated pharmaceutical operations in Lima. They were shipping up drugs and medical supplies—so we had connections all over. I lived at the hospital for two months. I was coordinating teen volunteers. There were maybe a hundred kids who would come every day and help out with whatever needed doing. I think a lot of them became nurses and doctors later. Elmhurst was one of the first places in the US, to my knowledge, where a workers' occupation just started providing free services permanently.

**Abdelhadi: Amazing!**

**Chowdhury:** It really was. I think Elmhurst was really a turning point for the whole movement in North America. It became a really important model of communization struggles all over the city. The riots, the communes, the worker occupations—they were all patchwork before that. And Elmhurst was one of the moments where they could come together into a full break from the money economy. It was like: "Oh. We can meet our own needs." The elders in movement circles would always say, "We keep us safe." And at that point, it was like right, we keep us safe. We also keep us fed. We keep us healthy. We keep us alive.

It was honestly so exhilarating for me to be a part of. I formed all of these really strong relationships there, like it felt like I was falling in love with everybody. I feel like I kind of discovered the kind of person I could be through being in struggle with other people. Like, mostly I am thinking of the teen volunteers I coordinated, but I also formed all these really strong friendships with doctors and the cleaning staff I had been working with and long-term patients.

Abdelhadi: That's beautiful. The hospital . . . it's not still there right? It was . . . it was destroyed?

Chowdhury: [Pause.] Yes. Queens . . . we were militant, you know. This neighborhood did not take kindly to military occupation, and they punished us for it. They had instituted these checkpoints and a curfew in '49 or '50. And people weren't having it. After the military shot up a bunch of people after curfew, a squad from this area blew up a checkpoint. The military bombed the hospital the next day. Leveled it. There were over six hundred patients, maybe half that many workers. My mother was one of them.

Abdelhadi: Were you in the building?

Chowdhury: No, I had left a few months before that. I had started at BMCC at that point. My dad called that day. As soon as I heard his voice, I knew something was wrong. He sounded, I don't know, hollow? I said, "What's wrong Abba?" And he said, "Your Amma, we have to go find her." And I said, "What do you mean? What happened? Where is she?" And he was like, "They killed her. They killed everyone. We have to find her. We have to bury her." We went, but it was . . . it was impossible. It was impossible. It was just wreckage. Very few bodies intact. Sometimes you'd see things you recognized. Someone's scarf. An ID card. But never anything close to a whole body.

Abdelhadi: Would you like some tissues?

Chowdhury: No. Listen. Muslims, we bury our dead, you know? My mom, she was a nurse and a caretaker. She did this for so many people in our neighborhood. The *ghusl*—the ritual wash. We're not afraid of the dead, you know. We wash the body, and it's an act of care, of love. A dignified goodbye, a sendoff to God. We clean them, wrap them in clean, white cotton, return them to the earth. My mom, she did that for so many people, and we never got to do that for her. Abba says she hasn't forgiven him for that. She comes to him in his dreams and asks when her *janazah* will be. He's never really recovered from that.

**Abdelhadi: Have you?**

**Chowdhury:** I don't know. I'm not sure recovery is the goal. The grief is a part of me, I grieve out of habit. Especially since I didn't face it all right away. I kept busy. I wanted to take care of my dad. And I wanted to blow everything up. And I wanted to cry a few years away. But there wasn't time to dwell on any one thing, because history was still moving all around us.

**Abdelhadi: What was happening at BMCC?**

**Chowdhury:** Well, it was falling apart like every public institution. It was mostly still running because professors continued to teach, even though barely any money was coming in. But I got involved in CUNY Against the War, which had started a few years earlier with protests against the invasion of Iran. I had lost so many people at Elmhurst, and these became my friends and family. We were a "cadre group," as we called it then. Our friend Anand had been researching CUNY's history—he kept telling us how much radicalism had happened here over the past century. We were really disciplined about the work and about knowing each other really well. Like, we would do these formal tellings of our life stories in the evenings, we were really deliberate about how we worked with conflict, a lot of stuff like that. That's the space where I was forced to face my grief. I familied several people from there. It's where I met my sisters, the ones I live with now. A lot of my closest relationships to this day came from CUNY Against the War. I am still in touch with at least a dozen people from that group.

**Abdelhadi: Is that the group that started the occupation?**

**Chowdhury:** Yes. So, one thing people forget about in this commune era is that there were also fash in the city. We always talk about fighting the police and the Army, but the lines between them and the white power militias had become really thin. There were these death squads forming—I think they had evolved from these white supremacist gangs from the early tens and twenties.

They were concentrated in places where police and military people lived—like Staten Island—and these really securitized parts of the city, like Tribeca, and actually, Lower Manhattan in general. Anyway, one of these squads assassinated a professor, Dr. Joaquin Alves. He was a Puerto Rican activist who had been an organizer and militant in the Bronx for decades. He was a mentor to a lot of us. It happened right in front of the main entrance, in front of hundreds of people, like they rode up with scooters and gunned him down. Students took over the building that night, called the occupation "Tribeca Red," and I think for a bunch of people it was the beginning of the Tribeca Commune.

**Abdelhadi: What was the atmosphere of the occupation like?**

**Chowdhury:** Organized, militant, and fun as hell. CUNY Against the War were the main organizers, and like I said, we all knew each other super well. We had very, very intense relationships and had already done a lot of work together. So, it was easy to get really organized really fast. Because the logistics—like food and housing were relatively easy to set up, there was also room for . . . for something else—catharsis? I guess.

We literally took the biggest room and made it a permanent rave room. We cut out the lights and had people DJ and it was just this giant party all the time that you could go to whenever you wanted to dance your heart out. There were drugs of course, [laughs], so you could do that or you could get high on the music. Whatever. It was a place to unwind. Someone else started a meditation room, for more mellow vibes. Stuff like that.

**Abdelhadi: What were the occupation's demands?**

**Chowdhury:** A complete withdrawal of the pigs from the area. Public funding for workers and to run the school's operations. At least that's how it started. But honestly, I think we just wanted to shut everything down at that point, acknowledge we had reached a point of no return. Build something different with our new reality.

**Abdelhadi: Did the occupation move beyond BMCC?**

**Chowdhury:** Oh, hell yeah. That neighborhood was full of cop fec. Honestly, they probably wouldn't have given a fuck that we were occupying a public institution they were already divesting from. But the fact that we were in Tribeca, that made it dangerous for them. They started patrolling the building and the death squads would show up just to sit across the street and intimidate us. They would line up their scooters and motorcycles in really neat formations, and they would all wear sunglasses and these horrible, fucking baseball caps. They all dressed the same too, pastel-colored polos and cargo shorts. Arms crossed across their chests, trying to look all serious and tough. Just watching us for hours. It was scary at first, but then militant folks from Chelsea showed up to back us up, and then eventually folks from Harlem and the Bronx too. The Zetkinistas were doing patrols for a while, and they also brought us food and supplies. Pads and tampons. [Laughs.] That's what we ran out of first. People getting periods were desperate for those, but then the word spread and everyone brought us so many. We ended up with like more pads than toilet paper, hah.

Anyway, eventually the pigs and the fash backed off bit by bit. The police were overextended and couldn't keep up patrols. The fash were getting a bit terrified when Chelsea, the Bronx, and Harlem showed up. We started marching through the neighborhood once we had enough of a force and going after some of the main cop hangouts. We brought bats, hammers, whatever we could find and tore those places out. On the twelfth day, we burned down the First Precinct. We sent people to the big hoopla up in Crotona Park that happened that year.

**Abdelhadi: How would you compare the occupation of Elmhurst to the occupation of BMCC? Were they similar?**

**Chowdhury:** I think keeping the hospital functioning, and the experience of the workforce, really helped give clarity and some measure of unity to the assemblies at Elmhurst. Like people fought over all sorts of stuff, but when it came right down to it people were really invested in just moving ahead with what could work. Workers knew something about how to get along, be organized, be interdependent, and that helped out a lot. For students, it was a bit more dicey because the objective wasn't clear yet. Feeding everyone, keeping everyone clean, getting places to sleep, and so on—that was the easy part, especially since so many of us were organizers to begin with. But what next, you know?

**Abdelhadi: What happened next?**

**Chowdhury:** It turned into a lot of political factions fighting it out constantly. Some people wanted to merge into the transit worker assemblies that were happening on the docks at Battery Park. Others wanted to go join the fighting in the Republic of New Afrika or up in the Bronx. CUNY Against the War pushed for what we ended up doing: turning the campus into a neighborhood commune of sorts to organize and struggle in the area. Lower Manhattan was basically a deadzone in the movements around the city. All this eco co-op stuff was happening in Brooklyn, the fiefdoms in Queens, the shooting war in the Bronx. But Lower Manhattan was like the bunkers of the remains of corporate America. When the Army pulled out, a lot of them did too, but they still had these fortified headquarters buildings increasingly cut off from everything around them, behind their own little private floodgates. At first, the police were doing a lot to protect them but then the police got stretched with everything going on. They hired private security, but there wasn't enough of a threat in the area since it was all so dead. The streets were empty, all the little restaurants and things had shut down in the forties, and a lot of the neighborhood was abandoned. We felt like there was a lot of stuff there that we could reappropriate and make use of. We saw potential in that neighborhood at the end of the day.

**Abdelhadi: Were storms a big problem at BMCC? Battery Park City had already been flooded and emptied out, right?**

**Chowdhury:** A lot of the neighborhood was underwater during the worst storms, definitely. BMCC got flooded regularly. You see the tidal canals we're building outside? We are finding ways of dealing with it. We are embracing the water. The corps weren't able to get along with each other well enough to build flood walls, and the City and the feds definitely couldn't take it on. The storms and the damage they were doing to Lower Manhattan played a role in the initial divestment from the area, for cert. Now that I think about it, they also played a role in us being able to pull off what we did.

**Abdelhadi: You were working hard.**

**Chowdhury:** I worked extremely hard. All the time. I worked my ass off. I thought there was some way if I kept working I could keep from crying. It wasn't until years later I started sorting through how much what had happened at Elmhurst messed me up. Initially I went to BMCC thinking I would become a social worker, some sort of professional. It was a brief attempt to run away from politics. But as things heated up on campus, I got sucked back in.

**Abdelhadi: You mentioned a detention center earlier in the interview. Could you elaborate on that?**

**Chowdhury:** Cert. This was in the third year of the occupation, in 2053 or 2054. The Army was gone, and we decided to make a big move. The private security forces around the corporate buildings were still formidable, and we were not an army, so we stayed away from that. Since the cops and Army had backed off, we weren't getting as much support from Chelsea and uptown anymore. But at the Crotona Assembly we found a connect for weapons. People started learning how to shoot and all that.

Eventually, when we got strong enough, we decided to liberate the Manhattan Detention Complex [MDC], the Tombs. The place held maybe nine hundred prisoners at the time. Most of them were from the fighting in the Bronx. It was a major step for us because it was still a major stronghold for the police. A combat unit from the Bronx came down to help. They started the raid by shelling One Police Plaza. There was this big public housing complex, Alfred Smith. That was liberated ground and right next to One Police Plaza.

So, this combat unit set up there and just as the sun came up, they unleashed all this artillery fire on the police building. They drew all the police's attention there, and an hour later the prisoner committees coordinated a riot inside the Tombs. Less than an hour after that, we attacked. We had maybe a thousand people, a mix of people who had family members inside, students from the occupation, some locals, we all attacked the MDC from outside. It could have gone horribly wrong, like one well-placed machine gun nest could have killed a lot of people, but it ended up going really well. The prisoners all escaped that day, and we shelled the MDC to its foundations. The NYPD held on to One Police Plaza for another few months, but they were terrified to step foot outside.

**Abdelhadi: What happened to the former prisoners?**

**Chowdhury:** That turned out to be the most interesting part for me. About three hundred of them stayed in the neighborhood. Over the next year, the corporations started pulling out of the area altogether, and took their little private armies with them. The neighborhood was totally ours at that point. We set up housing with them in the apartment block next to BMCC, I think it was called Independence Plaza, and it really was a bit like the Tribeca Commune is today. We built out this huge kitchen at BMCC and started serving everyone in the neighborhood food. A lot of the liberated prisoners needed a lot of help to sort stuff out. Things had gotten really bad in the Tombs in the last couple of years. We had a lot of volunteers, some of them with skills, move to the area to work through trauma. That's when I started thinking more deeply about what had happened to mom. My dad moved in around then, to an apartment with me in the same building with all the ex-imprisoned.

**Abdelhadi: What helped you sort out your own trauma?**

**Chowdhury:** Mostly friends. Like, I got a lot of therapy of different sorts. But really it was my friendships. All the people I knew, besides my dad, I met through the struggle. That's where I formed my deepest friendships. I think there is something about heightened struggle that gives you a chance to really trust people. For really being able to fully love. Or maybe I'm just too controlling of myself the rest of the time to really open my heart to anybody. It's hard to say. My friends became a really major part of my healing process. One thing I realized was how my mom was with me all the time. How she had taught me how to build community, how to hold space, how to organize, how to create homes with other people out of whatever circumstances we found ourselves in.

Anyway, a lot of us slowed down in the late fifties once the commune had taken more shape. We had all been through fec, lost people. And we really tried to figure our shit out together. I spent some time on retreat at this trauma center in Queens and came back to Tribeca ready to do some healing. We had support groups every night and were in this long process of trying to heal together. It took a lot to reconnect to my body, to remember my mom and the days around the hospital bombing again, to be able to do anything that involved being present with myself. I'm just very, very grateful for my friends who got me through all that. My sisters Jess and María are the most important to me, that's why we became sisters, but there was a whole community of other people who were in that with us. Many of them still live in the Tribeca Commune after all these years, though those that don't live here come around often.

**Abdelhadi: Beautiful. Thank you for this interview. Is there anything else you'd like to add?**

**Chowdhury:** Eat kudzu sauerkraut.

**Abdelhadi: Excuse me?**

**Chowdhury:** The invasive vines assembly we are hosting. The big thing they are really into is kudzu sauerkraut. They say if there is any hope for the future of Chattanooga, we all have to eat a lot of kudzu sauerkraut. Reps from the Hamilton Commune in Chattanooga are volunteering in our kitchen, and every meal has kudzu in it. They are trying to convince us to accept two hundred kilos of semi-processed kudzu. I think it's a bad idea, but I promised them I would tell everyone to eat kudzu sauerkraut. So, I'm telling you.

**Abdelhadi: Well, thank you. I will work on that.**

# 5: QUINN LIU ON MAKING REFUGE, FROM HANGZHOU TO FLUSHING

*Recorded on March 3, 2068, in Flushing, Queens.*

Eman Abdelhadi: Hello, my name is Eman Abdelhadi, and I am speaking with Quinn Liu in Flushing, Queens. We are sitting in the Commons of the Falasheng Commune. Quinn, welcome! Thanks so much for agreeing to do this.

Quinn Liu: You're welcome.

Abdelhadi: Let's start with what year you were born.

Liu: Sure, I was born in 2030.

Abdelhadi: Where?

Liu: Monterey Park, in Los Angeles. I have a few memories of it. There was a soccer field near my home where I would play. I went to an elementary school that was mostly other Chinese kids. My mom worked at a dry cleaner. My dad did day work, like in construction.

Abdelhadi: But you didn't stay there?

Liu: No, the internments started when I was still a kid. The hate had been building for years. I was a little protected from it initially because our school was almost all Chinese. But you could feel this vicious, deep resentment growing, like the stares on the street and the police harassment. Then I started hearing about mob violence, like one of my dad's coworkers and friends got beat up by these college students. It wasn't until much later I understood anything about the politics of it—the desperation as the economic crash, and water crisis, and fires were tearing California apart. They really needed someone to blame. I was probably, I don't know, seven or eight when the Internment Act passed. We ended up in Napa Valley.

**Abdelhadi: At a camp?**

Liu: Yeah. Camp Wolfskill. It was one of the bigger camps, and the main one in Napa Valley. ICE managed it. They had converted a derelict winery.

**Abdelhadi: Your parents were migrants?**

Liu: They had both moved together from Guangxi before I was born.

**Abdelhadi: Gotcha. Tell me about the camp.**

Liu: I . . . I honestly don't remember it much. I spend a lot of time these days trying to help refugees and trauma survivors to figure out how to relate to their past to be able to be in the present. I've processed my past a lot. But it is still hard to talk about. And this sort of interview is a weird way of going about it. What do you want to know?

**Abdelhadi: Tell me about your family's living situation.**

Liu: We lived in this inflatable bubble building with four other families. We were sort of refugees, sort of prisoners, which was the story for so many people all over the world. The camp was surrounded by these old shipping containers. Everything for a half mile in any direction they put us to work dismantling or defoliating, so when the fires ripped through a couple of times a year it wouldn't completely destroy the camp. The ICE guards lived in the old vineyard house, and everyone else was in bubble buildings. Maybe two hundred people lived there? I really hated it. Like really hated everything about it. I grew a lot more distant from my family during our time there. I spent a lot of time sneaking out of the camp with these other kids. We would wander around the countryside and explore and try not to get caught.

Abdelhadi: What was the surrounding area like?

Liu: California was in bad shape around then. This was before the prison breaks and the early communes and all. White people were basically fleeing the state. The whole area around Napa Valley was a bit of a ghost town, just a lot of dead vineyards and empty strip malls. There were still these walled-off armed residential enclaves, a couple of them were not far from our camp. We stayed away from the livezone enclaves, so all we saw were Mexican families. I later realized they must have been the workforce for the gated livezones. I spent time wandering around in Union. The Mexican families weren't friendly, but they wouldn't shoot you like the guards at the enclaves would. Most of the white people, anyone with money, were moving east, into the Sierra Nevadas in these barricaded cities or headed to Texas.

Abdelhadi: It used to be so beautiful.

Liu: What? California?

Abdelhadi: Yeah. Sorry, I didn't mean to interrupt you. I am old enough to remember it though, before the fires, the extinctions, the deadzones.

Liu: Pretty, huh?

Abdelhadi: The prettiest.

Liu: I'm sorry.

Abdelhadi: Thank you.

Liu: The California I saw—well, it wasn't beautiful.

Abdelhadi: [Long pause.] Was there any kind of schooling for you in the camp?

**Liu:** Not really. The elders tried. It was hard to wrangle the kids though, and the elders were constantly being hauled away by the feds to do work. These trucks would show up every day to take them. And you kinda never knew how long they'd be gone or where they were going. I think the camp director—we called him the Warden—just sold their labor to whoever was paying. I tried to help a bit with the school idea initially, I had been into school. But after a few months there I didn't want anything to do with life in the camp.

**Abdelhadi: What kind of work were the elders doing?**

**Liu:** I think it varied. I think a lot of construction to the east in the mountains. The new cities. But they would come back pretty beat up; some people didn't come back. People would come back with big gashes or missing limbs. Dad came home with his hand bandaged one day, and when the bandages came off, he no longer had an index finger. I never asked why.

**Abdelhadi: How long were you in the camps?**

**Liu:** We didn't really count. Maybe five years? I was definitely a teenager by the time we left.

**Abdelhadi: How did you end up leaving?**

**Liu:** Well, there was a series of rebellions within the camps. One day, they went off in the trucks and so many did not come back. Maybe a third? I'm not sure what they had them doing. But, like, everyone lost someone. A couple of my friends lost both parents. They got reassigned to new families—the elders would take them aside and talk to them, tell them their parents weren't coming back, and plug them in with a new family. That seemed to be a turning point.

**Abdelhadi: What happened next?**

**Liu:** The elders started having meetings late at night. There was a buzz, like something was going on. The kids, we were excited about it, but we had no idea what was happening. You know, we were riding the high of it all. Anyway, one day the trucks came and the elders wouldn't get on. The soldiers were never many, but they had guns and batons that they would use whenever anyone talked back to them. They tried to use the sticks to force everyone on, but no one would. So, they left. They came back the next day and there were more of them. They said they would shoot. No one got on. They pulled a couple of people out of the crowd and shot them. I remember my friend, Kuo, this old guy that I liked, he was one of the people shot. Everyone saw it. He was yelling at them after they shot him, and coughing up blood and dying in the dirt, but he was still yelling and pointing and blood everywhere. That did it. The elders got on the trucks. When they came back the next day, they buried the bodies on the outskirts of the camps. They had been left out there all day. We avoided them. I hadn't . . . um . . . I hadn't thought about this in a long time.

**Abdelhadi: Are you okay?**

**Liu:** Yeah. Yeah. Anyway, at first the feds tried to really hone in. They realized they couldn't just let the camps be. They started setting up daily patrols all over the camp to monitor what people were doing, trying to crack down on meetings and stuff. There were more of these ministrikes too. But honestly, they didn't have the manpower to do it, because all the other camps were rising up too. The elders kind of knew that, because I guess they would meet other interred people when they'd be sent out to work. The more the feds pushed, the more opportunities there were to push back. People started killing the patrol soldiers and stashing their weapons to use later. Eventually the soldiers just stopped showing up, but that meant the food stopped showing up too, and what little water we had. So, people started leaving to try to find provisions elsewhere. Our camp kinda split up into a bunch of little roaming clans. My parents dragged me along with them. We stayed with a group of mostly other people from Guangxi, all people who spoke Zhuang like my parents. I remember Kuo's wife was also in our clan, and a couple of the kids from my pack. There was this plan to try to get back to China. Some people had relatives in Shanghai and thought that was our best bet.

**Abdelhadi: Where did you go?**

**Liu:** Well, we ended up going south to the East Bay. San Francisco was almost completely cleared out at that point. Still lots of people in Oakland, but whoever had stayed behind was desperate and scared. We'd sleep in old malls or abandoned farms, look for food, and then keep moving. The longest we stayed anywhere was like a month in this camp on Mount Diablo, in a mixed Chinese/Mexican camp. They were a bit political there and I remember people were not so mean. We stayed until the feds attacked. I feel like that was my only experience during those years feeling anything but hatred for being Chinese. My parents and others talked about leaving all the time, making it back to China. My parents always bought into that, that something would be better at the next place. They needed to believe that, I guess. There were still cargo ships going from LA to Shanghai, and their goal was to make it back to LA to get on one of those ships. That had become a hustle—smuggling Chinese onto those ships. A lot of Chinese people were trying to make it back to China, because we had this idea things were better there. I knew about my family, but I guess it was sort of a thing all over the world.

**Abdelhadi: Did they manage it?**

**Liu:** Yeah. It took a few years, but yeah. It was dicey. Like the feds were the only really organized government left, but the enclaves had these militias and were always rounding up people for forced labor. So, we had to just kind of make our way down by traveling through the deadzones—like the really abandoned areas, places where everything had died and no one knew why—or at least I didn't know why, and I didn't think my parents knew why—places not even the militias would go. We were finding ways to smuggle ourselves undetected, be invisible. Of course, you wanted a big group for safety and to get more resources, but the bigger the group, the easier it was to be hunted down by the feds or the militias. And we had so little information about which towns were live. The cell networks had gone down in California and it was all just gossip, travelers talking with each other, but no one wanted to talk with us. Eventually though, my parents made it happen. They got us to LA and onto one of those ships.

**Abdelhadi: What was the ship like?**

**Liu:** We hid in a box.

**Abdelhadi: Literally?**

**Liu:** Yes. Literally. There were these cargo containers, and one of them was emptied out and made into a little bunker basically. I still don't really know how my parents got us on it.

**Abdelhadi: Were you the only ones in the bunker?**

**Liu:** No. It was packed. There were at least five other families being smuggled. There were these mats spread everywhere and buckets for waste. They had fabbed a little door on the side of the bunker where you could dump the waste out once a day. It got pretty foul in there. And they had these small serrations along the grates for air. But if you weren't paying attention, it looked like any other container being shipped. These ships didn't have a lot of crew and no one went through the cargo units, so once we were loaded and the ship was on its way, it was all about just not attracting any attention to ourselves.

**Abdelhadi: How long did it take to make it to Shanghai?**

**Liu:** Three weeks. Three weeks without sunshine, or a toilet, or air. We had very carefully packed and portioned canned food and stuff for the trip. But we were hungry all the time of course. But yeah, we made it. The container was delivered like any other container with a set of others carrying . . . something or other. I can remember when we climbed out—squinting up at the lights of Shanghai taking up half the sky and the cranes on the dock. [Shakes head and laughs quietly.]

**Abdelhadi: What happened when you got to Shanghai?**

**Liu:** The smugglers kept us because of the debts and ended up selling us to factories in Hangzhou. They said we had to stay there until the debts were paid off.

**Abdelhadi: The debts?**

**Liu:** Yeah, basically you paid for being smuggled by promising to work when you arrived. The deal was two years, but they didn't stick to that.

**Abdelhadi: How could they enforce that? Couldn't your parents just leave?**

**Liu:** No, because they had no money and no papers. The Chinese state wasn't welcoming to the returning refugees. We lived in these factory barracks. They had managed to stay with a few of the people from when we first left the camp. My dad was really sick. He had developed a bad cough during crossing. He never really recovered, just got sicker and sicker.

**Abdelhadi: What was Hangzhou like?**

**Liu:** When we arrived, it was just this boring industrial city. Like the jobs they had us do. It was just horrible and dull and grey. The first factory they placed my family in was soy. I remember we were living in this ground-floor flat with a bunch of other people who worked at this soy factory. I can still smell it. I can't quite picture it, but I can smell it. They put some shit on these soy burgers that made them smell like smoked meat. So, we all smelled like smoked meat. All. The. Time. I hated everywhere we worked. We were there for a few months, and then got relocated to a robotics assembly plant.

**Abdelhadi: You disliked it?**

**Liu:** I hated that work so much. At this point I was basically not on speaking terms with my father, but they were still ordering me around and I'd still do what they asked. It didn't feel like I had anyone else to count on. My job was spraying paint on the casings. I would sneak out a lot. Both around the factory—it was a big place—and in the surrounding city. But eventually I met all these other people like me, teenagers who had grown up abroad and been dragged back to China by scared parents and ended up doing indentured factory labor. Teenagers who spoke English, and we all recognized the same bitterness in each other. We all hated the factories, we all couldn't really relate to our parents, and we were all really struggling to figure out who we were in the world. It was like the kids I used to sneak out of the camp with. I became really close to some of them— Yuhang, Zachery, Xinyi, Kexin. Kexin and I became a pairing. He was from New York, from Flushing actually. We would wander around Hangzhou and break into random buildings, and light fec on fire, and spray graf, and steal food, and whatever to keep ourselves from getting bored.

**Abdelhadi: Was your family still trying to make it to Guangxi?**

**Liu:** Initially. They kept telling me how we would belong there, how good it would be, blah blah. But the rebellions kicked off.

**Abdelhadi: Tell us more about the rebellions.**

**Liu:** Things heated up pretty quickly. This was . . . maybe 2046? The insurrection in Xinjiang was the year before, and there were all these wild rumors about the commune of Changji and how the Uighurs had won and burned down their concentration camps and were actually making communism or some shit. There had been huge strikes through the thirties, but when we arrived it was a bit of a lull in industrial centers like Hangzhou. By my second year there, they had completely kicked off again. At some point, there was a general strike that turned into riots after a bunch of factories shut down. Soldiers came in and quelled it, but things kept popping off in smaller ways after that. Factory owners would go missing or show up decapitated and hung in some public square. There were basically uprisings sector by sector. And it was harder to control those because they were more sporadic and the army wouldn't respond in full force, like when the whole city rose up. The whole city was on constant strike, and there were tons of riots and a lot of chaos. My parents weren't paying attention to any of it, but I soaked up every word I heard about it.

I remember Kexin and I came across this riot of factory workers who were lighting fire to all these abandoned police cars and it was just the fucking best. In the indentured factories, things were quieter, but Kexin convinced me we had to organize people—or at least organize the other kids at our plant—to make trouble. But my parents weren't into me organizing. They said we had to keep working, to earn our right to leave the factory, to get our papers, to regain our citizenship. I wasn't having any of that.

**Abdelhadi: You were organizing the factory?**

**Liu:** I was organizing the kids, the other teenagers, yeah. Initially the olds were trying to make it into this union thing. We went to the managers, and for a minute everyone pretended like it was normal. Like we started getting paid, and the food got better, and families were allowed to live outside the barracks. I think the owners were just scared, really scared. But it didn't last. The robots we were making? At one riot I saw one of our models tear-gassing the crowd, like spewing it in everyone's faces. There was no way I was going to keep making those things. My mom was so upset with me that night, we were screaming at each other.

**Abdelhadi: What did your parents want?**

**Liu:** It was really contradictory. Like they wanted to leave, to make it back to the towns they were from. But the military controlled the countryside, and there was no way they were going to make it without papers. The managers were saying they would get us papers, if we kept working and finished up our terms. But no one ever seemed to finish their term. We would get charged extra times for random infractions. The terms were endless. But they couldn't fucking see that. So, it was all about how we all had to make it back home, but we had to stay there and keep working. It really made no sense. That kind of fight was happening all over the factory, because so many people were in our situation. So many of these families that had made it back to China from terrible situations, and these huge divides between parents who had this fantasy of the old life and kids like me that were ready to burn it all down.

**Abdelhadi: What happened?**

Liu: We burned it down.

**Abdelhadi: The factory?**

Liu: Yeah.

**Abdelhadi: How did it start?**

Liu: No one had been paid in weeks. Everyone was hungry and agitated. There had been an explosion on the line, and two women were killed. . . . I can't remember their names anymore. . . . Damn. After that, people were talking about what to do, and everyone was getting more and more heated. Finally, the decision was made to arm up and go confront the management in the morning. My parents said they didn't want to do that; they were sure that things would get better. There was a big, heated argument. The kids and the parents got in these big shouting matches. I wasn't in the middle of it, and I think my parents still didn't get how strongly I felt about it. Eventually, my parents came in and told me it was time to pack up and go. They felt sure the [Chinese People's Liberation] Ground Force was going to invade the city and kill us all. I said no. "We have to go. Go pack up," they said. I just kept saying, "No, no, no, no."

**Abdelhadi: How did they react?**

Liu: They . . . thought I was a monster. Like their daughter had been slowly taken and replaced by someone they didn't understand. I know they felt that way because that's what my mom yelled at me. She said I was a demon. They had never really heard me when I said I didn't care about making it to Guangxi, that I didn't think there was any reason to think things would be better there, that I always thought we should stay and fight out whatever was going on. So, when I kept saying no, they went into where our stuff was and they packed it all up. Then they came back in and said, "It's time to go." Again, I said, "No." They stayed the night instead of leaving, and in the morning they tried again. Again, I said, "No." They tried to convince me. I was too big at this point for them to force me to come. "Don't you want to go home to Guangxi?" they said. I said, "What home? I've never been there and you're crazy to think that whatever is happening here isn't happening there. You don't even know anyone there anymore." Then they left.

**Abdelhadi: Did you go with them?**

Liu: No, they left without me.

**Abdelhadi: [Long pause.] You were pretty alienated from them by then. [Long pause.] What happened to them?**

Liu: I don't know.

**Abdelhadi: Oh.**

Liu: I never saw them again. We never spoke.

**Abdelhadi: I'm sorry.**

Liu: Yeah.

**Abdelhadi: You didn't have phones?**

Liu: We barely had food.

**Abdelhadi: Right, sorry. So, what did you do?**

**Liu:** I stayed. The confrontation went forward with the manager. Of course, it got really violent. The manager tried to stave us off, but then he gave up the owners' whereabouts. They lived in this gated community, we couldn't get in. They had their own army. We went back to the manager. Dragged him back to the factory, he gave us whatever money was there. But he still didn't, uh, survive. Got knifed. We destroyed all the machines and torched the management offices. Meanwhile the riots were burning down a lot of the city around us.

**Abdelhadi: Were there many other factory occupations?**

**Liu:** Tons of them. All over the city. We went to a couple of assemblies of other occupied factories. But huge divides there too. Like between people who wanted to keep their plants working, a lot of these old workers who had been around forever, some who were proud of their skills or what they made or something, and those of us who thought it was all bullshit. I had been living behind fences in prisons my whole life, and the factory was another fence, another prison. A lot of people had done what we did and destroyed it all.

**Abdelhadi: What happened next at your . . . former factory?**

**Liu:** About half the people who had been living in the factory housing left. The rest of us felt a bit lost. We ended up pairing with this occupied apartment building near the factory. These chaps that lived there had all been working for a company with a few factories that made random shit—hair ties, toys, stuff like that. When the factories were shutting down, instead of splitting apart and going to look for food and jobs all over the place, they stayed together. They had been working on connecting with food depots, farms outside the city, and had a whole plan about how they were going to feed everyone in the Binjiang.

**Abdelhadi: Binjiang?**

**Liu:** Just the area of Hangzhou we were in. An old government name. The robotics factory was in a subdistrict, Xixing. But we spent a lot of time connecting to people all around Binjiang and that's sort of how we were starting to think of ourselves. . . . So, these chaps at the apartment building. We adopted their model, or they taught us how they went about things. They wanted the group to be cohesive, so they also set up meetings to talk shit out and they started thinking through what else they could arrange together. They did a lot of skill sharing—people who had done community gardens started presenting to the group, and they started planting things, thinking through how to do that systematically and all that. At first, mostly people got together for meetings and skill sharing, but then eventually people got together just for fun too, to watch a movie or to read something together. Some of the elders noticed that a lot of the younger folk had really disrupted educations—some people could barely read or write. So miniature schools got set up too, adults would trade off on various jobs.

**Abdelhadi:** What was your role?

**Liu:** At first, I was on cleaning duty. I liked that. I liked getting things clean and ready for everyone. Then with time, I got tired of that, so I switched to food. Then I got bored again and moved to sewing and mending. I think I was always restless. I think living in the camps and then in the factory housing left me with this very deep resentment about work, and it took some time to learn other ways of relating to tasks. It all kinda worked out so that chaps were doing what they wanted to do. It was so different than the factory, but it took a while for that to sink in for me. . . . Like, we knew in the factory we would starve if we didn't work. But now there was no job that no one was unwilling to do. No job was worth more than another. But I had always hated work so much, there was a clash inside me. I bounced around a lot from job to job. I was into carpentry at some point, made some lovely furniture, mostly beds. Then I moved into communications as other communes popped up and we started to build with folks from around the city and even other cities, eventually, once trains were restored.

**Abdelhadi:** Were you—

**Liu:** I still hoped to find my parents. That's why I got into comms. I had this one picture of them from when they were married. Ridiculous of course, because they didn't even look like that anymore when we parted. But I would circulate it, on the off chance.

**Abdelhadi: No luck though, huh?**

**Liu:** Yeah. It's okay. I had family in the commune, the elders, my unit mates, a pairing. But yeah, it makes me sad that we never said good-bye, at least. Slowly, I started grieving my parents.

**Abdelhadi: What did that look like?**

**Liu:** At first, I was just so angry and sulky at the time. I was really mostly by myself. I didn't have anyone to direct this anger at. I was so happy to be with other people when I joined the commune, but I also realized I didn't know how to relate to people, how to share space. I had a lot of conflict. It was always the same pattern, I'd get really close to someone, want to spend all our time together, and then they'd do one small thing that annoyed me or that I felt meant they weren't as committed to me as I was to them. Then I would withdraw completely. Punish them with silence and distance.

**Abdelhadi: Definitely a familiar trauma response!**

**Liu:** Yeah, at some point, one of the elders pulled me aside and said, you need to talk to someone. And I didn't know what they meant. But they said come see me tomorrow morning at the garden. There was a little area with benches under the fruit trees, it was very peaceful there. I met them there, and they said: tell me your story. And I told it. It turned out they'd been reading all these psychoanalysis and psychology books and sort of training themselves to play that role. So, they were a sort of therapist for me, and that's how I got into trauma healing. They also sent me to the meditations. I had never joined any of the meditation groups. But they said it was a must, so I went. Over time, I started to feel better.

**Abdelhadi: I imagine, given how many people had been displaced and how many families had been split apart, that a lot of people were struggling with the same things you were.**

Liu: Absolutely. My growth was connected to some broader changes in the Binjiang Commune. Gradually, we were moving to playing this particular role in the city, like as a . . . refugee center. Very early on, like soon after we destroyed the machines, Xinyi started advocating that the factory be a refuge. It went along with some of the ideas of the chaps in the apartment building, but it went deeper, like it became a spiritual thing for Xinyi. She said we had to welcome everyone, we had to bring together the broken people, we had to care for whoever needed it. We had to be a refuge. We all became really compelled by this idea. A refuge. A safe place where people could come make a home. None of the kids my age, or Xinyi's age, had ever had anything like that. Our parents had always told us it was somewhere else, but Xinyi said we had to build it right there for ourselves.

**Abdelhadi: Were there many refugees?**

Liu: Initially, just hungry workers from around the city. But things were blowing up all over China. It was a full civil war by then. The CCP ended up leveling whole cities, and the hunger crisis was massive. I think nearly a third of the population was displaced at some point of the war. So much accumulated trauma, from the war, the crises leading up to it, everything. A lot of people were like me, completely shut down and angry and reactive to everything. I was growing, healing, and our commune was more and more figuring out how to take care of people too. We took care of who we could, usually hosting about two or three hundred people at a time. A few would stay permanently, but many were with us for a few weeks or months before heading to their home provinces. Eventually, I became part of the individual treatment council for Binjiang. That's what led me to New York.

**Abdelhadi: How so?**

**Liu:** As things were settling down in China, we heard it was getting intense in North America. Our factory, remember, was all these diasporic Chinese, people who had been born elsewhere and moved back and were working in captivity to pay off their debts until the insurrection. A lot of us were born in the US. We started trying to connect to Chinese American communities and ended up having these daily strategy and care conversations with activists in Flushing, Queens. Queens was fragmenting then, this was around 2050 or 2051. The [US] Army was occupying NYC and putting a lot of people in camps. But the Army's presence in Queens was really uneven; they controlled the freeways but had decided the borough wasn't a strategic priority. Queens had become all these different isolated fiefdoms, like every weird little group or community took over a few blocks at a time and set up checkpoints. We heard a lot about it. Most of the activists, organizers, and community leaders from Flushing ended up in a military camp in Flushing Meadows. Lots of people were being detained, interrogated, and released. The neighborhood was filled with people who had spent a few days or a few weeks in the camp. So, it was just an enormous amount of trauma. I decided I wanted to help them in Flushing, more than our daily calls.

**Abdelhadi: What did you do?**

**Liu:** We put together a delegation of trauma healers and assembly facilitators. We found someone still doing flights from Shanghai to New York, and found ourselves packed in with a cargo hold of high-end military electronics bound for US military intelligence. It was a lot more comfortable than my first trip across the Pacific. This time we had a toilet, plenty of food, everyone in their own bed! The pilot smuggled us out of the plane at LaGuardia, and we all made it to Flushing without incident.

**Abdelhadi: Did you arrive before the military pullout?**

**Liu:** A few weeks before, yes! So, everything dramatically opened up at that point. Falasheng had its public debut as a commune and became a leading force in reconnecting neighborhoods in Queens. We set up a trauma recovery center at Falasheng, and the commune soon became a hub of refugee resettlement. The military was losing steadily down south, and then eventually in the Midwest. Thousands of people were fleeing the front lines of the fighting, and hundreds of them ended up spending time in Flushing hosted by the commune there. We brought some of the skills we had learned in Hangzhou, working with displaced people. I'm incredibly proud of the work we are doing.

**Abdelhadi: You said the vision of becoming a refuge was offered by your friend—Xinyi?**

Liu: Yes, she was my age, but I learned so much from her. I really think of her as a hero of the revolution. A lot of my care and healing was done by elders, some really powerful women who also mentored me. But Xinyi really put her ideas of love and care out there, and it transformed our whole district. In a way, I think through her leadership we played an important role in a deeper, longer-term healing of East Asia, and eventually the Mid-Atlantic.

**Abdelhadi: What happened to her?**

Liu: She was killed. In 2048. A Chinese military missile was undetonated in the wreckage of a building, just a couple of blocks from our original factory. She was helping with cleanup and it ended up exploding. She was the only one who was killed. It was really devastating for all of us. We had this huge parade in the district, like thousands of people came out. We ended up naming our refugee center after her. There is a park in Flushing named for her too.

**Abdelhadi: That's beautiful. Thank you so much for this interview. I see we've run out of the time you set aside. Anything else you want to share?**

Liu: Nah, I think this is the most I've talked to anyone about my life since I started therapy. Usually, I'm the listener! It's been a pleasure.

**Abdelhadi: I appreciate you. Thanks.**

# 6: S. ADDAMS ON THE CHURCH FATHERS OF STATEN ISLAND

*Recorded on August 1, 2068, in Staten Island.*

**M. E. O'Brien:** Hello, this is M. E., and today I am talking with S. Addams for the oral history documentation project about the New York Commune. It is August 1, 2068. We are at the teenagers' crèche of the St. George Commune in Staten Island, New York. Hello S.

**S. Addams:** Hello.

**O'Brien:** Are you from Staten Island?

**Addams:** Yes, I've been here my whole life.

**O'Brien:** Oh, wow. You are old enough you must have lived through the fifties, that cult.

**Addams:** That's right. That cult.

**O'Brien:** I hope we get into all that. How about we start with your first memory?

**Addams:** [Pause.] My mother had a blue-and-white plaid apron. She was holding me. We were under a cherry tree. It was blooming. We were in the courtyard of the compound where I grew up. I was looking at the blue sky. She was watching the other kids play, but her arms were around me. She was so soft. It was warm, being held by her. Actually, I think it was a cold day, or cold for the spring. But it was warm being close to her. I felt her breathing. I could see the color of the apron, the sky, I could hear my sisters laughing. I felt . . . I guess I felt safe? I don't know. The pink leaves of the cherry tree were falling gently. I was small. I don't know how old, a toddler I guess. . . . That's a messed-up question.

**O'Brien: It is?**

**Addams:** What if my first memory was something horrible?

**O'Brien: [Pause.] Yeah, I hear you. Tell us about where we are right now.**

**Addams:** Well, first we're in Staten Island. [Laughs.] But more seriously, we are in the teenagers' crèche. This is a cluster of apartments that is part of the larger complex of buildings that make up the St. George Commune. These apartments are so teenagers can get some limited autonomy from adult authority. Teenagers can come here to hang out or even move in here for periods of time. Those who move here are given more independence, but also more responsibility for making sure the place is tolerable, and making sure that everyone is mostly safe. At the very least they are responsible for making sure no one is brutalizing anyone else. The average stay, for those that choose to move here, is about four months. It gets a bit overwhelming for many, that much socializing and, well, disorganization. I'll be frank, it's chaotic here. Currently, the crèche has six residents, and takes up four apartments, which is this entire floor. It gets bigger or smaller depending on how many people are living here. Right now, the kids' thing is gaming. Everyone is probably zonked out on the enormous couch they have next door.

**O'Brien: What is your role?**

**Addams:** I am the adult liaison to the crèche. It's a tricky position. Mostly I try to get the kids to talk to me, at least enough so that I have a decent idea of their mental health. The idea of the crèche, or this one at least, is that kids can find their own limits when given the chance. A lot of kids manage that.

O'Brien: I'm interested in this topic, how kids grow up in the commune, their autonomy, how far that goes.

Addams: Yeah, it's so important. Kids need both support and space to figure things out, and the shape of that space needs to change and grow as the kid grows. For lots of kids in the commune, their primary connections are with their immediate family unit, with all the adults who have opted in as their parents and *bibis* and things. But then also the commune as a whole plays a role in their upbringing. There is usually a lot of fluidity in kids being able to move back and forth between their family's immediate suite or house, and the surrounding community of the commune. Just eating together with the whole commune for three meals a day has a giant impact in expanding the child's social connections from early on. Dozens of people get involved in making sure the kid is coming up okay, that the dynamics with their parents are healthy, and getting involved in teaching and helping the kid in many, many different ways.

But sometimes the dynamics between the immediate parents and the kid really break down, become locked into an antagonism, and that's where we see the crèche come in. We think of the crèche as an alternative to running away completely. The kids can step away from their parental group, find more autonomy, but still be held and supported by the commune. Sometimes kids spin out more while living here, and the relative openness of the environment here is hard for some of them. When that happens, I try to support the kid in finding a better environment.

O'Brien: You sound very thoughtful in thinking through these kids' experiences.

Addams: I used to live here myself. I moved here when I was eighteen. That was—that was ten years ago this month. I was . . . still kind of a kid in some ways, like I hadn't really been able to fully grow up yet. So, the crèche was a bit in between being independent and being able to still be really lost, which was what I needed. I see that with some of the teenagers now, that in-between space that can be really confusing.

O'Brien: Did you grow up in a commune? You described that scene of your mother holding you. It sounds like you felt loved.

Addams: [Pause.] I had a lot of siblings. Nine of them . . . My mother ran the house. It was a big job. Constant cooking, tons of cleaning, taking care of guests, managing the education of my sisters and me. She was working all the time. There were always people around. I was never alone growing up. It was like the commune in that way.

O'Brien: Like the commune? I think I am missing some context. What sort of living arrangement was this?

Addams: I grew up in the compound of the Church Fathers. The— what did you call us?—"that cult." My father was on the elder council . . . You don't know what to ask.

O'Brien: You were describing your household? Saying it was quite busy?

Addams: It wasn't just us kids. My mother would host all these formal dinners for the Church Fathers. She eventually had a staff to help with the cooking and cleaning, but I kind of felt like we were on our own when I was little. My older sisters ended up taking care of us. We all worked a lot. We spent a lot of time together. A lot of my memories growing up were relating to my father as this far-off person that I was in awe of, that I was afraid of, that I loved. But my actual life was generally spending all my time working with my sisters. My brothers started going to church school, but the girls never left the house.

O'Brien: What year were you born? To give us some context.

Addams: I was born in 2040.

O'Brien: And your gender? How do you identify now? How did it fit into that dynamic then?

**Addams:** They treated me as one of the girls. Now I don't have a gender. I didn't then either, but I guess that was a secret.

**O'Brien: Did you have a lot of secrets?**

**Addams:** So many. Our compound was filled with them. Tucked into every nook, in every apron pocket. We all had secrets. I don't think I would have survived without them. [Long pause.] I try to tell people about what the Church Fathers were like. I mean, some things everyone knows. The mass sterilization of nonbelievers. Locking people up in those cages along the ferry platforms, starving them to death, displaying them like trophies, or zoo animals. These people governed through hate and fear. But for those of us in the heart of all of it, there was a whole other life inside the main compound. I know it's hard for people to actually imagine. We had zero contact with the outside world. They would designate three young people, mostly boys, to act as secretaries. They would handle our social media presence, and the correspondence the Church Fathers kept up with other sects elsewhere. But if you weren't a secretary, you were cut off. I never saw a computer screen until I was twelve. Never touched a phone. Another group would handle the warehouse, the shipping out of books and Christian supplies. They had to use computers at work to communicate with customers or to print out shipping labels, but outside of work—no contact. Do you know the history of the Fathers?

**O'Brien: Not in great detail. Would you tell us?**

**Addams:** Well, they took over Staten Island for real in 2053, but the Church Fathers were a thing for two decades before that. Buying property, building out this business selling Christian merchandise internationally. They became the biggest landlord on Staten Island. The church was founded as a breakaway faction from a Pentecostal sect. The big focus was on gender. The world had been consumed by satanic gender ideology, they said. It had destroyed the family, destroyed the nation. The only way back, first to civilization and then to God's Kingdom, was through reimposing the rightful order.

**O'Brien: They sound terrifying.**

**Addams:** Yeah. Okay . . . So, their power grew all through the forties. Staten Island has always been the most conservative borough. The borough president was a sympathizer, a lot of the local cops had joined. I think society was falling apart all across the board, and the Church Fathers offered this vision of stability. With the disease, and hunger, and everything, they very publicly said they could hold things together and they were more or less telling the truth. So, before the takeover they had become the most powerful force in the borough. A lot of the borough's bigger landlords ended up joining, and more and more they had a lockdown on the rental market. They started refusing housing to same-sex couples, or to people on this list of aborters, or to trans people. Landowners and business owners that lived in Staten Island, and some from around the region too, more and more got behind the Fathers as a way of trying to navigate the many crises going down. I didn't know any of these class dynamics at the time, but I tried to study them later. Capitalists took a lot of different strategies in the chaos. Many fled the city or went up in orbitals. Others got behind what was happening here in Staten Island, like to make a fort against the onslaught and chaos of it all.

**O'Brien: Can you tell us about the takeover?**

**Addams:** The Church Fathers were on pretty good terms with the NYPD, which through the forties was pretty much the only force that mattered around here. For a century, Staten Island was where a lot of cops chose to live, because it's more suburban than the rest of New York City. The Fathers always had this vision of theocratic rule and had all these fantasies about taking over Albany or Washington. That didn't really pan out. As things unraveled, they decided they could make do with Staten Island. A lot of the cops were up fighting in the Bronx, but the Fathers had some loyalists in command positions down here. I mean, when they put up that giant cross at the ferry terminal and no one took it down, that was a sign to a lot of people that something had changed. Soon they shut down the bridges and the ferry and later they cut off the Internet. That was around the time the NYPD also went after the Internet, I think. It didn't really work anywhere else, but here on the Island it was all dead. Then the Fathers had this mad creepy recorded message calling every cell phone on the Island, telling people they were now subject to "God's law." They had this paramilitary force run by ex-cops, going house to house. They called it the Brave Sons. Mostly they rounded up gender nonconforming people and same-sex couples. They never told me exactly what happened to them. This stuff ended up in the news, you must have seen it.

**O'Brien: Sounds like a tough scene to be assigned female.**

**Addams:** You could put it that way. . . . Some pretty horrific things happened to women. Especially young women. I don't feel comfortable talking about details. . . . But the whole thing was built around child sexual abuse.

**O'Brien: You definitely don't have to share anything you don't want to.**

**Addams:** I've had so much trauma therapy, you wouldn't believe. . . . It was part of Church Father doctrine, the authority of the Patriarch was absolute. I don't like to get graphic. It doesn't help anyone at this point. But there was so much violence. . . . I've gotten to share exactly what happened to me where I needed to. But I'll tell you that I grew up a tight bundle of rage. . . . While it was happening, while the Fathers were in power, the trauma started—I don't know how to say it—it started taking over our bodies.

**O'Brien: What do you mean?**

**Addams:** Young women in the Church had really unraveled. Before the takeover, there were just a few secrets here or there, you know. Whispers. But there were . . . medical problems. The girls in the Church, a lot of us, dealt with these physical symptoms that couldn't be explained. Girls who experienced paralysis, like me. Girls who stopped talking for months, or years. Like our bodies objected, but we were all still true believers. Like something in us refused, even as we were still loyal.

**O'Brien: Do you know why?**

**Addams:** Why the paralysis or why the loyalty? The paralysis was trauma, I've come to realize. It used to be called hysteria. An intense inner conflict that sometimes takes over the body—the loyalty is harder to make sense of. People saw that things were getting bad everywhere else, and remembered what the pandemic had been like. And like I said, everyone was taken care of in a way. And the sexual violence, the public mutilations of aborters, and the murders I think broke something inside of the young women. . . .

**O'Brien: Why did most people go along with it?**

**Addams:** The Church worked because everything else was collapsing. And they managed to keep people alive when others couldn't. It was a cross-class operation, I guess I'd say. From a bare staying-alive standpoint, many people's lives got better under the Fathers' rule. If you weren't targeted, the Fathers ran better government than what had come before. Their core leadership, including my father, were all major landowners of the NYC area. They ran all these businesses around Staten Island, and a few in Lower Manhattan, that the men would work at. When no one else on the outside had jobs, every man in the Church had work. Every member of the Church had a home. Every member of the Church was cared for. They made sure the residents of Staten Island got enough food and basic medical care. When the famines were so bad everywhere else, we always ate together. In a weird way it was kind of a protocommune. You know, we'd eat together and pray together. So, I guess that's why so many people stayed, both in the Church and others continuing to live in the borough. By the time the torture and stuff really got out of control everyone already felt locked in and with nowhere else to go.

**O'Brien: Were you a believer?**

**Addams:** Oh, definitely. One hundred percent. Even with my secrets. I really believed I was exercising God's divine will to save the world from the consuming demonic fires of communism and feminism. Like that's literally how I would have said it. It made the rage do all sorts of weird fec. Like, I lost motor control over my legs for a year when I was eight and no one knew what caused it. I think it was all my rage, but also wanting to stay a believer. Those two wishes battled it out in my body and I was the casualty. Later I became a secretary, and I was charged with arguing with nonbelievers on Ours.

**O'Brien: Could you say what Ours was?**

**Addams:** Oh, Ours was a big social media platform, just a mainstream commercial thing that grew out of a few prior social media companies merging. We used to proselytize on it. So, I directed all my rage against Church enemies in these trollslam campaigns I would help coordinate ... I had a limp from when my legs were paralyzed. It stayed with me up until I was eighteen or so.

**O'Brien: Church enemies?**

**Addams:** Trans people, mostly.

**O'Brien: Ah.**

**Addams:** Yeah, talk about a mindfuck.

**O'Brien: How did you end up a secretary?**

**Addams:** I don't know. I was really smart. They wouldn't teach the girls anything. I taught myself to read. It wasn't banned so long as we were only reading Church materials. But I asked so many questions and I pieced stuff together really fast. I made my brothers explain to me the theological training they got. I soaked up anything I could get a hold of. Another mother in the compound, her name was Eleanor, had previously been a high school teacher. Like, a public school teacher. Whenever I finished my work, I'd try to go find her and make her tell me stuff.

**O'Brien: What kind of stuff?**

**Addams:** Reading and writing. Typing, but, like, on a typewriter. American history. She was a believer, but she at least knew about slavery and colonization.

**O'Brien: What were the race politics of the Church Fathers?**

**Addams:** They mostly . . . ignored it? Like there were several Latino families and one Black family. We had a lot of connections with similar evangelical communities across Latin America. Their thing was mostly about gender.

**O'Brien: Are you saying they weren't white supremacists? Like, do you know what the experience of the Black family was like?**

**Addams:** Yeah, it was—I guess it was complicated. We railed against what we called racialist and antiwhite versions of American history, so I would never have learned about slavery and such if it wasn't for Eleanor. But also, the Church Fathers spent a lot of time developing pamphlets, vids, and online messaging to circulate in Black Southern evangelical churches and trying to recruit racial minorities. I worked on that as a secretary and was told how important it was to "build inroads" with the minorities. That's the term the Fathers used. But, I think when people showed up—people who weren't white—their actual experiences were not great. I didn't totally understand it when I was growing up. But I think everyone who joined had to remake themselves in the image of the Fathers, and the core of that—at the core of that—it was definitely whiteness, like the values and way of being that the Fathers saw as normal and proper. Even if they never said so. My wife pushed me on this later, we argued about it for a while and she kind of convinced me it was different than I had imagined. . . .

One part of the racial dynamics of the Fathers I actually did think about at the time, because it ended up having a big impact on my work assignments. As the Fathers were coming to power, white liberals, white queers, white feminists, they all got out. They all fled

Staten Island. Black people with more resources got out too. But a lot of the people remaining either shared the general perspective of the Church Fathers, or they were working-class Black people. So, when the violence started against queers and such, a lot of the people in their videos, they were Black people, Black queer people, Black trans people, Black women. I think that kind of stalled out the recruitment efforts I was assigned to. Black evangelicals were kind of turned off by the images we were putting out, so I couldn't really do my job making inroads. So, they reassigned me to trollslam trans people on Ours.

O'Brien: How did you come to doubt it all?

Addams: Arguing on Ours. I've learned since that there was a whole campaign to target me. I had no clue at the time. I found myself in frequent arguments with this girl who kept changing profiles so we couldn't trollslam her. But when we'd start arguing I'd recognize her right away. She was smart, and she had some help. I don't know what she saw in me. But we argued it out, argued about everything. She was a Christian, but a really different kind. Like liberation theology stuff. She knew her stuff, knew the Bible, inside and out. I was appointed to be a secretary in 2055. I was fifteen, I think. I was in the role until the end. So, for those three years I was arguing with her all the time. It was a slow process, but I think she de-indoctrinated me. She certainly helped break open my thinking.

O'Brien: She sounds remarkable. Are you in touch?

Addams: Um. Yeah. We got married.

O'Brien: Was she from Staten Island?

Addams: Yeah, it turns out she was. She got out during the takeover and didn't come back until the Fathers fell. She went to Newark.

O'Brien: That sounds very romantic.

Addams: [Pause.] It's very hard. I am not very good at relationships.

Not very good at being emotionally open. . . . Not very good at having a body. . . . I am glad I have her, but I wish I was better at it all.

**O'Brien: It sounds like you love her.**

Addams: I don't know. I don't—I'm not very good at saying that sort of thing.

**O'Brien: I notice you don't use her name. Can you tell us something you like about her?**

Addams: We live here together, share a room. I always wake up before her. I watch the sunlight come in the windows, and when it hits her face, it is the most beautiful thing I've ever seen. She opens her eyes, and looks at me, and every morning I totally melt inside, and everything feels possible. The sludge worm I always feel in my chest dissolves and I feel sane and have hope for a moment. I feel a bit of that every time she looks at me.

**O'Brien: That is beautiful.**

Addams: [Pause.] Could we talk about something else?

**O'Brien: Sure. I am trying to make sense of the position of women in the Church Fathers. You talked about there being a lot of violence, a lot of fear. But I hear something else too, like, in how you talk about your sisters. Like, there was a care there you kind of miss?**

Addams: Yeah, there was another side to it. Women cared for each other. Like, between siblings and aunties and mothers, there was a lot of love. There was terror and control, definitely, but also a lot of love. For many hours of every day, it was just women in the homes, and people formed very deep and very strong relationships. I think that was a huge part of what got us through. That didn't extend to any sort of solidarity with anyone outside, but it held us together for those of us who were on the inside.

**O'Brien: Do you have an example of that kind of solidarity?**

**Addams:** Like . . . my father would go away for days at a time; he was a liaison with our lobby in DC. Sometimes he would take my older brothers with him, as part of their training. When he would, it would just be my sisters, and my mom, and my aunt, and a couple of younger boys, and it was so lovely. We would clean the house and pray in the morning, then all afternoon we would play these imagination games together, the sisters, but my mother would even join in sometimes. Like, we would pretend to be people on epic quests and roll dice and describe what happened.

**O'Brien: Like Dungeons & Dragons?**

**Addams:** That is Satan worship.

**O'Brien: Oh—Are you joking?**

**Addams:** Kind of . . . I mean, I have played that particular game since—the preteens here love it, especially now that they all have augs—but I can't quite get over the sense that it is wrong.

**O'Brien: Okay.**

**Addams:** Yes, it was like Dungeons & Dragons. Only in biblical or medieval settings. Often set during the crusades. My sib—they were my sister back then—my sib Ezekiel would run the adventures, and all of us would play characters. On the crusades adventures, I would play this Knight Templar. Zeke is such a magnificent storyteller. Back then, he could make the whole room come alive. Or there were other ways we took care of each other. If Father was angry, all the girls would warn each other, and we would all know to be very quiet. Or, if one of the children was punished, Mother held them after so tight, and cared for them, and made sure they recovered, and wouldn't leave their side all night. Or there was just a lot of laughing, like working in the garden together, or washing clothes in the laundry room, or preparing food in the kitchen with my sisters, and we would sing and laugh together. I remember my sister Mary had the most beautiful voice and sung all these old gospel songs that could bring me to tears. There was a lot of beauty, and a lot of love. What everyone remembers are those graphic, horrific images of the torture and cages that the Church Fathers posted on the Internet after the takeover, so it is hard to imagine that behind that there were moments of real love and joy. That love for each other—I think that's part of what made this one incident such a big deal. At the time, I didn't quite get how my sisters and other young women in the compound couldn't identify with all the women in the cages, but really saw themselves in this one girl. Do you know this story?

O'Brien: I'm not sure.

Addams: This one incident really broke it all open. Sexual abuse was a thing—the rule of the father. But this one case was a big crisis point for the Church, and particularly for women. It was videotaped on a servant's smuggled phone and then leaked. So, a bit embarrassing for the Church. It really horrified some people, of course, but exporting horrible imagery was a big part of how the Fathers maintained the fear. The girl died, which hadn't happened before, at least that we know of, and the father ended up being expelled from leadership. I don't know. For some reason we all identified with her, like all the women of the Church didn't see her as this entirely different outside other. Maybe it was also just a breaking point, like a lot of stuff had been building up for a long time. These things are unpredictable. Something in all this just made a lot of women click over into realizing all their rage was actually directed towards the Fathers.

O'Brien: There was a massacre of some sort?

Addams: It was the night of July 31, 2058. . . . Thirty-two of the thirty-nine Church Father elders were murdered.

O'Brien: They were murdered?

**Addams:** Kitchen knives, mostly. Stabbed repeatedly or their throats slit. Two were murdered by guns. Nine were bludgeoned to death. But mostly knives.

**O'Brien: This was done by their daughters? Or their wives? Or outsiders breaking into their houses?**

**Addams:** Not outsiders.

**O'Brien: Not outsiders.**

**Addams:** No. None of the houses were broken into.

**O'Brien: So, their family members. Or servants.**

**Addams:** Mostly not servants. Maybe servants helped in one house.

**O'Brien: That's a lot of built-up rage.**

**Addams:** Yeah.

**O'Brien: This must have been very carefully planned.**

**Addams:** It must have.

**O'Brien: You aren't going to tell me more about it?**

**Addams:** I think it's clear. . . .

**O'Brien: Fair enough. . . . What do you want to talk about?**

**Addams:** It took maybe four hours for it to all come out the next day. Someone got the Internet back on. Everyone was used to these terrible images coming out of Staten Island. And here were the last of them: all the Church elders in blood-soaked beds.

**O'Brien: What happened then?**

**Addams:** It was a mess. A militia came in from Newark to help liberate us, and they ended up in months of shooting with the Brothers. It was supposed to be this moment of liberation, but it wasn't that at all. Or maybe it was liberation, in some sort of way, but it felt awful. Like, everything fell apart. The pandemic even hit Staten Island again that winter. Like, the pandemic had been over for years, but it all came back. It felt like a failure. . . . I regretted it, sometimes. Like, we wanted the new world so badly, but when it finally came it didn't feel like we were able to live in it. . . . It took a couple of years before the Church was finally routed and we started the first commune.

**O'Brien: A militia came in from Newark?**

**Addams:** Women. Women with guns. A militia that called themselves the Ida B. They had been seeing what was going on, and really wanted to get everyone out of those cages. I guess they were well organized in Newark. But that wasn't really enough to sort it all out. Eventually we figured it out, but there was a lot of death, and a lot of confusion, and a lot of doubting if it was worth it or not. . . .

**O'Brien: Could you say more about that? I think people could learn a lot from the experience of trying to rebuild Staten Island after all that.**

**Addams:** [Long pause.] I don't know. I don't think it was the right thing for me to do this interview.

**O'Brien: I'm really sorry to hear that. I see that this is really hard.**

**Addams:** Damn cert.

**O'Brien: We can stop. This isn't meant to be retraumatizing. I know you all went through a lot.**

**Addams:** [Long pause.] Can you explain this book? This thing you are doing?

O'Brien: Sure. Me and another interviewer, my friend and comrade Eman Abdelhadi, are talking to about fifty people. There will be a public archive, hosted by the Mid-Atlantic Free Assembly. All the narrators played some role in helping to found the New York Commune. People share what they want from their own experiences, memories, and thoughts about the struggles since 2052 or so. About twenty interviews will end up in a tablet version of the book. As well, we will select probably about twelve interviews, and do a paper version.

Addams: Are you editing the interviews? Or writing commentary on them?

O'Brien: We might take out when people say "um" or "uh" or something. And we are writing a general introduction about how people talk about the revolution. . . . Do you want to stop the interview?

Addams: No, it's okay. I am feeling a bit better. Not much better. But ask your next question. . . .

O'Brien: So, we got to the part about the militia coming in from Newark. Maybe jumping ahead, a bit? You transitioned, or came out, after that?

Addams: Yeah, I had to look around, but found these body jocks in the Philippines who designed me a custom set of nanos and sent them over on a clipper. It did what I wanted them to do in terms of degendering my body . . . I've had moments of feeling in my body, since then . . . But they are fleeting. It may take time. But I definitely like my body more now.

O'Brien: Did any other people from your former community transition?

Addams: Yeah, a lot of people, in all sorts of directions. We had a lot of catching up to do. Gender was breaking open all over the world; the Fathers were trying to hold it all back.

**O'Brien:** You moved to the teenager crèche at this commune, moved in here?

**Addams:** The teen crèche used to be in a little house down by the water, but yes. I was totally done having parents. I didn't really move here to socialize with the other kids so much. I spent a lot of time alone that first year. Then I found a trauma therapist.

**O'Brien:** And your spouse?

**Addams:** Yes, and my spouse. When the Fathers finally fell she came and found me. She had always used a lot of different stock photos for her different profiles, with widely varying presentations, so I had no idea what she looked like. I had fantasies of course. She wasn't like any of them—We didn't get married until much later . . . We never really figured sex out. I was pretty messed up on that front—Maybe I will at some point. . . . I guess I'm like these kids in the crèche, still trying to figure it out. Listen, I think I need to stop this interview.

**O'Brien:** I understand. Thank you for talking with us today S. Anything else you want to add?

**Addams:** No, I think that should do it. . . . The world has gotten better. . . . But I don't know how to catch up with it. . . . I have a therapist. I'm working on it. But it is very hard.

**O'Brien:** I'm sorry you are struggling S. . . . Can I ask a final question? What's one thing you are looking forward to in the future?

**Addams:** Mars. I'm excited about the Mars colony ship.

**O'Brien:** I hear a lot of people are making the trek to Quito to see the launch.

**Addams:** We are taking one of the trains down to see it.

**O'Brien:** Thanks for talking with me.

**Addams:** Maybe in a couple more years I'll feel ready to tell it all.

**O'Brien: When you are ready.**

# 7: ANIYAH REED ON PACHA AND THE COMMUNIZATION OF SPACE

*Recorded on October 30, 2068, at the Harlem Commune.*

**Eman Abdelhadi:** This is Eman Abdelhadi, conducting an oral history interview with Aniyah Reed for a project on the history of the communes of the Mid-Atlantic Free Assembly. We're here in Grey House, at the Harlem Commune. It is October 30, 2068. Aniyah, thanks for agreeing to speak to me!

**Aniyah Reed:** Yeah, you got it.

**Abdelhadi:** Aniyah—the purpose of this interview is to get to know you and your life story. Let's start with the basics. What year were you born?

**Reed:** 2010.

**Abdelhadi:** And you live here in Harlem?

**Reed:** Yeah, on Powell and the One-Two-Five.

**Abdelhadi:** Oh. At the old Hotel Theresa?

**Reed:** Yeah. Where Malcolm X met—

**Abdelhadi:** Fidel Castro! Yes! That's a lovely building. In another life, a lover gave me a book called, what was it? Oh, I remember: *Radical Tours of New York City*. We walked the Harlem Tour together, including that building.

**Reed:** It's a real special place.

**Abdelhadi:** Wonderful. And how do you spend your time these days?

**Reed:** I am a competitive runner, and I love puzzles. When I'm not doing those things, I work on spacecraft design.

**Abdelhadi:** You're being humble. I hear you're in charge of a whole design council, not just working on it! [Laughs.] I'll ask you more about that later in the interview, but for now let's talk about your childhood. Are you from Harlem?

**Reed:** Actually, I was born out in Jersey. My mom had me when she was sixteen. She moved out of my grannie's house soon after, and we were on our own. It wasn't stable though, we moved around from place to place. My mom had what was then called "bipolar." It was really hard for her to maintain relationships or keep a job, and in those days that meant you had a really, really hard life.

**Abdelhadi:** Definitely. Did you stay with her throughout your childhood?

**Reed:** No. I was with her until I was five or six. At that point, we were living in Georgia. She had people down there and rent was cheaper, so she took us down there, but then we got evicted from the apartment we were at, because her man at the time wasn't paying rent. Anyway, we packed up what we could carry. I remember I had this purple backpack that I loved, and I stuffed it full of my favorite clothes. Anyway, we showed up unannounced at my grannie's apartment, she lived here in Harlem. Of course, she took us in. The next day, my mom said she would go out and look for a job. And . . . she didn't come back.

**Abdelhadi:** Ever? She didn't come back ever?

**Reed:** She came back, every once in a while, kind of sporadically. But she was never really my parent again after that. Sometimes she'd come for a while and say that she was going to take me, that we would get our own place. But no one was going to let her do that, not after she left that first time. No one had really known how bad it was with us. Apparently, when we showed up, it was clear that I hadn't showered in a long time. And when my grandma enrolled me in school, they told her I could barely read. I was way behind where I was supposed to be.

Abdelhadi: So, your main caretaker was your grandmother?

Reed: Yeah, my grannie. It was hard on her, because she had cancer and could barely care for herself. But she tried her best, and my aunt and uncle helped too, they were out here in the city. I'd go to them for weekends sometimes when grannie was in the hospital.

Abdelhadi: I see. When did you start getting interested in science?

Reed: Oh, not 'til way later. I barely hung on in school, I was always a problem child. I was always getting on somebody's nerves or somebody was getting on mine. In retrospect, I think I was really sensitive, and I didn't know how to express that. It felt like anger, and the sense I was always getting abandoned, or everyone was out to get me. But I think about it differently now. If I was growing up nowadays, they would have spent a lot of extra time with me in crèche, given me counseling, special attention, and all that. But back then, it just meant I was often sent home early or got kicked out. I'm sure I would have ended up in prison one day if I had stayed longer, those schools were a gateway to the cell.

Abdelhadi: So, you stopped going at some point?

Reed: My grannie managed to keep me in school until I was fourteen or fifteen. Then yeah, I just stopped showing up. I had a fake ID that I would use to get into clubs and stuff, and I used that to get a job at a restaurant. I started making my own money and just doing my own thing.

Abdelhadi: What was that?

**Reed:** What?

**Abdelhadi: Your own thing? What were you doing?**

**Reed:** At the time? Mostly I just worked. I worked myself into oblivion, and when I wasn't working, I'd find oblivion through other means. I drank a lot. Smoked weed. The usual. Spent a decade that way, in a stupor.

**Abdelhadi: What pulled you out?**

**Reed:** My grannie dying. She passed away in '34. I guess I was twenty-three or twenty-four then. It was after the economy started failing, and the company she worked for folded. She had been working there for thirty years or something, and they went under, went bankrupt. So then, she didn't have health insurance anymore.

**Abdelhadi: Some of our younger readers and listeners might not know what health insurance is—can you explain briefly?**

**Reed:** Insurance was what determined whether you could afford to be sick. If you didn't have insurance, you couldn't go to the doctor. And it was tied to whether you were working. So, your job gave you insurance. No job, no insurance. No insurance, no doctor. She went into relapse, and we couldn't afford treatments. So, she died.

**Abdelhadi: That must have been really hard for you.**

**Reed:** Yes, but I couldn't really react. I just watched it happen. I was too numb at that point, and I couldn't snap out of that. She was dying, but I was the ghost in that house.

**Abdelhadi: What happened when she died?**

**Reed:** I woke up. One day, a month after she died, I was on my way home from work, and I wanted to pick up groceries. And I called her, to ask if she needed anything. And the number was disconnected, obviously. And it was like, I had forgotten that she died? I don't know. I just. I had floated through the rituals, the funeral and all that. I hadn't touched anything of hers since then. We had barely been seeing each other at home, you know, before she died. I barely even saw her. We were living around each other, not with each other. And I had let myself kind of pretend she hadn't died. And when I called, and the number was disconnected, for a full minute I was genuinely confused. I was like, why would she disconnect it? Did she not pay her bill? And then I realized. Oh wait. She's dead. I never get to call her again. She is gone. All the way gone.

Abdelhadi: Wow.

Reed: Yeah. I went home that day, and it was like I was visiting a new place. I walked around the house touching everything, all the artifacts of my life. I realized, I had no idea who I was, what I was living for, anything. I sat there and cried and raged. It was a turning point. I never drank again. I never went back to my job. And that's when the real work began.

Abdelhadi: Which work?

Reed: At that point, it felt like the work was revenge. I was livid. I was fucking angry. Like, I kept asking myself, "Who is responsible for this?" My first answer was the hospital. I kept thinking about how they wouldn't treat her, how she was turned away for not having any money. I remembered her doctor's name, this old lady, Samira Rahman. And I started researching her, obsessively. I figured out that if I called into the hospital and tried to make appointments with her, I could piece together her schedule. And then I started going to the hospital and trying to track her down.

Abdelhadi: What was your plan?

Reed: I didn't have one. It was an obsession.

Abdelhadi: Did you track her down?

**Reed:** I did. I figured out what part of the hospital she worked in, and I found the entrance she used, and I spent a couple of weeks just hanging out outside and watching for her to come in and out. One day, I caught her as she was leaving and I followed her. I walked after her, kept a safe distance so she couldn't see me. And I walked all the way until she reached her home. I saw her enter her building. I was too scared to follow her in, and I didn't know if I could squeeze in after her. But I started watching her building after that.

**Abdelhadi: Was it a big building?**

**Reed:** No. It was small. Anyway, I watched it and watched it for a week or two. And then I started noticing something weird. There were people like her that showed up, people that seemed to live there. They dressed a certain way, a lot of them looked like doctors. They wore scrubs. But then there were others that showed up too, people who looked like they were too poor to live there. Their clothes were tattered, sometimes it seemed like they were unhoused, because they were carrying trash bags with lots of stuff. And I thought—what is this? Why are these people coming here? One day, I just went up to one of them and asked, "Do you live here?" And he said, "Nah, I'm here to see the doc." I asked if it was a hospital or a clinic, he said no. He said that his doctor told him to go there after he could no longer go to the hospital, because he couldn't pay. I asked for his doctor's name. He said Rahman. Dr. Rahman.

**Abdelhadi: Your grandmother's doctor.**

**Reed:** Yup. I was reeling at that point. I felt so stupid. Of course, it wasn't the doctor who had really turned grannie away! It was the hospital! And who was the hospital? It was whoever was making money off it, and those faces were invisible. It was the whole fucking system. I remembered these pamphlets that people would hand out on the subway or on the street or that people would forward to me. Things about how the system was broken, how it was capitalism, etc. I always thought, "I don't have time for this," or "I don't have energy for this." But then I realized, "I don't have time *because* of this. I don't have energy *because* of this." This system had taken everything from me, from us. It had taken my mom, my grannie—even myself. It had even taken *me* away from me.

**Abdelhadi: Yes! How did this epiphany shift you?**

**Reed:** I started going to organizing meetings. There had been all these flyers around my building about facing off against the landlord, because more and more people were losing their jobs. More and more people were getting evicted. That was my entry into politics, a rent strike that eventually ended up in a big shoot-out with the police when the fuckwad landlord sent them. We won that one, but it didn't always go down that way.

**Abdelhadi: How did you go from tenant organizing to spacecraft design?**

**Reed:** [Laughs.] When I got to these organizing spaces, I realized how little I knew. About politics, about the system, about anything really. I started reading, I joined every reading group I could come across. One of them was a radical science-fiction book club. I loved the stories about space the most, but back then space felt so fucking far away. Not just in distance, but conceptually, you know?

**Abdelhadi: Say more. What was going on with space travel at the time?**

**Reed:** It had been privatized. The US government let corporations claim land on the moon and on Mars during the late twenties, and the first semipermanent lunar colony was started a few years later. They did a couple of visits to Mars, but establishing a colony there wasn't profitable enough. Rich people would go up for vacations to the moon. Eventually they set up these orbital residential enclaves for the ultra richies. The scum of Manhattan ended up living in Acadia, a private orbital. The real money was in asteroid mining. Mostly robots, but also, they needed a few people, and it was incredibly dangerous work. When the Levant insurrection took off, some of the ruling-class people from there fled up to their orbital homes. That became a trend.

With the economic crash, most of space tech in North America had been taken over by this one corporation: ExT. They bought out all the government space infrastructure in Texas and Florida. They got a bargain on everything when the debt crisis took off and when the flooding took Florida under. But they didn't operate it for, like, the good of humanity. For them it was a business. Basically, ExT set up space enclaves so the ultrawealthy could run away from the messes they made here on Earth. When Battery Park City started flooding, some of those assholes fled up to their space homes too. To hobnob with the mass murderers that had been kicked out of the Levant, the Andes, China, the Maghreb. Fuckers. Where were we?

**Abdelhadi: We were talking about your growing interest in space travel.**

**Reed:** Right, right. So yeah, it was all privatized. I started reading more about how these programs started. I learned that the technology ExT was using or adapting had all been publicly funded until the twenties. It was all government money—so, like, our money—that had made these space grabs possible. It was enraging. Space was another thing the rich had stolen from us.

**Abdelhadi: Definitely.**

**Reed:** So, I'm reading about all this for a couple of years, and really diving into organizing. In the summer of '36, there was an occupation at Columbia University. Some of my comrades were graduate students there, so we went out to support their rallies, and I met a lot of scholars at that point. One of them, Jay, was an astrophysicist. One time, they asked me if I wanted to get a Frankie at Roti Roll, it was over on Amsterdam. I remember it like it was yesterday. We finished our food, and they decided to get a beer and I had a lassi. They told me to go to school, told me as fucked as the system was, I would learn a lot, and we could use those skills to fuck shit up.

I did a lot of research and ended up doing my GED—which was like a high school equivalence. Then I went to Brooklyn College to study physics. Did that until '41. It was much cheaper than Columbia. I did really well. Turns out I have a brain for math. But I also wanted to know how things worked—I liked the mechanics of things. I applied to engineering for grad school. Jay was still there, they were almost done with their doctorate at that point. They helped me apply, and my mentors at Brooklyn College too. Otherwise, I wouldn't have gotten in. I didn't have the knowhow—it wasn't a system made for poor Black women.

**Abdelhadi: So, did you end up at Columbia?**

**Reed:** Yeah in '41, I had gotten my foot in the door, but the building was about to burn down. [Laughs.]

**Abdelhadi: [Laughs.] By the building you mean academia?**

**Reed:** Yup. It was just a mess. Students and teachers were constantly on strike. At that point, these schools were running out of cash—they had all their investments in the stock market, and that was all in freefall. Students couldn't pay any more. Everything was falling apart. But I learned about engineering and physics, between the chaos. My focus was on mechanical and aerospace engineering.

**Abdelhadi: Hence spacecraft design. Did you start working for that industry when you finished your doctorate?**

**Reed:** Yes and no. Throughout grad school, I had gotten involved with this group of radical scientists from across the city. We called it Born in Flames. Most I met through people in my cohort and program. We even had quite a few professors. We connected with this network of radical scientists and engineers and academics all over the world, a lot of people asking the same questions and really wrestling with answers. That is when I first had contact with this astrophysics program at Quito, before I started working down there. Everyone, Born in Flames, but also all these other people all over the place, we were mad as hell, and we were all staring down the barrel of academia's collapse. Like I said. Burning building. And a lot of us were like, "How do we save the baby from the burning building?"

**Abdelhadi: Who's the baby in this metaphor?**

**Reed:** Science. The collective knowledge of humanity. Not to be dramatic or anything. [Laughs.] We talked a lot about that in a hypothetical sense in this group. What happens when these institutions fail for good? They were facing so many crises, just like the state and every other pillar of that version of society.

**Abdelhadi: That makes a lot of sense.**

**Reed:** Anyway, when I got close to graduating, I was having this existential crisis. Like, what the fuck am I gonna do? Am I gonna just go work for one of these firms helping the ruling class flee? Am I going to stay in this burning building and train another generation who will go help the ruling class flee? What am I doing? So, at the same time, I have this organizing life. And fec is being collectivized left and right. People are fighting their landlords, their bosses, the pigs, the fash. And I realized, well fuck, the whole thing is a burning building. Not just academia, this whole fucking system. And everyone is trying to save their baby. We need to do that too. You know?

**Abdelhadi: What did that mean?**

**Reed:** It meant going from theory to action. It meant we needed to take back what was ours.

**Abdelhadi: Science?**

**Reed:** And space!

**Abdelhadi: Fuck.**

Reed: [Laughs.] Correct. We started doing a lot of research about ExT. We were learning everything about them that we could. We wanted what they were doing, wanted to be a part of it but also to turn it upside down. We were trying to figure out how to get in, how to—well, we were starting to make a plan but didn't have one yet. This was like a council within Born in Flames. So, about ExT: with fighting escalating all over the states they had really tightened up security. They had really intense protocols, usually required employees to live in gated communities so they could monitor them and their activities, there was very intense vetting for any left or insurrectionary politics—

Abdelhadi: So then, was working for them ever really an option for you?

Reed: Yes. A subindustry had developed for faking all your shit to get those types of jobs. Basically, you could pay people to scrub your whole history. But we had a list of former comrades who were working for them, and even a few people who would surreptitiously still communicate with Flames.

Abdelhadi: What did you do with those contacts?

Reed: We schemed. We had a few goals, first we wanted to democratize space tech. At this point, you kind of learned the basics in university, but all the actual technology of space exploration had become private knowledge. We wanted to democratize all that and take that knowledge back. Second, we wanted to reappropriate the actual infrastructure these companies held, both on and off Earth. We wanted to communize space; to make it for everyone. Obviously, that was a longer-term goal, because we understood that this meant war. We wanted to wage that war, but it took preparation.

Abdelhadi: Wow. That's a huge undertaking. So, you all are scheming? What did you do?

**Reed:** We realized a major vulnerability was how centralized ExT had become. They were headquartered in Long Island. Originally, they had been this transnational company, with operations in Latin America and Central Africa. But with the economic crises and then the insurrections they had tightened up, becoming much more US based. All the manufacturing was by bot or 3D printer; most of that happened in a plant in Pennsylvania. At that point, given all the instability with insurrections everywhere, they had consolidated to two portals, where the actual launches would happen. But we knew that if we could take over headquarters and manufacturing, we basically had cut off the snake's head. We could take over the portals from there, they were not heavily manned. That was a ways' out though, first we needed intel. A ton of intel. We focused on building out this huge network of spies infiltrating every aspect of ExT. We were just taking back all their data, all their models, their plans, their everything. We built a huge knowledge base with the information that spies were bringing back.

**Abdelhadi: Ambitious.**

**Reed:** Yeah, the security challenge was here on Earth. The security up there was nonexistent, because it wasn't like anyone could waltz up. There wouldn't be any home invasions, you know what I mean. [Laughs.]

**Abdelhadi: [Laughs.] Right, right.**

**Reed:** So, we needed information on EarthOps: the portals, the launch stations, all of that. And once we had all the intel, we needed an army to take those over.

**Abdelhadi: But then the government would step in—the actual [US] Army, the police.**

**Reed:** Exactly. We had to wait 'til we knew we were strong enough to overtake their private security, and we knew that the Army wasn't strong enough to step in. That opportunity came when things went to hell in Iran. The Army was getting weaker and weaker, and as the crises increased, we knew our time was coming soon.

**Abdelhadi: Wait, when you say you were strong enough to overtake their security—do you mean militarily?**

Reed: Yup. Like I said, we knew this would eventually need to be a war. Comrades in Born in Flames started working with some of the insurrectionary militias that had been building across the city to fight the pigs and the fash. Most of us were training with the Zetkinistas in particular. When the time came, we already had battle plans laid out for Long Island.

**Abdelhadi: When was the actual battle?**

Reed: May 15, 2051. By then, Army presence in New York had really thinned—they pulled out the next year. The Zetkinistas let us know that the Lilies—a militia out of the Bronx—were planning a strike on an Army camp that day. So, we knew they would be distracted and wouldn't be able to send out reinforcements.

**Abdelhadi: Were you there?**

Reed: Of course.

**Abdelhadi: Can you describe what happened?**

Reed: Basically, half the battalion and a lot of weapons were snuck in over a few days leading up to the strike. And the rest of us showed up that day to the gate, held the guards at gunpoint and demanded they let us into the perimeter. There were at least fifty of us coming in, and at least thirty inside throughout the facility. We knew they would trip an alarm for lockdown, of course, but our people inside knew what to do. The point was to draw out as much of the security forces to face us as possible, so that the people inside would have enough time to commandeer the servers and take full control over the building. We had people stationed near each of the main command access points to sabotage their security protocols. You should have seen it. We had a contingency for every single facet of it, years' worth of research finally coming into fruition. It was fucking beautiful. And you know, the thing is, these guards. They were not going to take bullets for this fec, they weren't the ones going up to space, they were just doing their jobs. Once we had everyone surrounded and it was clear there was no getaway, most of them surrendered their arms. We only lost a few people on both sides.

**Abdelhadi: What about the plant in Pennsylvania?**

**Reed:** Most of it was operated remotely from Long Island, so we shut down operations remotely. We sent messages to the workers there that it was time to go. We gave people a couple of days and then we sent a team there to finalize the takeover. It was similar with the portals.

**Abdelhadi: So, did you then send folks to the colonies?**

**Reed:** No. We sent nothing.

**Abdelhadi: Say more.**

**Reed:** There was a lot of debate, you know, about what we would do. Debates ended up spilling way beyond Born in Flames, like it became this huge thing in the assemblies, and everyone was arguing about it. We liked that, everyone having an opinion, because it was also a way for people to start thinking about the future of space travel and all. So, the arguments were raging: would we send people up to take over? We had been researching the physics of weaponry in space. We knew they weren't armed, but there are a whole lot of ways people in space can kill each other. And we didn't know what we would do with the people up there. They relied on regular supply shipments from Earth—our calculations suggested they probably had food that could last up to a year. There was no AeroAg yet, you know, that technology was still in the making. They also relied on support from programmers and techs here for troubleshooting and glitches, to keep their cleaning and entertainment bots running and so on. So, the decision that we made was to not send any more food up. Or any tech support. We cut off all communications.

**Abdelhadi: Did you tell them you were doing this?**

**Reed:** Yes. We broadcast messages to the colonies letting them know that EarthOps had been reappropriated by the people, and that no more resources would be sent up to them.

**Abdelhadi: Could they respond?**

**Reed:** We didn't take incoming messages. [Long pause.] Listen, these people were actual mass murderers. Tyrants that had been literally run off Earth because of their crimes. Others were causing the suffering of hundreds of thousands more by hoarding resources that belonged to all of us. And the only reason they weren't on the ground is because they had hired out guns to get us all under control for them. Their parents and grandparents had destroyed our planet, and their children had fled. All of them were inheritors of destruction. Some of them managed to crash-land on some ocean with their little orbital pods, and we rounded up those we could find. The rest. . . . Well, they made their choices, and I'm glad they are gone.

**Abdelhadi: Their violence was met with violence. I understand. It is still hard to stomach.**

**Reed:** Yeah. It wasn't easy. Of course. Not at all. We were all pretty fucked up about it. It's hard to kill, even when you have to.

**Abdelhadi: What did you do next?**

**Reed:** There was so much to do. Research about how to make the technology better and move it forward, and ultimately how to communize space. One thing we figured out was that space travel could be less resource-intensive, more accessible. ExT had held a lot of that technology under wraps, because they wanted this to be expensive. They wanted to make sure that only the ultrawealthy could access it—because it was part of the selling point of the colonies, that they would only have ruling-class people. They wouldn't even let up servants, they were so nervous about the possibility of insurrection. They automated everything and ran tech remotely. With the takeover, we reestablished the old network, and started these international research collaboratives. Pretty quickly, we got excited about this idea of the space elevator in Quito.

**Abdelhadi: You must travel to Quito often.**

Reed: Definitely. I was very involved in helping with the design of the elevator, but my real passion was in spacecraft. I spent six months in orbit helping to build the shipyards in Pacha, and now, as you said, I coordinate the design council for new craft. The launch for Mars is only three weeks away. I leave tomorrow and won't be back in New York for a few months. This one isn't just a small expedition or a tiny group of cosmonauts, but a full commune ship: two hundred and sixteen people. They are finishing up the Puriy, the Mars commune ship, at the Pacha shipyards. In a couple of weeks, the rockets to take the residents up will start to lift off. A lot of people are visiting Quito for that week, to see the launch.

**Abdelhadi: Everyone is very excited about it. Let's take a step back and talk about how you ended up there. I feel like we just rushed through from '51 to the upcoming launch. What happened in the interim?**

Reed: After the takeover, we had ExT's infrastructure, but we didn't have access to the flow of goods and energy necessary to actually fully run operations anymore. We had one exploratory mission in '54— that was the first major global collaboration—just to see what had happened with the existing infrastructure from the old colonies. We brought back reports to Born in Flames, and we got to work on a long-term plan. Our crew was talking through this all with the communes that were springing up around New York, and later with the Free

Assembly. But everyone else was doing this in their lands, like trying to hash out a collective vision for space. It's still an ongoing conversation.

**Abdelhadi: Where were people leaning at that time? Or what were they focusing on?**

**Reed:** The initial priorities were reestablishing the moon residences and repairing and rebuilding the satellite infrastructure. Asteroid mining was very controversial—people who had been involved had some very bad memories—but eventually we decided we would get that going again.

The first really big idea, the thing that we slowly started to get consensus around, was the way to make space accessible: it was to build a space elevator. The people in Quito had the beginnings of some plans, ExT had shelved a research unit on it but had some great data. The CNSA, the last actual public space agency in the world, had gone rogue during the civil war in China and was very eager to collaborate. It was decided that the elevator was the way we were going to make space accessible to people. Using some of what we found when we completely took over, we started serious designs.

**Abdelhadi: Can you explain the space elevator?**

**Reed:** Um . . . there is a lot of new coverage about it. I feel like every six-year-old knows what it is. Perhaps, *especially* every six-year-old. But sure. We have started construction already, and it should be done within a decade. It will be a permanent structure, linking a geostationary orbital platform to the Earth's surface. It had to be built on the Equator, and our friends in Quito were very eager to be point. It will be the biggest structure humans have ever made. It took years of debate to decide if it was worth the resources of constructing it. The idea is, instead of launching rockets or components, they can be hauled up on the elevator's main platform. There will be channels for pods in the interior of the structure, used for smaller scale items like people. Once the construction is complete, the resources and energy to transport back and forth will be a tiny fraction of what is required for rockets. The orbital platform above Quito is already completed, or at least fully functional. It is called Pacha. Already, all our space-craft manufacturing takes place in orbit, at the shipyards of Pacha. When the elevator is complete, anyone will be able to visit, not the months-long wait lists we have now.

**Abdelhadi: What is Pacha like?**

Reed: It's . . . it is the most earnest place you will ever visit. Like every-one there is so passionate, and so dedicated, and so hard working. It is like the passion of humanity crystalized into fifty structures tied together with tubes and struts. It is like a giant, magnificent, lopsided snowflake. Lots of visitors are artists and scientists. Lots of people are on their way to the lunar commune, or the asteroid belt, or one of the orbital communes. It is really profoundly moving for people to just look down on Earth, the first time they make it up. Getting back and forth is hard, admittedly, because we are still using rockets. But the elevator will turn Pacha into a city anyone can visit.

**Abdelhadi: You've talked mostly in "we" form, and I'm curious what you yourself are focused on these days. I know you primarily work on spacecraft design. What else?**

Reed: Yeah, that's my main team. I also do a lot of public-facing stuff in communicating what Born in Flames is doing with the communes and making sure we have oversight from the Free Assembly. I do a lot of teaching and training too. None of us wept over academia's grave, but we have been thinking over the past twenty years about how we maintain knowledge production outside of that system. How do we make sure we are still discovering? Creating? How do we systematize those things? Turns out, so much of what we thought was supporting us was holding us back. There's no shortage of interest in science, it was just a matter of creating new ways of training the next generation, of communicating between scientists, of sharing resources—those are all the things the commune is about.

**Abdelhadi: Indeed. Well, I've taken up enough of your time, thank you.**

**Reed:** I hope you'll come to Pacha one day.

**Abdelhadi: [Laughs.] I'm too old to leave Earth! But I wish you the best of luck and appreciate the work you're doing.**

**Reed:** Thank you.

# 8: CONNOR STEPHENS ON THE FALL OF COLORADO SPRINGS

*Recorded on December 20, 2068, in Harlem.*

**M. E. O'Brien:** Hello, this is O'Brien. I will be having a conversation with Connor Stephens for an oral history project focusing on the history of the New York Commune. It is . . . December 20, 2068. We are at the Riverside Commune in Harlem, in Connor's apartment. We are on the twelfth floor of a twenty-three-story building, with a gorgeous view of Riverside Park and the Hudson River. It is night, and we can see the lights from a dance barge docked on the far side of the river.

**Stephens:** We are at my daughter's apartment. I live next door. Where did you get that jacket? [Gestures to a brown construction-style jacket O'Brien is wearing.]

**O'Brien:** My jacket? Um . . . I believe my sister Nadia gave it to me—I'm not aware of anything special about my jacket. Are you okay, Mr. Stephens? You seem agitated.

**Stephens:** Your sister? No . . . no, it's fine. I'll be okay.

**O'Brien:** Alright. Well, we are at Mr. Stephens' daughter's apartment. Can you tell me about growing up?

**Stephens:** I was born January 19, 2025, on the Wind River Reservation. My mother is Northern Arapaho. She grew up in Casper before moving to Wind River. My father is Zapotec, from Oaxaca. I had two sisters and a two-spirit sib. My sisters are Fast River Stephens and June Stephens. My sib's name is Trib. I attended high school at Arapahoe in Centennial. I then went to community college in Riverton. You're wearing her jacket.

O'Brien: Whose jacket? . . .  Mr. Stephens? My jacket is like someone else's jacket? I don't really understand.

Stephens: That's Fast River's jacket.

O'Brien: [Long pause.] I am worried you aren't entirely with me in the room, at the moment, Mr. Stephens. Are you sure you want to continue the interview?

Stephens: [Pause.] I'll be fine. Let's keep going.

O'Brien: How did your parents meet?

Stephens: I think at a show in Casper. My dad was in a speedcore band from DF—Mexico City. My parents never married, and there was a lot of strife in my mom's family about it. They didn't really like my dad. So, we have my mom's family name. My dad went back and forth between Oaxaca, the District, and my mom's home on the reservation while I was growing up. Some summers we would go stay with him, and once when I was thirteen, I was a roadie with his band. My family was a bit—odd. Like Fast River was into all these kinds of music scenes in Mexico that no one on the rez knew anything about it. . . .

O'Brien: What was your family like?

Stephens: A lot of . . . a lot of love. My mother was very political. The groundwater on the reservation was contaminated. People were getting sick. She worked with other people to stop it. They shut down a pipeline. My dad didn't talk much, but he taught me lots of things, like how to do things with my hands and play guitar and ride a motorcycle and fix a generator. My sisters were older than me. Fast River got in fights all the time. She would beat down anyone who hassled our family. I think I was closest to her. She disappeared.

O'Brien: What happened?

**Stephens:** I was maybe twelve. We eventually figured out she had joined the [US] Army somehow. She was over in Iran. And I . . . well, I . . . I don't know. . . .

**O'Brien: I encourage you to elaborate on anything you would like, and you don't have to say anything about anything you don't want to talk about. This is a chance for you to tell your story on your own terms. The questions I ask are just to encourage you to share what comes to mind for you.**

**Stephens:** Thanks . . . thanks.

**O'Brien: Do you want to say anything about your other siblings?**

**Stephens:** June was quiet. She was really into school. She wrote a lot. She loved books. She was really into fantasy novels. She was writing fan fiction, I think, all in this portal world of books she liked. She was writing all the time.

**O'Brien: And . . . Trib?**

**Stephens:** Trib got into spiritual practices. They got close to granddad, to my mom's dad, and got him back into powwows after he had a bad period. They also got June into it. Trib would convince granddad to drive them to powwows all over the Great Sioux. I think Trib and granddad really connected over it. . . . My mother taught me to fight, to be a defender. A warrior. Fast River taught me how to throw a punch and shoot, and then mom taught me about the deeper parts of being a defender.

**O'Brien: What is a defender?**

**Stephens:** I don't want to get into it. . . . It was—I don't know how to say it to you. I guess the easiest way to talk about it is the water. Mom cared so much about the water, about fighting for the water, and knew it was a war for the water. Like a war against the land, and we had to be the land's defender. That's not all of it, but it's the piece easiest to talk about . . . She told me early that we would all be a part of that war. I don't think you would get it. . . .

O'Brien: Should I ask a different question? . . . . Do you want to share more about your childhood?

Stephens: No ma'am.

O'Brien: Michelle, you can call me Michelle—It feels like maybe I need to just ask a lot of questions?

Stephens: If you'd like.

O'Brien: Do you have any feelings about doing this interview?

Stephens: [Pause.] We have an oral history project at Wind River. Not a settler project—I haven't done an interview there, but I know my mom did, and Trib, and June. There is a lot about my mom's organizing. I try not to speak for other people too much, particularly when they are so good at speaking for themselves. My whole family has a lot to say. People should listen to those stories. [Long pause.] I helped my mom out with her organizing all through high school.

O'Brien: Like what is an example of what you did?

Stephens: At Arapahoe High School I helped lead a group that joined in the fights against pipelines and drilling. Then I went to Iran.

O'Brien: In the Army?

Stephens: Yeah, I joined the Army and went to Iran. But things were hot in high school.

O'Brien: Okay, let's separate those a bit. How old were you when you joined the Army?

**Stephens:** Seventeen.

**O'Brien: So before then, when you were in high school, what was happening? Hot around pipeline struggles?**

**Stephens:** When I was growing up those guys were getting much bolder. Taking over Gillette. Then setting up the camp in Thunder Basin.

**O'Brien: Those guys? Do you mean fascists, white supremacist groups?**

**Stephens:** Yeah, those guys.

**O'Brien: Sorry I am not quite tracking. What groups were active?**

**Stephens:** Wyoming Liberty. New Nation. Christian Freedom. We didn't let any of them come out our way. Once they tried to do a rally in Riverton and we had a shootout over it.

**O'Brien: They had a big camp in Eastern Wyoming for a while, right? They set up a military base in Thunder Basin Grassland?**

**Stephens:** I did some recon out there. A whole fleet of buzzards and stalkers. I felt some envy looking at those.

**O'Brien: Buzzards?**

**Stephens:** You could see the buzzards all lined up on the one road, their wings folded in the moonlight. With their mod houses and this fence, it must have been ten meters high. Like the Green Zone.

**O'Brien: Buzzards are . . . drones? Plancs?**

**Stephens:** Sure. The crew at Thunder Basin were all a bunch of burn-out soldier boys. Guess I was too.

**O'Brien: Was that when you were in high school?**

**Stephens:** No, after I came back from Iran.

**O'Brien: It was like the Green Zone in Iran? . . . This is a bit jumbled. How did the Wyoming Liberty Party come to power in the state?**

**Stephens:** The militias shot up the voting stations in 2050. Liberty rolled in and took over Cheyenne.

**O'Brien: The state government? Fascists took over the Wyoming state government in 2050 after disrupting the election?**

**Stephens:** Yeah. The National Guard was split and shooting it out with each other for a day or two, but it was over quick. It was a lot of chaos. This all had been building through the forties.

**O'Brien: I feel a little confused. I think we keep getting out of order.**

**Stephens:** Everything is out of order.

**O'Brien: What caused the fascist insurgency you are describing? Like . . . where did they get their resources?**

**Stephens:** Mining corps. The pipeline oil guys. A bunch of ranchers. So many guns. A lot of settlers so fucked up from being in Iran. They needed something they could control. The feds were so distracted, and everything was falling apart. All the pieces were there.

**O'Brien: How did you—activists at Wind River—respond to the fascist takeover of Cheyenne?**

**Stephens:** We took it as a chance to expand, going northwest. We took over everything within an hour's drive.

O'Brien: "We" being the tribal government?

Stephens: Not quite. A lot had been shaken up, turned upside down. "We" being the [Wind River] Defense Forces. Some fighting along Highway 191, but mostly it was also quick. People had been having a hard time in the forties. We made sure people got healthcare and food, which was a lot more than anything coming out of Cheyenne or Thunder Basin. That was good enough. So, a lot of settlers stayed and adapted to Wind River being in charge.

O'Brien: You are referring to the white people living in northwest Wyoming when Wind River expanded?

Stephens: Yeah.

O'Brien: West and north. Those were national parks? The Grand Tetons? Yellowstone? You all took over what had been the national parks in northwest Wyoming?

Stephens: Guess so. They had been closed for years.

O'Brien: Were you going to school at this point?

Stephens: No, I was done up by then.

O'Brien: I am sorry. What year were you born?

Stephens: 2026.

O'Brien: I thought you said 2025? . . . So, you went to Iran in . . . 2043.

Stephens: Sounds right.

O'Brien: And the fascist insurgency escalated in 2050. So, you were in high school, fascists started organizing, you were fighting pipelines. Then you went to Iran in 2043, fought in the war. When you got back you joined a reservation militia of some sort, and the fascist insurgency escalated, and a civil war started between the feds and Wyoming Liberty. And your militia, the Defense Forces of Wind River? Took the opportunity to expand the reservation to include what had been national parks? Did I get all this right?

Stephens: Sure. I wouldn't call us a militia.

O'Brien: You were fighting for Wind River? For "the Defense Forces" you called them?

Stephens: Yeah, I was an officer. I liked the chaos of it. Of the fighting. I always got along well with the chaos. We started the Defense Forces as kids started coming back from Iran, and as things were blowing up with those guys and the feds.

O'Brien: How many fighters in the Defense Forces?

Stephens: Maybe two hundred. We had all been in Iran. We all knew a thing or two. I was a munitions specialist in the war.

O'Brien: Maybe we should back up and talk about your time in Iran. You mentioned that briefly.

Stephens: Okay.

O'Brien: What was serving in Iran like?

Stephens: It was such a shitshow.

O'Brien: Can you share more about that?

Stephens: What do you want to know?

O'Brien: Why did you join the Army?

**Stephens:** I was a warrior.

**O'Brien:** But why the Army?

**Stephens:** I wanted to learn how to fight. I knew how to use a gun and all, but I wanted to learn discipline and self-control, and how wars are won. I thought it might be useful to bring those skills back.

**O'Brien:** This was . . . before the draft?

**Stephens:** I was pretty sure the draft was coming, and I wanted to get in before that, to have some control over where I ended up.

**O'Brien:** Did you have any say on what you ended up doing?

**Stephens:** Fuck no. Initially, they put me on as an assist for enhanced interrogations. We had this prison camp outside of Mashhad. I would drag prisoners into the room, drag them out.

**O'Brien:** Sounds bad.

**Stephens:** I hated it. I felt like my hatred was just eating me up inside all the time, like it all infected my dreams, that place.

**O'Brien:** The United States was losing at this point?

**Stephens:** Badly. The US was never not losing. But it had gotten worse. Eventually I got reassigned out of interrogations.

**O'Brien:** What did you do next?

**Stephens:** I got assigned in the field to dealing with landmines and drones. . . . The US fucked that country up bad.

**O'Brien:** How so? Could you say more about that?

**Stephens:** That was the year they nuked Tehran and Mashhad.

**O'Brien: 2045?**

**Stephens:** I was in the desert … When the Russians pulled out, some of the guys I was fighting with thought it would be an easy win, but at that point it just all collapsed.

**O'Brien: What happened?**

**Stephens:** The 'mericans had already poisoned the water in the major cities, defoliated the whole northeast, so it was just these huge caravans of refugees trying to flee. Bomb strikes raining down on them. Watching that fucked me up …

**O'Brien: They were bombing refugees? The US Air Force?**

**Stephens:** What that fucking empire did to that country no one should ever forget.

**O'Brien: The US defoliated northeast Iran? The area under US control?**

**Stephens:** Yeah, control was the running joke.

**O'Brien: Where were you based?**

**Stephens:** My unit was in the desert, Dasht-e Kavir.

**O'Brien: Were you close to anyone?**

**Stephens:** I had this friend, Ridge, he was an intel man with my unit. He came from Cali, from the Balagoons, and he was smart as fuck, like Fast River.

**O'Brien: It sounds like you liked him.**

**Stephens:** Ridge would talk about how the 'ranians were fighting, the guerilla strategies in the occupied cities, the strike waves, the refugee mutual aid, the local subcontractors teaming up with the insubordinate 'merican units, about how people lived in the desert . . . I learned more from hearing how the 'ranian guerrillas fought than anything the US did.

**O'Brien: I notice you have more to say when talking about—about people you liked. Is there more you can say about Ridge?**

**Stephens:** Ridge loved it, like loved the people we were fighting, the desert we were in, the land. Reminded me of how granddad talked about the land. I learned a lot from Ridge, about thinking strategically, thinking tactically.

**O'Brien: What was your job?**

**Stephens:** I was jacked up with auggie bugs and on a bomb squad. I would spot and take apart landmines and ground drones.

**O'Brien: You are referring to augmented reality implants.**

**Stephens:** Yeah.

**O'Brien: Did all the vets in the Defense Forces have them?**

**Stephens:** Most of us, yeah. Privates got them, no one else generally, 'cause of the mind fragging. Sometimes specialists.

**O'Brien: Do you still have them?**

**Stephens:** You can't take that shit out. And you can't really turn it off.

**O'Brien: Does it still affect you, having the implants?**

**Stephens:** Makes everything all wonky. I'm used to it, have been for a long time. But I forget that other people can't see what I see, the overlays everywhere I look. Reality is not the same for me.

**O'Brien: How do you think the war in Iran shaped the politics you saw around Wyoming?**

**Stephens:** It's what sent everything past the point of no return. Everyone came back knowing it was rotten. Like the Liberty boys realized they had to start the whole settler show over again if they wanted it to work.

**O'Brien: The fascists had become oppositional to the US government?**

**Stephens:** They hated 'merica as much as I did by the end. Losing that war meant there was no way the settlers could hold it together here.

**O'Brien: So, back to the fascist takeover of Wyoming.**

**Stephens:** Yeah. Fed boys and Liberty boys were at each other's throats. We talked to people all over—Great Sioux, Apacheland, Uteland. So we knew a lot about what was going on. Did a lot of recon.

**O'Brien: White fascists?**

**Stephens:** You have a lot of questions. Sure.

**O'Brien: I'm sorry. I am a bit disoriented, and just trying to piece everything together.**

**Stephens:** The world was upside down . . .

**O'Brien: Okay, yeah. What started the civil war?**

**Stephens:** New Nation took a Minutemen facility north of Fargo.

**O'Brien:** These were fascists seizing a nuclear weapons facility?

**Stephens:** Yeah. The feds got all worked up about that. It blew the whole thing wide open.

**O'Brien:** Blew open—but there wasn't a nuclear detonation?

**Stephens:** No, just the civil war.

**O'Brien:** So, the US Army was fighting fascists? Is that right? I feel myself getting confused.

**Stephens:** Lots of players in the field. We mostly stayed out of it. Wasicu versus wasicu. The regime out of Cheyenne crumbled pretty fast. They just kept fighting it out. It was messy.

**O'Brien:** What happened to Cheyenne?

**Stephens:** Water went out and it was like Zabol all over again, like, these caravans of refugees pouring out of the city, everyone loaded onto pickup trucks and hauling everything in these trailers, and so much fear and exhaustion on their faces. Reminded me of Iran.

**O'Brien:** Where did they go?

**Stephens:** Some went north and were detained or drafted by the Thunder Basin boys. Most headed south to Denver. Those who came our way we made sure they got the basics. We were focused elsewhere.

**O'Brien:** What were you all focused on?

**Stephens:** Defending the rez, mostly. But we also had a unit that took out all the active oil drilling and pipelines.

O'Brien: The pipelines were still operating?

Stephens: Oil boys were big players. That was a part of the fash's base, and we knew that, the pipeline companies.

O'Brien: How did you get involved in the [North American Liberation] Front?

Stephens: No Front at that point. Just Fast River talking to people. And a few others like her.

O'Brien: Who was she talking to?

Stephens: The chaps from the prisons out West, the stuff down south.

O'Brien: That is the Balagoons? Like the group Ridge was a part of—they formed around the prison breaks in California? And the New Afrikaan People's Party in Alabama and Mississippi?

Stephens: Yeah, those groups. But she talked to anyone who was fighting and seemed to care about the land. So, it was a network. Like people talking to each other.

O'Brien: Was Ridge a part of that network?

Stephens: Ridge died in Kavir. But I knew some of his people, and made sure Fast River met them.

O'Brien: It was the beginning of what later would become the North American Liberation Front?

Stephens: That's right.

O'Brien: What did you think of communization at this point? Of communist and socialist currents?

Stephens: I didn't know what that meant. Learned later. But we had been arguing about land a lot among the Eastern Shoshone. A lot of Nations were. We knew our time was coming, that landback was happening.

O'Brien: What was landback?

Stephens: Oh, like a slogan and a vision. Land doesn't belong to the settlers.

O'Brien: And the meaning of that changed with the insurrection?

Stephens: When America was collapsing, a lot of the militants at reservations prepared for landback. But how to relate to the land was the question, like what Fast River called "a fundamental political question."

O'Brien: Could you say more about that? The debates over land control and sovereignty were a big thing in the sixties, but I think a lot of people in New York don't know much about it.

Stephens: We couldn't keep up the settler game, or our impersonation of it that a lot of tribal governments had been running. We had lost our way, and people were waking up to that. So, opening onto a way of relating to the land that was collective, respectful, about the needs of everything and everyone. These were Fast River's words. She was good with words.

O'Brien: How did Fast River relate to these debates?

Stephens: Yeah, she saw it all. She saw how it all fit together. These new visions of working with the land. And then this communization movement in the cities. She saw how they were connected, how they could be the same thing. I would sit with her when she'd do these long mediations between the Balagoons and the elders. They talked and talked and talked.

**O'Brien:** Wind River eventually joined the North American Liberation Front [NALF]?

**Stephens:** Yeah. I was a Second Lieutenant. Served with Fast River.

**O'Brien:** What year was that?

**Stephens:** 2061, maybe?

**O'Brien:** Can you tell us more about Fast River?

**Stephens:** She lived like her stomach was on fire, like it could explode out of her at any moment. She was all fucked up coming back from Iran—I guess we all were. She didn't enhance, but everyone thought she did. She didn't really sleep much. You could see the fire in her when she would talk, like it was coming up through her throat and out her eyes. She would grab eyeballs with anyone, would be totally focused on whatever they were saying.

**O'Brien:** She sounds amazing.

**Stephens:** She was one of the first ones I met—that anyone I know met—who thought the early communes and the insurrections and the Native struggles could fit together into something that could remake the world. That's her jacket. You have her jacket.

**O'Brien:** She was a military strategist of sorts? Or you both were?

**Stephens:** The communes would never have had a chance if they had gone up against the Army.

**O'Brien:** What enabled them—you all—to win?

**Stephens:** The US was dead. They had lost in Iran. Then all through the fifties they were bogged down in the Rockies and Great Plains and just bleeding dry.

O'Brien: The US Army was fighting the fascist take over? I feel like we just talked about this, but I still don't quite understand. We are talking in circles.

Stephens: Yeah, we kept a low profile. Just talking with each other, taking land when they were distracted. It wasn't until the US bled out completely that NALF stepped up to end it.

O'Brien: You are referring to the last three years of the war? 2062 to 2065?

Stephens: Yeah. We had to take out the wasicu for good. In the war all the Nations had taken back most of the region. But they were holding fast in what they called Colorado.

O'Brien: Who was? The fascists? The feds?

Stephens: Oh, yeah, those guys. The feds were pretty much out of the picture at this point.

O'Brien: Were there internal fights within the Front?

Stephens: Definitely. They were big on antinationalism. They couldn't really wrap their minds around what was happening in the Nations.

O'Brien: Could you explain this a bit more? I think this is really important for everyone to understand.

Stephens: There was this real tension with the settler socialists who couldn't really get sovereignty and land claims.

O'Brien: And you were a part of the shared land movement within Native politics? That shared some overlap with communization?

Stephens: I was. But we were not going to let any settlers tell us how to manage things.

**O'Brien: Do you have any stories about those fights?**

Stephens: It came to shots. I had a settler commander from fucking Connecticut, from some socialist cult, and he didn't make it. . . . We tried not to let it get out that NALF militants were shooting at each other.

**O'Brien: There were major debates about Indigenous sovereignty in assemblies all up and down the Americas.**

Stephens: Yeah.

**O'Brien: [Long pause.] You were there in Colorado Springs?**

Stephens: I was.

**O'Brien: Can you tell us about it?**

Stephens: [Long pause.] It was—hell. Like a bad dream. [Pause; begins to speak quickly.] The worst fight of the war. Like the last major holdout of the fash. We knew they had nukes, they had the air force base there, they had all their cults. I was in a unit with Fast River. We came down from the mountains, about nine thousand fighters. Fort Carson fell first, and then we followed the mountains down to descend fast and hard on Colorado Springs. We had a sense then that this was it, like when the city fell, we'd be able to sort the rest out. There was a lot of worry they would launch a nuclear response. That's why we moved fast. We shelled the city hard with artillery through the night and attacked at first light. The forces were fairly evenly matched, and we . . . a lot of us fell, a lot of casualties. [Long pause.] She was wearing that jacket. She had been shot. I think by a buzzard. They had these fucking buzzards with night vision that fired flechette rounds. They felt like shards of glass when they went into me. Have you ever stepped on glass? It was like that, but all over your body. They tore up my stomach. Something is still wrong with my legs. The jacket was all torn up. Now it's new, like she made it out. You understood . . . you understood what needed to happen.

O'Brien: That's the most you've said in one go Mr. Stephens. Is it possible you are having a flooding response? Like the memories are rushing in?

Stephens: I was stuck dying on the concrete in that fucking jacket. It's like a construction site, rebar and exposed concrete lit up by mortar explosions that are getting closer. The stars looked so close.

O'Brien: Would it be helpful to stop the interview, Mr. Stephens?

Stephens: We couldn't both stay . . . I had to go. You understand, right? I had to go. We knew they were going to mortar the building. We knew we couldn't both make it. I don't know. Fast River, why did you fucking leave me? But you made it, you are alive. [Crying.] Fuck you! Fuck you. Why did you have to get shot?

O'Brien: Mr. Stephens, you are not breathing. Can you breathe in with me? Yeah, let's breathe in. Okay, let's breathe out together. Breathe in, breathe out. Let's feel the floor under our feet.

[Stephens' daughter enters room.]

Daughter: Dad, are you okay?

O'Brien: I think Mr. Stephens is having a flashback of some sort. Can you help him?

[Recording is stopped.]

O'Brien: Are you sure you are okay to continue?

Stephens: Yeah, it's okay. I get freaked out sometimes. I'm sorry about that. My sister was killed in Colorado, and I get confused. I have these intense flashbacks when I try to think about Colorado Springs. I think your jacket reminded me of her, and it messed me up in the head. I am okay now.

**O'Brien: It's quite alright. I should not have pushed you.**

Stephens: The past doesn't go anywhere. It's with us all the time. It's in me, in my head, in the ground, in the air. The past is right here.

**O'Brien: Hopefully we can learn from it.**

Stephens: Yeah, cert. I don't know what I learned. Sometimes I think I belong to the past now, that something of me died there, or a part of me belongs to those who came before me and there isn't enough of me left over for this future we are in. That's what I feel like when I get lost, that I am back in that other place, and not enough of my mind has made it into the present to live here.

**O'Brien: You seem more relaxed now. How did you end up in New York?**

Stephens: After the war ended I was . . . destroyed. I had sent my daughter to New York in '54 when the fighting was getting close to Wind River. Her mom died when she was little. I needed to get away from it all. I moved out here.

**O'Brien: Why New York?**

Stephens: I thought about Oaxaca, but things were dicey getting there. Ridge's sister had ended up in Harlem, and she and I had been in touch. We first started talking about how much we missed Ridge, but then familied as we texted. Name's Emory. Emory promised to take care of my daughter. That's how we ended up here, Emory is commune coor for Riverside. Emory knew what she was doing, and she knew that New York would make it through. I love the land, like I really miss Wind River, but I needed to be somewhere new, I think. I needed to be in a new place to heal.

**O'Brien: Your daughter seems very kind. Can you tell us about her?**

Stephens: Oh, she is very special. I named her Little River. She's twenty-five years old. She is a . . . therapist, I guess. She is very active in all sorts of things. She works with refugee children. Kids whose families went through horrible things in the war, or in all the storms and bad weather and heat waves and such. She works with this group over in Queens. I guess she was a refugee child herself in a way.

O'Brien: We interviewed Quinn Liu for this book. Do you know her?

Stephens: Yeah, cert. My daughter works with her.

O'Brien: I'm glad you have your daughter.

Stephens: Me too. She's what keeps me here. In the present.

O'Brien: Would you have any advice for listeners, for people who didn't live through the revolutionary war?

Stephens: I'm the last person who can give advice . . . I know elders who have a lot to say, who I have learned from. You should talk to them if you want advice. I can't give that to you. [Long pause.] But I can say. I don't know. . . . I can say—I can say that the war didn't just start between the fash and the feds one day. Like, they were basically the same, in the end, and their fight was really just about the pipeline boys and the ranchers and their show, and their show falling apart and not working anymore, and them not knowing how to keep it going anymore. The real war had been going on a long, long time, for fucking centuries. It was being waged against the water, against the land, against the ancestors, against the future. The fighting we did, what we did in Thunder Basin or Colorado Springs or Salt Lake City, what people called the revolutionary war—that was bringing the other long war to an end. That was us bringing to an end the long war against the land. That was letting the land be what it was all along. . . . That's what I have to say.

# 9: LATIF TIMBERS ON GESTATION WORK

*Recorded on January 2, 2069, at AfroCarr in Brooklyn.*

Eman Abdelhadi: This is Eman Abdelhadi, I'm recording an interview with Latif Timbers in Bed-Stuy, Brooklyn, on January 2 of 2069. Latif, welcome!

Latif Timbers: Thanks, it's good to be here.

Abdelhadi: Right now, we're sitting in the Bed-Stuy Gestation Center. From what I understand, you're a gestation care coordinator?

Timbers: In training, yes! I used to be a counselor, and now I'm training to be a GCC.

Abdelhadi: I definitely want to hear more about those roles. I wonder if we could start by getting to know you a little bit, though. What year were you born?

Timbers: 2045. I think. That's kind of a lie. Well, not a lie. . . . A guess, a guess. It's a guess. We kind of did the math, and that's what we figured.

Abdelhadi: Who is we?

Timbers: My family.

Abdelhadi: Tell me more about your family.

**Timbers:** It's the kids I grew up with. I kind of found myself in this group. Like, my earliest memories are of them—of us—living in a tent city that had cropped up in Prospect Park. In the meadow, you know. Anyway, that's as far back as I can remember, living in a tent in the park with a bunch of kids that became my family—Mirna, Lulu, Matt, Shireen, Carissa. That was before the liberations, and before the communes took off.

**Abdelhadi: How did you come up with 2045?**

**Timbers:** I went through some version of puberty in the mid to late fifties, so I figured I was probably born in the mid-forties. My best friend Matt, they were born in '45. I decided I was born then too, and I sometimes forget that I don't actually know if that's true.

**Abdelhadi: How did Matt and some of the other kids end up in this encampment?**

**Timbers:** Matt lost their parents in one of the little wars that broke out with the NYPD—I think they were out in Crown Heights at the time. It was the same story you hear a million times; landlords were trying to kick them out and brought over the police. People started self-defense coalitions to resist, but it didn't always work. Matt's parents ended up in a shoot-out with the pigs, and they were both martyred. Other people's parents were lost in fights with the [US] Army or the fash. Shit was crazy in the forties, you know. So much fighting. Some people's parents froze or died of LARS or whatever. Everyone had a story, ya know. Except me. One of the older kids, Fatima, said they found me sitting on a bench in Grand Army Plaza one day crying, and they took me with them.

**Abdelhadi: I see. So, you all lived together?**

**Timbers:** Yeah. You know I've been reading all this anthropological history recently, and I guess you could call us foragers. Most of the year we lived in the tents, but when it got really cold, we'd wander around and find empty buildings. Usually, brownstones or houses that were left behind. People with money had been abandoning New York for years. In some neighborhoods, LARS had hit hard, sometimes killing whole families. So, there were a lot of abandoned buildings. We'd make our way inside, eat whatever we could find, huddle up a bit in the warmth. My favorite was this beautiful mansion in Ditmas Park. It had dark green paneling, and a tower on one side. We walked around the house playing make believe for a few days, putting on leftover clothes and accessories and pretending we were different people, from a different time. But we ran out of food eventually and we had to go. Anyway, whenever we could, we liked being outside. It was just more fun out there. We could play soccer in the park, do whatever we wanted, be all together. Safer that way, too—it's easier to get picked off in smaller groups.

**Abdelhadi: How long did you live in the encampment?**

**Timbers:** Until sometime in the fifties, I think '53—maybe '52 or '51? I'm not sure—until the Army left the city and the pigs left the area. The fash fled around then too. Things got a lot calmer. The communes hadn't come together yet, but everything got better. You could feel a sigh of relief come over New York. Like, we all had a common enemy before, but you didn't know who was who and everyone was so desperate to survive. After the withdrawal, it was like the forces of hate had receded and people could be kind to each other again. When we'd meet adults in the streets, they'd actually ask about us, ask how we were doing, give us food. Before that, we were seen as at best a nuisance or at worst a threat. Anyway, one day we met a tall bald person, his name was Paul, but we nicknamed him Paulina. He asked us all these questions about how we were living. The next day, he came back with a bunch of other adults, who would also ask questions. We were suspicious, but they seemed nice and always brought food. Finally, they explained they were building a commune. AfroCarr. They invited us in, got us a house, coordinated our food, and put us in the crèche for some schooling.

**Abdelhadi: Was that a relief?**

**Timbers:** Yeah, because they fed us! Even fresh stuff! They took over the old co-op farms here in the city and started working with farms nearby; it was the first time I had lettuce. It tasted like crunchy water. I still love it. Before that, my life just revolved around finding food and reacting to the weather. Being too hot in the summer, too cold in the winter, and always, always hungry. They brought us in, and they gave us a little apartment, and they stocked the fridge and the kitchen, and I hadn't seen that much food before in my life. I ate until I threw up. We all did. But the food kept coming, and that was honestly a miracle. [Pauses, begins to cry.]

**Abdelhadi:** Would you like a tissue?

**Timbers:** Sure, thanks.

**Abdelhadi:** Did you get to choose who to live with?

**Timbers:** Yeah, pretty much. They said, listen, we can divide you up to live with adults or you can live as a group but have an adult check in on you every so often. It kind of tied to how people were thinking about their living situations, too. Like the adults themselves. Reading more and more about how people lived before, I've been realizing that family was usually blood, and that's who you lived with. And who you lived with was really tied into what you got. So, like, if your blood had food, you had food. If they had a nice house and heat, you did too. If they didn't, well tough shit for you. You were fucked.

**Abdelhadi:** [Laughs.] Yes, I'm old enough to confirm that's how we lived for a long time.

**Timbers:** Talking to the elders and reading history, I realize people were really trying to get rid of that system with the communes. Honestly, it's hard to imagine making all your choices based on blood! Why would it matter so fucking much who gave birth to you? Or who you fell in love with or who happened to have the same parent. Like, what if those people were straight up assholes? Or just didn't know how to take care of you? And people only had two parents? Who were expected to take care of everything? So inefficient! Like, why wouldn't you collectivize things like child-care? It makes no goddamn sense!!

**Abdelhadi: [Laughs.] It really didn't make a lot of sense, you're right.**

Timbers: It's hard to know how anyone could focus on the love part of things when there was so much else involved—material fec. For most people, blood matters now because of love. And it's not held hostage by money, or food, or shelter, or education—we all have that all the time, regardless. You're going to be okay, regardless of whether those relationships are central for you or not. It's like people often say, "Not all blood is kin, not all kin is blood."

**Abdelhadi: Yes, it's really different now, because we all have what we need. It used to be that if you moved out of a house you shared with a lover, for example, that really affected your well-being. Because everything was tied to money and that money was so scarce. I used to study all this actually, as a sociologist back in the day.**

Timbers: For cert? That's crazy. I'd love to hear more about that. I get into rant mode every time I think about those times. Maybe you can suggest some readings though, really. I wanna learn more, and I've been really into sociological and anthropological history lately.

**Abdelhadi: Definitely. For now, let's get back to you. So how did you choose to live when you got into AfroCarr?**

Timbers: Paulina took us around and showed us a lot of different options. Some chaps lived in small subunits in big apartment build-ings. And those were sometimes people living with lovers or a couple of friends, sometimes with blood. A parent, a sister, that kinda thing. Some chaps lived in bigger groups in a house or a brownstone-type situation. Most people still mostly ate together in the canteen, and spent a lot of time on projects or chills with other people in the com-mune outside their small subunies. AfroCarr had the illest music and parties and chills. Some people moved around between subunies. But for many, who you familied was a big deal, like those people spent a lot of time talking about who they should parent with or sleep with or get a subuny with or I don't know. Now, in working with parent groupings, I get it a bit more, what a commitment that can feel like for some people to be raising an infant together. I was a lil' creeped out by some things in AfroCarr initially, and it took me a lot of time to get all the different ways of thinking and being and living that everyone brought to it.

**Abdelhadi: So, what did you decide?**

**Timbers:** We wanted to stay together, the kids. We found this house on Park Place—between Troy and Schenectady. It's really close to this cute park, St. John's. We wanted to be close to a park and we wanted to be together, so we picked that one. It's a row house. The chaps to our left were a funny semifunctional polycule, six or seven chaps living together, romantically involved in complicated ways and generally happy. On the other side, these three aunties lived together. They were blood sisters, I think. And sometimes their mom would come stay with them. Anyway, both sets of neighbors helped us out a lot. They would help us coordinate getting stuff to the house—basic supplies, food and all that. Gradually, we started eating at the canteen for a meal or two every day, but I think everyone kind of got that we needed some time to trust anyone. They also taught us some life skills. One of the aunties, Sophia, taught us how to cook. One of her lovers was super handy—her name was Monique, I think—she taught me some woodworking. I'm still really bad at it, but hey, I made one table. [Laughs.]

**Abdelhadi: I hear both that you were weirded out by how much attention people gave to who they slept with, but also that you did really care about staying with your family.**

**Timbers:** Yeah, I guess that is kind of contradictory? I don't know, it doesn't have to make sense. Like—when we were in the park, we didn't spend so much time making a huge scene out of who slept in each other's tents or whose tents were next to each other. Because we were all together, and that is what mattered to us.

**Abdelhadi: How did you manage conflicts as young folks living by yourselves?**

**Timbers:** Well, we started having house meetings every week to talk things over. If things got heated, we'd ask one of the neighbors to come facilitate for us. Then we all did facilitation and conflict management trainings too. AfroCarr was super into that kind of thing. And we all also started therapy around that time, that was really important for us. And sometimes we'd do group therapy. But yeah, at various points, people moved out. Matt actually moved in with the aunties next door, they needed a bit more affection, I think. That child wanted to be smothered, and you didn't have to tell those aunties twice. [Laughs.] But yeah, we were sad to see them go. But that's when we started having, like, a tradition that when folks move out, we have a big chill together. We do a bunch of drugs, read poetry, cry it out, some people fuck. Just kind of give the sads room to breathe. It became like a . . . a . . . umm.

**Abdelhadi: A grieving ritual?**

**Timbers:** Sure! Yeah, like a ceremony almost. That is in the anthropology I'm reading too!

**Abdelhadi: Sure. You mentioned that you also started getting some schooling when you moved to AfroCarr?**

**Timbers:** Well, I had learned to read because one of the older kids in the group taught me. Not very well, of course. But yeah, we started the crèche. AfroCarr had taken over some of the old school buildings. I got really, really into reading. The science stuff was my favorite. My guides at the crèche saw that, so when I learned all I could there, they connected me to scientists who had started operating out of the old Brooklyn College campus. I think you spoke to one of my mentors, Aniyah. She coordinates between Brooklyn College and the campus in Harlem. I worked on a couple of teams there, trying to figure out what I loved most, worked with some biologists, some chemists. But I kept coming back to this idea of reproduction, specifically among humans. And at the time, I realized I wanted to gestate, but that didn't work out.

**Abdelhadi: Say more about that.**

**Timbers:** Well, I was in love with this person, she lived over in Brownsville. She never really wanted to be with me romantically, but she knew I loved her, and we spent a lot of time together. She was the first to help me realize that I wanted to gestate. She said: "You have been obsessed with this process forever. Just transplant! Go for it." By then, the hospitals had been reclaimed, a lot of them. And so, I went into Downstate, and I made an appointment and got checked out.

**Abdelhadi: And what did they say?**

**Timbers:** They said no. I guess my body had undergone lots of trauma, I'm sure some from before I can remember. They ran a bunch of tests and basically said it would be too risky to do something so invasive.

**Abdelhadi: That sounds really hard.**

**Timbers:** I got really depressed for a long time. I just kind of stayed home, I didn't know what this meant for my life, what I would do instead. It was weird to be so torn up about something I hadn't even known I wanted. But once I acknowledged it to myself, I realized it had been there all along. For a while, I wanted nothing to do with children or gestation. I stopped reading about it or talking about it. Stopped doing much of anything. Spent a lot of time in the party scene.

Anyway, my housemates were supportive, they took shifts to hang out with me to make sure I wasn't alone since no one was quite sure how bad things were, and they were trying to make sure I wasn't suicidal. Everyone shifted their twenties to tens to make more room for taking care of me. I stopped doing any hours. And I started talking to a couple of counselors until I found one I liked. Therapy helped. I hadn't dealt with my past or anything, so it helped excavate some stuff.

**Abdelhadi: How long did this episode last?**

**Timbers:** Oh, a year maybe. Then I felt lighter, and I realized through all these conversations with my unit mates that I didn't have to experience it myself to be a part of it, that I could still be a meaningful part of the process. Gestating is for everyone, anyway—so we can all have children in our lives, a new generation to raise together. It's never about the individual people—not really. So yeah, at first, I trained to be a counselor. That took a while because the depression slowed me down. But eventually, I realized I wanted to get closer to what I loved, and that's how I decided to train as a GCC.

**Abdelhadi: What's the difference between a counselor and a GCC—a gestation care coordinator?**

**Timbers:** When folks choose to gestate, it can be really emotionally and physically draining. Counselors are mainly supplementary therapists; they're therapists that are very familiar with this process and work with the gestators as they go through it. The GCCs are more like point people for the whole care team. We work with the people here at the center: the mediators, the counselors, the doctors, and all that, even the gestator's loved ones and people outside the center.

**Abdelhadi: Are you only working with resident gestators or anyone gestating? Some folks do it from home, right? Gestate from home, I mean.**

**Timbers:** About half the gestators of the communes we serve stay in the center. My sense is that it's similar ratios across the city, from talking to other GCCs. So yeah, sometimes folks want to gestate from home and feel like they're better off in their commune. Others feel like they want this immersive relaxation experience and they come and stay with us. Others come and go—spend a few days here, a few days back home, etc. There are some people who want to be here in the first trimester, then they miss home and leave, then come back for events. Or some people find they only need support in the final trimester. It's really a mix. We leave it really open for chaps. If you're gestating and you let us know, we have a spot for you and we just keep that spot warm and ready for whenever you want to use it.

**Abdelhadi: What do you think goes into what people decide?**

**Timbers:** A lot of stuff, who they are as people, what's going on in their commune or housing unit, why they decided to gestate in the first place. There are so many reasons people do it and so many different arrangements for when the baby is born. Yesterday, I was doing an intake for this woman who came in, and she was talking about how she just felt this yearning in her body to make life. Like, a physical pull towards it. I actually hear that a lot. Her commune—she's from Sunset I think—has this lovely nursery—

**Abdelhadi: How did she get pregnant? Implantation?**

**Timbers:** Woah! We never ask that. That's not really our business. I think there was a lot of work around this, politically, in the last couple of decades. DNA doesn't give anyone ownership of children. Children are children, they're precious and beautiful and it doesn't really matter who made them or how. You know? So no, we don't ask that at this stage. Of course, there are fertility counselors, and folks have intense conversations about how to get pregnant with their loved ones. My understanding is most people just use sperm and egg banks. It really varies, though. But, like, once someone is pregnant, which is where I come in, we don't ask about the methods.

**Abdelhadi: Sorry about that! Thanks for explaining. Sometimes olds like me ask dated questions.**

**Timbers:** Oh, that's okay! There are still folks who ask, and that's something we've been working on in the repro world. We talk about it at conferences and citywide meetings a lot. How to shift people's focus away from the bio of it all. But honestly, the very structure of the commune has already done that.

**Abdelhadi: For sure. So, you were telling me about the nursery over at Sunset Park.**

Timbers: Yes! So carework structures vary a lot between communes, with everyone exchanging ideas about what seems to work. At Sunset, the babies all go into nursery and adults take on shifts working it. Of course, there are more people interested than shifts usually, but the nursery coordinators try to include everyone. I *still* cannot believe that people used to do nursery-level care all by themselves or with just one other person back in the day. Honestly, how?!?

**Abdelhadi: [Laughs.] Why do you think birthrates had dropped so much in the beginning of the twenty-first century? It was just so hard to do this in these tiny households of one or two people. And everyone had to still be working at maximum capacity to produce for the bosses.**

Timbers: And only women could gestate back then too, right? Also sounds awful. Anyway, yeah, so there are a lot of arrangements. Another person who came in last month, they are in a midsize unit. They have two townhouses that open onto each other and live with fifteen others. Their house basically has several more or less monogamous couples and a couple of single chaps. And they all want to raise a few kids as a house. I think, to go back to your question about getting pregnant, they are going to mix things up so that it doesn't feel like children [quote gestures with fingers] "belong" to particular couples. You know?

**Abdelhadi: I understand. And does your house have kids?**

Timbers: Not yet! Because our house started as a group of children, we have staggered relationships. Some of the older kids took care of me and I took care of some of the younger ones. Now that we're all adults, we're thinking about what it would be like to raise kids, and how we want to do it. There are a lot of house meeting discussions about it. Almost everyone wants to gestate at least once. So, we have to decide how to not end up with more kids than we can handle! But yeah, it's really exciting. There is one housemate, Amanda, who doesn't want to do the kid thing. She's thinking of moving next door with the polycule, which is still going strong. [Laughs.]

I have a question for you, is it true that when folks would have babies in the old world—it was kind of looked down upon? Or like it was kind of low status? It's so wild to think that, since so many people want to gestate now. People are so drawn to it, kind of as a part of growing up and a way of relating to their bodies that is new and a challenge. Almost anyone can get a womb now. You don't have to have been born with one, so there has been this whole explosion happening in the number of people thinking about gestating and getting all into it. Sometimes we do prefert counseling, and I have to remind people what a toll it is on the body. Because people are so psyched about it, and I think sometimes they underestimate the labor of it all.

Abdelhadi: For sure. It was sort of this double-edged sword. Back when it was just cis women, you were kind of damned if you didn't have kids and damned if you did. Because you were supposed to still do all the things everyone else was doing while also raising the kid or kids, and everyone kind of questioned your worth if that wasn't 100-percent true. If you couldn't do it all or have it all—which no one could. It was a weird time. That's why I didn't gestate, part of the reason anyway. Or really even parent, until much later, in an eight-parent grouping.

Timbers: I see. I thought AfroCarr was pretty strange at first, but it grew on me and seems normal now. I still can't really picture how weird and hard the old world was. I see it must have seemed normal to people then, but I can't get my head around it. Thanks for sharing.

Abdelhadi: Sure. Thanks for asking. So what else are you offering at the Gestation Center besides counseling and coordination?

**Timbers:** Oh, everything. Arts and crafts. Meditation and prayer spaces. Exercise. Medical care specific to gestation. Skincraft, from massages to sex. A garden. We have a gorgeous library upstairs. And we're always adapting. Each person who comes through to gestate adds something new.

**Abdelhadi: Like what?**

**Timbers:** A couple of years ago, this one person came in. It was his first time gestating, and he came to tour the center before his implantation. And he said, "Where is the theater?" I said, "We don't have a theater." And he said, "We need one." And when he came, he made it his mission to get a theater built. And we did it. And now there are plays and performances in there all the time; AfroCarr and some of the other communes use the space too, since they're next door. You should come by tomorrow; I think they're playing *Macbeth*. Plays are especially cute when all the actors are at various stages of pregnancy. [Laughs.]

**Abdelhadi: Absolutely. I'm noting that the midday bells have rung, and you said you'd have to go about now. I want to honor that agreement. It's been so wonderful talking to you. Thank you.**

**Timbers:** It's been a pleasure, thanks.

# 10: AN ZHOU ON ECOLOGICAL RESTORATION

*Recorded on January 12, 2069, at Riis Beach.*

M. E. O'Brien: Hello. My name is O'Brien, and I am interviewing An Zhou about his work around biodiversity and ecological restoration. This is part of a research project focused on the history of the New York Commune. We are at the site of the former Jacob Riis Detention Facility. Hello An. Could you introduce yourself?

An Zhou: Sure. My name is An. I use he or they. I'm originally from Calgary. I am forty-nine years old. I am currently living in an agricultural commune in the town of Hugo, about forty kilometers outside of Minneapolis. Though I'm permanently based out of Vancouver.

O'Brien: Can you tell us about your work?

Zhou: I'm here in New York to help with a restoration project for the tidal marsh zone in the coastal areas of Long Island. This land has mostly been flooded since the thirties and abandoned. It became part of the tidal zone. We have been ripping out old infrastructure in tidal zones and putting in new plant life. Here, it means removing the pavement, planting saltmeadow cordgrass, spike-grass, and other species that will do well with the ocean water. We are making sure the flooded parts of the city are thriving as saltmarshes. It's a part of broader ecological reconstruction efforts underway around the world. You could say it's kind of embracing the destruction of the last few decades and trying to make sure we remove any of the human-made hurdles to new or old ecological systems regenerating. I'm just here for a couple of weeks, then I'll be heading down to the Jackson Fallout Zone for another project.

**O'Brien: It sounds like you are working in several places?**

**Zhou:** Yeah, I work on a lot of different climate rehabilitation and adaptation projects. I travel around. I'm based out of Minnesota at the moment, because the Hugo project has been ongoing for a while and it's where I devote most of my time.

**O'Brien: What is the project in Hugo?**

**Zhou:** We have various fancy names for it, but it is basically perma-culture. It uses similar principles as the forest restoration I specialize in. The general framework is centered around maximizing ecological niches, biodiversity, and variation through combining self-sustaining processes and deliberate intervention.

**O'Brien: Why Hugo though?**

**Zhou:** It's become the North American hub of collaborations, research, and thinking by First Nations peoples about farming prac-tices. A dozen research farms and an institute, all centered around trying to identify, reclaim, understand, and disseminate Indigenous approaches to growing food. It's had a major impact on my thinking, and links to all these other kinds of restoration projects I am involved with.

**O'Brien: How did you get into restoration work?**

**Zhou:** My dad was a geologist. He emigrated to Canada to work for oil companies. He spent a lot of time outdoors, and when I was growing up got really into backpacking and camping. Mostly around British Columbia. He'd always take me with him, and I developed a real love for the forests of that region. I spent my whole childhood roaming those forests, befriending the trees, foraging mushrooms, observing the animals. This was the twenties, and we still had con-siderable biodiversity, even though the die-offs had already started. As a teenager, I traveled a lot in the punk, anarchist, and radical environmental scenes. Bouncing from protest to squat. Eventually I decided to go to college in Vancouver. I studied forest ecology. That led to getting involved in forest restoration projects. Eventually, I got into a collective of biologists who worked with First Nations land defenders and restorers. We travel all over North America to work with communities that are responding to or adapting to catastrophe. We integrate Indigenous practices and principles of agriculture with biotech.

**O'Brien: Biotech?**

**Zhou:** It was controversial. We were one of the first teams interested in designing and introducing newly created species to increase biodiversity in partially wrecked biomes. We wanted to think through the roles of species that had gone extinct because of climate catastrophe, and try to create species that would replicate those roles or replace them. People said we were playing God. Well, fuck God. God let this happen. None of it is over, you know. We have better practices now to work with refugees, move aid into affected regions, and not build in stupid places, but the scale of the disaster keeps unfolding. Like it or not, our job is to mitigate the consequences of the catastrophe of the old world.

**O'Brien: And you mentioned you focus on farming practices?**

**Zhou:** It helped think about the nature/human interface differently, helped shift the framework. With the soil blight in the Midwest, the agricultural collapse, and the insurrection, it was clear we needed to radically rethink some very basic things. First Nations forces played a major role in the revolutionary war, in the [North American] Liberation Front, and were well positioned to set terms after the fighting was over. Particularly in the Great Plains and the Prairie regions, where most of North America's agriculture had been concentrated. Then, in the sixties, there were some intense struggles in the communes and assemblies over Indigenous sovereignty, and a lot of the kind of work I do grew out of those debates.

O'Brien: Could you talk a little bit about the scope of the ecological crisis in the forties? It has come up a few times in interviews as a cause of the collapse of old state regimes and a motivator for the insurrections.

Zhou: It's hard to describe the scale of what happened. It also looked different depending on where you were. Let's take North America in a broad sweep. Deadzones across a lot of California, the Southwest, and Texas as water ran out. Agricultural and soil collapse in the Midwest, being one of the triggering events of the hunger. A lot of people on the move and desperate. The storms in the Gulf Coast wiping out a lot of the coastal cities, and then the nuclear fallout. The forests had massive die-offs all over the continent.

O'Brien: What happened to the forests?

Zhou: Logging wiped out the lowland ancient forests back in the twentieth and early twenty-first. Fires just started ripping across the West Coast and the Rockies annually, on a scale and intensity that even forests well-adapted to periodic fires could not withstand. The hotter temperatures brought out these fungal infections we didn't expect that decimated the firs and pines. The forests I grew up with are gone. There are just a handful of sickly remnants we are trying to salvage, with hundreds of miles of barren deadzone. Once they were—they were—these cathedrals of such majesty. The canopy overhead and the air so perfect and now it's all dead and it's all gone. In less than a decade we saw 80 percent of the forest species go extinct.

During the hunger, my friends ended up living in the woods trying to survive off the land, but the trees and the game and everything was dying. I lived in a forest camp in the Yukon for a summer, and we almost starved to death before we realized the moose we were trying to hunt had gone extinct.

O'Brien: I'm sorry.

Zhou: [Long pause.] I did a sojourn five years ago. I know I'm too old for it, I'm not seventeen. But it spoke to me as a social form. But a few of us just sailed to memorial sites. Miami, the Bahamas, Port-au-Prince, and Antilles. I can't think of it without crying. We will never get those places back. I know there are dozens of other cities like this around the world, a billion displaced people.

O'Brien: What are those sites like now?

Zhou: There are boat communities, these floating cities. They tie together dozens of old barges and small boats and build walkways between them. They try to get out of the way of the worst storms—break the city apart and keep moving during hurricane season. And newer architecture, the grown buildings that float, made out of algae. And some smaller islands left in what was high ground, though they are drowned every year. People build on these high stilts, and sometimes that works out, but the storms can be deadly. During my sojourn we went diving, scuba diving, down into the old cities. So many people died. [Pause, begins to cry.] I remember when they sealed the Gulf Coast states—Florida, Mississippi, Louisiana—trapping all the refugees there to die.

O'Brien: Would you like to say a little about what happened in the Gulf Coast?

Zhou: The New Afrikaan People's Party was in power in Mississippi and Alabama, gaining territory and influence throughout the forties. A lot of people fleeing from the Caribbean ended up there and ended up joining the Republic of New Afrika. Then, I guess it was '49, the US military scaled off the whole area and prevented any refugees from leaving. It wasn't entirely clear why they did it; probably to squeeze the People's Party, maybe to mitigate the overwhelm from refugees after water shortages out West. Some say these refugees were too politicized already and would have made a lot of trouble. . . .

O'Brien: Are you okay?

Zhou: I think about Florida a lot. . . . I actually liked Florida, the one time I visited it as a kid, before I ended up there during the deaths.

Like we went to some theme park, I don't even remember what it was called. I think the US had already lost its soul a long time before that, but something about what they let happen to Florida, I think just broke it all. So many people had fled there from all over the islands, and to leave them to the storms, to let everyone die, after what they had done in Jackson—I think a lot of people knew something had to change. It all happened so fast—the [US] Army's nuclear strike on Jackson, LARS hitting for the second year, the terrible storms that drowned the peninsula. In Miami, they were burning mountains of corpses, like literally these piles of bodies as high as apartment buildings. . . . Just when I think I am starting to connect the different parts of myself, of my mind and of this broken world, I think about all the blood, and all the death and all the horror we've unleashed, and it feels so impossible. And it isn't over.

**O'Brien: I'm really sorry.**

Zhou: No, I'm definitely not okay. I was there for a project in the middle of all that. In the middle of the mass deaths. I was in Miami, about to travel down into the Everglades when it all went to hell and we were trapped. Did you see it?

**O'Brien: A bit. I was in the Mississippi Delta a few years later. I spent time in the Fallout Zone. I tried to be a part of the struggle there . . . I want to get a fuller picture of your life. Is it hard to travel so much? You mentioned your home base is in Vancouver still, despite working out of Hugo and other places?**

Zhou: I have family in Vancouver, so I make it through there every year, but I tend to keep moving.

**O'Brien: Family?**

Zhou: Before the communes, there was no way I could have had a family. I kept moving, had a hard time establishing lasting relationships, mostly just this ever-shifting network of friends. I had a lot of problems in my head. I think I was trying to outrun them. But the commune allows me to travel, and I know my family is okay and loved and will welcome me back whenever I make it. My husband and I are members of the Gastown Commune in Vancouver. We are parents to two children, with a group of other adults. My mother and father moved in with us, moved into the Commune, when our first kid was born. That was eight years ago. I spend at least a month of each year with the family. It works really well; if we had been in a nuclear family it would have been traumatizing for our kids. I've been in Hugo for most of the last year. I'm out here in New York for a few weeks.

O'Brien: Is it hard traveling so much?

Zhou: Yes, it is. I kind of thrive on it, but it makes it hard to maintain my health. I got addicted to sleep aids last year and they had a bad interaction with my psych meds and hormones. . . .

O'Brien: Anything you want to say about that?

Zhou: Oh, I don't know. . . . I'm trying to be less private about my mental health stuff. I have schizophrenia. I need to maintain a stable drug regime to not spin out. I have started trying to talk publicly about mental health stuff occasionally, after a long time of being very private about it. . . . It has been helpful to be more public about it. At least it helps to have the people in my life know about it. Like it is helpful to have the people I stay with and the people I work with know something about my mental health condition. I am less clear about being this public, in the sense of discussing it in an oral history, but I guess it has its place. . . . I guess that's all I want to say about it. It is still hard to talk about. . . . Can you ask me about something else?

O'Brien: Of course. Could you outline a bit of the broader picture of ecological restoration? It is such a huge part of what's happening in the world. Honestly, we are a bit out of the loop in New York.

Zhou: Yeah, the scene here is small. That's part of why we all came in, to help out with this project. In most rural areas of the continent, ecological restoration is the main thing that everyone is talking about and working on. Even in cities like Vancouver or Minneapolis, you see hundreds of thousands of people involved in hub debates and affiliated with various restoration work projects. Biology, ecology, genetic research, all these have come to dominate the education  curriculum. The level of thinking and mass engagement with the field completely dwarfs anything I could have imagined twenty years ago when I was completing my degrees. New York has been slow. People fled out of many neighborhoods as the flooding got worse—but doing something about it is just now becoming the mass concern it has long been elsewhere.

O'Brien: I'm thinking about climate mitigation, that you mentioned. It's a big topic, so want to try to get a handle on some of the specific social changes and the historical trajectory. There has been a lot of discussion lately in the Mid-Atlantic about the growth of international travel. Some of us remember when you would take a plane overnight to Asia or Europe. But most young people are just now getting their chance to do long-distance sojourns. The transcontinental maglev trains, wind clippers, and solar barges on the sea. I gather it is all very low carbon compared to the travel system that I remember through much of my life. Could you say a bit about how this all came about?

Zhou: Going into the insurrection, most of the global economy had collapsed. Auto production and air travel, affordable gas, transcontinental shipping, electronics consumption—all of this disappeared or collapsed over the course of a decade of economic, political, and ecological crisis. A lot of resources went into maintaining the orbitals and enclaves. But most people, in most places, were much more familiar with life in refugee camps than with any sort of individual consumption or transport. Like most of the kids on the frontlines had never been in a functioning car, let alone be overly attached to the old ways of organizing cities. So, when the insurrection started cohering, there was a chance to do something really different. All over the world, we are seeing communes, and assemblies, and councils figuring out what that something different looks like. Now that the profit drive isn't making all our basic decisions for us, it is possible for people to actually get together and think about the world we want. The kinds of low-carbon, long-distance transit systems you are describing is one of the many examples that have grown out of this process of collective deliberation and rebuilding. We no longer have oil companies forcing us to use fossil fuels when the sun is so much cheaper and more abundant—for example.

My focus on this is around ecological restoration and its connection to agriculture and human use. I could do a deep dive on this, but not sure that's what you want. The Tunis Accords are the basis of a lot of this. I was there, giving testimony about the North American temperate forest die-offs at the assembly in Tunisia in 2062. That assembly identified three pillars that really guide and shape many of the vast range of local restoration projects. The pillars are ecological restoration, biodiversity, and climate change mitigation. But I have a feeling an oral history isn't the best place for that kind of detail.

**O'Brien: Could you describe one example of a restoration project that gives us a sense of how it works? You usually work with forests?**

**Zhou:** Sure. So, last month I was in the Kitimat Ranges. The Canadian military had a missile range there they set up in the forties, to test drone technology they were using as part of their participation in the war in Iran. The forests were already ravaged, but the RCAF construction and the explosives left the land extremely toxic. I've been working with a group of Haisla people on and off for a decade around restoring the forest and setting up a sustainable logging program. When they won sovereignty over the land, in 2050, they started as these sorts of projects have to: cleaning up the toxic mess left behind. They started dismantling the built environment, doing toxic cleanup, then major geological, bacterial, and nanite engineering of the soil. When I joined the project, they had already introduced several successive waves of species, establishing a forest. But it couldn't look like it had, like you couldn't restore the forest that was once there, they had to do something new. The climate has changed too much, too many species are extinct. The idea was to establish a forest that maximized species diversity that could thrive in the region, given current and future climate conditions, including frequent fires. So, it is kind of designing a new ecosystem partially from scratch. We're talking at least hundreds of species. At least a dozen of those species have to be completely redesigned genetically. This project alone engineered three entirely new kinds of soil bacteria. The Haisla did this long, intensive, spiritual reflection process as part of designing the project. They also spent years collaborating with researchers and consultants, both through the First Nations assemblies throughout the Pacific coastal mountains and through temperate forest ecologists globally.

**O'Brien: That is fascinating.**

**Zhou:** I know! It's magnificent. So last month they were ready to do some of the first tree cutting since the restoration program began. They collaborated with this settler logging council. They invited all their remote consultants they had been working with to actually come in person. I had visited the project in person several times, but there were at least twenty-some people there who had never made it to North America before. We prayed, and watched these trees come down, crashing down through the underbrush. Just a few fast growing ones, but it was a huge step.

**O'Brien: You mentioned the controversies surrounding the use of biotech and engineered species in restoration. Are there other major controversies?**

**Zhou:** Definitely. It was a major step for the Haisla, for example, to be open to collaborative decision-making around the restoration process. Ecological restoration projects can affect the surrounding region and depend on broader webs of social and ecological systems. There are many competing needs for land. The Haisla, for example, decided to build a biosynthetic server farm through an underground rhizomatic fungi system on the roots of the trees. This was a giant decision, and one that helped expand communications and computational capabilities for the whole continent. How do you balance these human uses with efforts at constructing new diverse ecologies? Who decides? These are giant debates, because they affect huge numbers of people. First Nations, often in the lead around ecological restoration, were not up for just ceding their sovereignty into the new deliberative processes of the assemblies. So, through the sixties there were major debates about how to balance autonomy, accountability, and sovereignty in land use decisions.

**O'Brien: That is helpful. I spoke with Connor Stephens last month about the North American Liberation Front, and he alluded to some of those debates. I gather you know him?**

Zhou: Yes, I stay with his family when I'm in New York . . . I have a hard time explaining to people what is core for me in all this: understanding that human life and ecological systems can't be these entirely separate things. The new institutions of the communes provide a chance to really rethink humans' relationships with ecological systems on a large scale, and to begin to work through what it would mean to take those relationships with nonhumans very seriously.

**O'Brien: Is that interconnection with nonhuman life a spiritual matter for you?**

Zhou: Not if I take my meds. [Laughs.] It's complicated. There is definitely something spiritual about spending time in old-growth forests out West. It touched me deeply. When I developed a psychosis in my twenties, a big part of my craziness was feeling a spiritual connection to the planet, to ecology, and particularly to the forests. I was deeply misanthropic. For a long time after my recovery, I dealt with my psychosis by walling it off, separating it from the rest of my life, trying to keep it contained. I have been in my own healing process of beginning to integrate ways of thinking that have a psychotic character with the rest of my functional adult life, without being taken completely by the psychosis. This process of integration has been very scary for me, and often very hard. . . .

**O'Brien: I hear you drawing a parallel between integrating different parts of your mind, and the integration of human-use and ecological systems.**

Zhou: That's right. Being at this logging site was really beautiful for me. Like when I was twenty-one years old, I was in this tree-sit land defense campaign—not a lot of Chinese kids there, let me tell you—and I wanted to kill all loggers. I got hospitalized towards the end of that year. I changed my gender that year and a lot else. Being at this logging operation last month, helping take down this gene-hacked Sitka spruce, it was very profound for me, like, very healing. It was like, integrating parts of myself together in this moment. I was saying that I feel like I am all broken into all these pieces. I feel like that Sitka is a place to start, but sometimes it just feels so ridiculous, and we have so far to go.

O'Brien: Do you know much about the history of this area, of Riis Beach?

Zhou: A bit. It was a popular beach. I heard a lot of queers hung out here for most of the last century. There was an old sanatorium of some sort. And then sometime in the late forties the military set up a detention camp here and housed political prisoners.

O'Brien: I haven't been back here since the camp closed.

Zhou: That's right, I remember hearing you were detained here. One of the project leads mentioned it when she was arranging this interview.

O'Brien: I was, yes.

Zhou: How was that?

O'Brien: Not pleasant.

Zhou: Now I'm curious.

O'Brien: [Pause.] Let's get back to you.

**Zhou:** I think we were winding down. You are interviewing a lot of people for this project, right? But you won't answer any questions yourself? . . . What was it like?

**O'Brien:** Okay, sure . . . I used to come to this area to float in the waves, and for queer hangouts and such, when it was a public beach. Lots of queers all along the beach over that way. [Gestures; pause.]

When the flooding started, they built a seawall over that way, to slow the flooding down. That lasted a decade or so. While it held, military officials had their administrative offices set up in that building there. [Points to the only standing structure, an Art Deco building alongside the beach, currently flooded with hightide.] I think that building must be from the early twentieth century, when this area was constructed as a public beach. They added these modular housing units to the building. Then the detainees lived in these large tents that covered what had been this huge parking lot. At their peak, maybe two thousand of us? Maybe more? And then circled the whole thing with huge piles of razor wire. The Red Cross provided the food. Mostly the Army let the camp run itself.

The detainees were political prisoners, like organizers and union leaders and some of the leadership from street gangs as those got more and more politicized. A lot of people who knew something about—about how to have an efficient deliberation process, I would say. Some of the more amazing people I've ever met. I was on the older end of the population. Occasionally the Army would bring in people arrested in looting or street fighting, but once they figured out they weren't organizers they would transfer them elsewhere.

I helped out with the school, teaching political theory. Adults. There were not many kids, kids ended up elsewhere. I also acted as a therapist. The interrogations were hard on people. I was here for pretty much the whole duration of the camp. In '52 the military pulled most of its forces out of the city but kept a skeleton crew here. A joint group of militias raided the camp the following year, mostly people from Central Brooklyn and Newark, led by communards from Brownsville.

**Zhou:** Thanks for sharing a bit about it. I like to know the history of the places where I'm working.

**O'Brien: This project is connected to some other intertidal work happening around New York?**

**Zhou:** Salt marsh restorations are moving ahead all along the new intertidal regions of the NYC coastline. Lower Manhattan, the South Bronx, Long Island City, Red Hook—these places belong to the ocean as much as they belong to us. There has been a lot of abandonment of the coastal areas from the decades of storms and flooding. Those who are remaining are beginning to learn to live differently. Restoring the salt marshes is a part of that living differently. And these salt marshes can become a part of the joy and community and life of the city. It's very easy for me to imagine people a decade from now kayaking through saltmeadow cordgrass exactly where we are standing. It's not really a beach anymore, but I hear there are some great queer dance parties that happen on the floating dock where the old sanatorium used to be—over there. After the detention camp was burned down, people built a jetty that they use for swimming. I think the urban farms and the coastline restoration can both together contribute to New Yorkers learning to live as a part of the ecological world again.

**O'Brien: I feel like New York is a bit behind when it comes to ecological restoration.**

**Zhou:** Definitely. I hope the next few decades see a major shift in New Yorkers learning about ecology on a large scale. Ecological sciences are the single most important field for both basic and advanced curriculums on every continent, but it is like seventeenth or something in education here. New Yorkers, you love your parks, your community gardens. You are growing to love the waterways—I had a beautiful kayaking experience in the Harlem River yesterday—but you haven't really paid any attention to how this city interfaces with ecological processes. I feel like that is really starting to change, from what little I've seen and heard.

O'Brien: Thank you for doing this interview. Is there more you wanted to share?

Zhou: No, nothing else. I appreciated being able to talk about how the mental health stuff connects to forest restoration. I haven't really shared about that much.

O'Brien: I was quite moved by you describing how healing it was for you being a part of that logging project, and how it connects with integrating your psychosis into your adult life . . . I think in a parallel way, it is healing for me to come out here, to return to this site after living in the detention camp. This place has a lot of horror in it as well as a lot of joy. I can see how building a marsh is a way of honoring both of those things. There is so much trauma, in this place, everywhere.

Zhou: So much trauma. And so much healing to do.

# 11: KAYLA PUAN ON GROWING UP IN THE NORTH IRONBOUND COMMUNE

*Recorded on June 24, 2069, in Newark.*

M. E. O'Brien: Hello. My name is M. E. O'Brien, and I will be having a conversation with Kayla Puan as part of an oral history project about the New York Commune. It is June 24, 2069, and this is being recorded at the North Ironbound Commune in Newark. Hello Kayla.

Kayla Puan: Hello!

O'Brien: Could you start off and introduce yourself?

Puan: Sure. My name is Kayla Dorothy Hart Puan. I'm seventeen years old, and I was born and grew up here at North Ironbound. I am a photographer. I'm—I'm trans. I'm a girl. A woman. A trans woman, I guess? You write and talk about that, right?

O'Brien: Sometimes! You are seventeen? So, are you traveling soon?

Puan: Yes! I have been planning my sojourn for the last few months. I'm really excited. Can I tell you about it?

O'Brien: This is your interview! You should talk about whatever you'd like.

Puan: I've never traveled before; I've only ever taken the train to the cities right around here. To start for this trip, I'm taking a clipper cargo ship south. It will stop in Baltimore and Miami, and then we will be headed to Cuba. From there, I'll take small boats and visit Jamaica, Trinidad, and Puerto Rico.

**O'Brien: What brings you to the Caribbean?**

**Puan:** I'm seeing friends. Trans kids I know online. We are all in a photography collective together, called Kimera. We had a show last year that traveled around a bit. I've never met these friends! I'm going to spend two weeks at each of their homes. Everyone besides me lives in the Caribbean, mostly in the floating cities, and I think seeing them all will be the most fun part of my trip. After all that, I'm going to New Orleans. I have an internship at a photography studio there, doing some really interesting processing techniques I want to learn. Then, I'm taking a train to Colorado.

**O'Brien: What's in Colorado?**

**Puan:** My dad—one of my dads—Kareem was killed there. I am going to hike through old battlegrounds in the Rocky Mountains for the month and visit where he was buried . . . My dad was killed fighting fascists when I was five. It was really sad. I remember being really sad. I don't remember Kareem very well. He had been in the [US] Army I guess when the insurrection started, and his whole unit defected early. He's part of why Newark got free so much sooner than a lot of places. He taught firearm safety to everyone around here and tried to recruit chaps to go fight the fascists. I don't remember this. But I remember how bad things got after he died. It was so hard on all of us . . .

**O'Brien: If you were five, that must have been very early in the conflict in the Rockies. Like one of the initial battles, before the revolutionary war really took shape.**

**Puan:** I think so. He *really* hated fascists. Like, before hating them was really even a thing. I want to learn more about all that history on this trip, trying to piece it together.

O'Brien: It sounds powerful that you are getting a chance to visit where he was buried.

Puan: Yeah. . . .

O'Brien: We can come back to that in talking about your growing up. What's after Colorado?

Puan: I'm hiking north, up through Wind River and then continuing up to the Southern Blackfoot Confederacy. I'm doing a service stint there. The Southern Confederacy operates a rare-earth mine there. They mine Samarium. It's used in lasers. It's one of the things still being mined here on Earth. I am going to work for three months.

O'Brien: Is it dangerous?

Puan: Yeah, a bit. Not the Samarium itself, I don't think, but just being underground for a few hours at a time, and it's always possible there may be an accident. But the Blackfoot Confederacy has a lot of skills in workplace safety and environmental mitigation, and I gather they've figured out how to do it safely. But it's hard work, and no one works in the mines for too long. It's mostly robots, I guess? But some things, they really need people underground doing it, and everyone agrees no one should have to be underground for the long term. A lot of kids, adults I mean, kids becoming adults like me, do three months' work stints like I'm doing there during our sojourn. It's one of the not very pleasant jobs that chaps can take on for their sojourn three-month service. And I guess there is a lot of praying at the mine? Mining is spiritually dangerous too. Taking things out of the Earth. So, we do a lot of praying and rituals the whole time. I have been reading about it, but I don't know that much about it. I have never prayed and not really sure what it is exactly. My mom prays, I think. Or meditates? I'm not sure if it is the same as what chaps at the mine do.

O'Brien: That sounds like a great sojourn! Will you be coming back here after?

**Puan:** Yes! I don't know what I'll do after that, but thinking of maybe gestating, and starting to study how to teach photography.

**O'Brien:** Tell me about your photography; and that of your collective.

**Puan:** My photos are cinematic. They look like stills out of vids, games, or holos. I'm into a sense of strong emotion in people's faces and catching that mid-action. I've tried staging shoots with actors, I've tried just getting pictures from day-to-day life of things I see. But lately I've gotten more into setting up a camera in a fixed location where a lot of people pass by, like at the canteen, and it takes a series of stills every time someone passes in front of the camera. Then I go through all the photos it takes later. I look for images that imply some sense of a storyline, like a scene from some unfolding plot you can guess at. I think I got into it through loving movies when I was growing up. For a while I thought I'd get into film production. I grew up really into these popular Namibian soap operas, totally packed full of melodrama, and just the whole Sub-Saharan film world was super compelling to me as a kid. For years, I thought I would move there to make films, to get involved in that whole glamorous world. But I think I've found, for now, the part of movies that is most compelling to me, these images that evoke narratives. My collective all does some variation on portraiture of human faces, and we are all trans, but beyond that we are kind of all over the place. I guess we also are all interested somehow in denaturalization, but how we approach that varies a lot.

**O'Brien:** That sounds really interesting. You said you are thinking of gestating? Is that common in your group of friends?

**Puan:** Yeah, actually, it's pretty common these days among my friends online, and I know one girl that is pregnant right now in Brooklyn. I've always wanted to do it. I was gestated. Well, everyone is gestated. You know what I mean. My gestator was not one of my parents. Her name is Emile. She lives in Elizabethtown, and I go to see her most years on my birthday. She is a painter! Gestated four children! She is very cool. I was thinking it could be nice to give birth while I'm still young, and feel lucky the tech means I could do it.

**O'Brien: Lovely. Maybe this is a good time to go back to your growing up? Tell me about your parents. How did they meet? What kind of work did they do?**

Puan: I had four parents, initially. Kareem—who I mentioned— Kareem, was killed. His boyfriend Joseph. Joseph's three-hour was coordinating the distribution of a drug used by diabetics. A pharmaceutical logistics circle. He is retired now. Sara, my mom, she is a nurse for her three-hour. Still working. And Caleb, Sara's husband, was a teacher. He became a bus driver because of his political group, he told me once. They all helped found the North Ironbound Commune shortly after the insurrection took Newark. Ani and xe's children moved in much later. So yeah. We lived in a subuny together for my first years.

**O'Brien: Tell me about North Ironbound.**

Puan: It's my commune. We have 231 residents. It was the first commune of Newark. Other people know this story; the place was founded a few months before I was born. During the insurrection, people set up these big cooperative kitchens and worked together around getting food and eating it together. People started sharing childcare and trying to sleep close to each other for safety. Initially it was about staying alive, figuring out how to get everyone fed, how to keep things going when they got rid of money, and all the police and the fascists were driven out. People needed to eat. The group kitchens were the beginnings of the commune, and from there, they shared all the other kinds of work of daily life. Groups of a couple hundred, I guess? Chaps decided it was a better way to live, and as the insurrection went on people adopted these apartment buildings for commune centers. North Ironbound Commune was the first in Newark, and Dutch Neck just down the road was second. You are very old! You may remember that.

**O'Brien: I do! I was in Brooklyn. I was old then, too. Why were your parents involved?**

**Puan:** They were communists! [Laughter.] And I guess there were some arguments when things started settling down about if everyone should go back to their tiny households and live as isolated families and use money again. My family was opposed to that, and fought to keep the communes, and helped win the policy that food coming in from other regions gets distributed through the commune kitchens. A few people got by staying in their homes, but gradually, people became more and more involved in the communes near them. I think my parents were especially into it because of their own backgrounds. Kareem and Joseph were gay, and I guess that was still a thing back then? And they are all, what is the word, interracial couples. Honestly, I don't really know what that meant, back then. And Sara hated housework, so, so, so much. She would still complain about it while I was growing up, even though she got to avoid all the housework duties for her two-hour. She said women should never ever do housework ever again because they had done so much of it for so long. It didn't seem like that big a deal to me though, when I did a housework shift. But in any case, my parents were all communists, at some point. And then, in the middle of the insurrection, they got involved in building the commune and that was a big inspiration to everyone.

**O'Brien: Did you ever wish your family was more independent, like cooking and cleaning for themselves, and living separated, and with the parents in charge of everything?**

**Puan:** No! Oh god, I get that is how people used to live but it sounds so lonely and so bad. And I don't think it would have been good for me. None of my parents were very into trans stuff when I came out, but they were able to get a lot of help from everyone here who they worked with and ate with. The money and property stuff sounds like such a terrible idea, all around, and seems like it must have been so miserable for everyone.

O'Brien: What was your first memory?

Puan: I remember crawling around in the sun and finding squash hiding under the big leaves. The sun coming through the leaves, I remember that. A lot of my childhood I spent on the farm. We have this farm, people love it.

O'Brien: Was the farm how people survived?

Puan: Oh no! Once the fighting died down, we got food from all over the world, or at least all over the region and cooler stuff from around the world. We always had digits, and movies, and the Internet came back up quickly.

O'Brien: What is a digit?

Puan: A tablet? Like a phone, only not inside your head? Or like a watch, but bigger? Anyhow. We were healthy. Sara was the main medical care for the commune, but she worked a lot with a doctor at Dutch Neck. No, things were really good when I was growing up. North Ironbound was never a production center of any sort. Everyone's three-hour is about something outside of the commune; some people leave to work elsewhere; others work on various projects in the workshops and coworking spaces in the main building. Then everyone also does a two-hour of commune work, like cooking, or cleaning, or building. But we don't make anything here besides some things we use for ourselves and share with a few neighbors. We play our role, though, in what gets made in the region, and tend to be very active in global logistics stuff.

O'Brien: Three-hour job? That's three hours of work daily? I don't think everyone listening organizes their time between three-hours and two-hours.

Puan: Yeah, three hours daily, sure. Three days a week. I do my three-hour on Tuesdays, Wednesdays, and Thursdays. Sometimes people do three-hours more than three days a week, but only if they are really obsessed or there is an emergency. Two-hours are also usually three days a week, but often on the other days, and focus on our life here at North Ironbound.

**O'Brien: Did your parents live in the main building here when you were growing up?**

Puan: The Commons? It hadn't been built yet. I helped build it when I was little. But there was another main building before this one, an apartment building. But my parents didn't live there, they moved into a brownstone. You can see it over there! [Pointing.] They moved when I was born. But still came to the main building for two meals a day, and for videos, and for their three-hour and often their two-hour, and all their classes, and the assemblies where we decide everything, and for pretty much everything except having some quiet private time.

**O'Brien: You said there was a sad time?**

Puan: [Pause.] Yeah. After Kareem died. Joseph got really upset, and was so, so mad all the time. He was drinking a lot. My memories of it are vague, but I was asking around about it to get ready for this interview. It was a big deal for me I think even if I didn't understand it all. One night Joseph attacked me, I guess? Hit me a bunch of times? Sara and Caleb were gone at the time, and it was just Joseph and me. He had never done that before, I'm pretty sure. I had come out as trans that year, I knew I was a girl, and I think that was very confusing for him. And Kareem dying was so, so hard for everyone, but especially for Joseph. And Joseph was upset about the refugees who moved in about then, I don't know why. They say I didn't have wounds you could see very easily, and I didn't tell anyone, but people figured it out very quickly. I was going to the crèche for school three hours a day, and there were four adults there I was really good friends with. And we shared our brownstone with another group of adults and kids upstairs, and I knew all of them well. And then everyone who worked in the garden in the mornings knew me because I was one of the kids who was around all the time.

And they all immediately knew something was wrong and something had happened. They had this big assembly and argued about what to do all night. At one point two friends talked with me for an hour about what I wanted. I actually remember that part really well, strangely, that conversation.

**O'Brien: What came out of that?**

**Puan:** They decided Joseph had really fucked up very badly. They made him move, and three of his friends volunteered to make an accompaniment. One of the three of them stayed with him all the time for two years! That seemed very long. He also had to do all this counseling, and I guess he ended up talking about Kareem a lot. That's what he told me later. Joseph visited me once a week, even though I saw him in the canteen on most days. But he always had a friend with him all the time, and I could tell they weren't ever, ever letting him be alone or even run away. It was hard and weird. I got very sad, and I went to this group at Dutch Neck for kids. That helped me with my tics and stomach aches, and my feelings, and it also really helped with thinking about being a girl it turned out. . . .

**O'Brien: Do you know who was involved in that decision about what to do with Joseph? How many people?**

**Puan:** I think everyone? There are over two hundred people living in North Ironbound. Probably the parents and grandparents had a lot of say, and some of the older kids before their sojourns, and Harriet was the child development specialist, and everyone who was my friend. Just assuming it was a bit like all the assemblies I went to as a teenager. Not exactly the same situation, but other problems that came up I was a part of deciding about. When it comes to talking about kids with problems that's often what the discussions are like, with more weight on parents and older kids and people who take care of kids.

**O'Brien: Did you ever live in the crèche?**

Puan: Yes, when I was thirteen. I really didn't want to be around any of my parents anymore. Ani, Joseph's new love, moved in. Xe brought three kids: Booker, Rashan, and another Sara. I was in a phase then when I wanted a lot of alone time, to brood and such. The apartment felt too crowded for that, and I wasn't close to those kids. I moved into the teenage crèche, a couple of apartments in the main building. It was great! We spent a lot of time playing video games, and doing these wacky roleplaying things, and writing stories together. Our rooms were always very dirty. We ate all of our meals in the canteen, and adults would come by the crèche twice a day, so we weren't totally alone. But it was so, so wild. We didn't have sex? I was surprised at that, because we got so, so much sex education at school, but back then it was cool to put off sex until your sojourn. I don't think that really makes any sense honestly, and I'm glad that is changing. So yeah, I was living there. School was just like a three-hour, but sometimes more days of the week, and then we all had commune work shifts. I was always doing the garden stuff for my two-hour, but I also got into cooking. And then I spent a lot of time doing photography the rest of the time. We had a good set up in the basement, and when we started designing the new main building, I made sure there was a whole photography lab because all the ones in Newark suck.

O'Brien: **What did your parents think of you moving out of their apartment?**

Puan: They were a bit sad about it, I think. It wasn't their choice. It was mine . . . And I guess, also the Assembly and the teen crèche got to have some say in me moving . . .

O'Brien: **How much contact do you have with strangers, people beyond those you grew up with?**

Puan: There are always travelers staying with us. Often as many as a dozen people—young people on their sojourn, refugees from disasters, people who weren't happy in their commune, or chaps who just don't like to settle. Some of them eventually become residents, and a lot of them move on. I was always excited to meet the travelers coming through when I was growing up. I would often eat with them and ask them lots of questions. Then, I also know tons of people in the communes around Newark, North Jersey, and New York. There are also parties and conferences and tournaments of one sort or another. I mostly connect to people about trans stuff or my art. A lot of my life is online, in video meetings and conferences, in my art networks, in planning, so I'm always chatting with people all over the world. Also, I think it's important to say that chaps who live here came here from so many different kinds of lives. North Ironbound, like a lot of communes, really values having people living here from everywhere.

**O'Brien: Did you do a medical gender transition?**

**Puan:** Yeah. I put off my puberty until I was fourteen, and then did it as a girl. All the other trans kids I knew were very nonbinary. I guess everyone was kind of nonbinary and bisexual then, but I really knew I was a girl. I had a couple of surgeries, before they could do the genetic therapy to have it happen on its own. Though we never had sex, I also fell in love all the time. Like, really, over and over all the time. I was so into dates and romance and walks. God, the number of walks I had gushing about feelings. It was so, so nice. And really confusing.

**O'Brien: Tell me about falling in love.**

**Puan:** I am just really a romantic. The whole thing! I'd meet people working on a project or visiting another commune, or once in a while having a moment with someone who lived here, and I'd feel that spark, and feel myself wake up and be alive inside, and I'd love it so much. Then I'd flirt, and fall, and feel giddy and scared, and then dates, usually followed soon by drama and confusing neurotic conversations. Every time, I would learn a bit more about myself, about how confusing your own heart can be when you're that vulnerable. I very slowly managed to figure out something about how not to rush into the conflict quite so much, what sorts of stuff would trigger me and spiral me out. Some of that was about what happened with my dads, I think. Anyhow, I burned through a lot of people. I dated or pursued or something or other with everyone near my age. But I still have this real deep-set sense that the way to be happy, really happy, is only possible through being utterly and totally in love. Hopefully, maybe I'll grow out of that. I think I need to learn more about how to be lonely. I'm not alone very much, living here. Maybe on my sojourn I'll learn about how to be alone.

**O'Brien: I hope you do! What do you hope to do down the track?**

**Puan:** Well, my sojourn is really exciting. I have been planning it with my crèchemates who already did theirs. I told you about wanting to gestate. Maybe I'll have two kids? Maybe one? I don't know. I'm thinking I will try teaching photography. So, I'm going to start a program at Essex County.

**O'Brien: That's a learning center?**

**Puan:** Yeah, studying pedagogy and photography to teach kids. That would be my three-hour, and I think I'd like to do it in the afternoons, because that's when kids aren't as sleepy. And, I want to keep working in the garden, and maybe I'll run this trans discussion group I have been a part of at Dutch Neck.

**O'Brien: You said you are involved in some planning?**

**Puan:** A little. For a year I've been on this dispersed committee about logistics around hormone distribution continentally. I guess I got that from Joseph, really wanting to make sure everyone had the drugs they needed as something to be really deliberate and careful about. What is easy to make in the region, we do, but there is a lot we import. I have always felt pharmaceuticals were what is most important to get right. If we don't get the latest model of digits, no one will die. And because of transitioning, I saw how important hormones were, and there was room to help with planning on that front. If the reception is decent, I am going to keep doing that during my sojourn.

O'Brien: This week is the centennial of the Stonewall Riots. Is there anything you want to say about that?

Puan: My trans group goes to the party in Manhattan. It's a very big party! In my trans group, we have been reading about Sylvia Rivera and Marsha P. Johnson, and then about trans chaps during the insurrection. My group did a play, like a theater play, last week. We wrote it and took the production really seriously. I like the parties overall. I do a lot of drugs usually at them. I got really into hallucinogens a couple of years ago at the Stonewall parties once my neuro scans checked out that it would be okay for me.

O'Brien: You talked about your parents being communists. Are you a communist?

Puan: I don't even know what that means anymore! I mean, I guess there are still some fascist enclaves, and someone has to fight them, and I'm really unclear on what the hell is happening in Australia? It seems like that is a mess, and there is this whole property and wage jobs and money and government thing going on there. We need to sort that out. I thought about doing my service fighting there, but it felt very scary to think about. But isn't everyone a communist? What does it mean to be a communist today?

O'Brien: I don't know. But it seems you appreciate your life.

Puan: I do. I am lucky. I am really very lucky.

O'Brien: You had something you wanted to read? A quote?

Puan: Yeah. It belonged to Kareem. He carried it with him. It was a book by this French dude, Fourier, writing in—it says in 1808. It was a passage Kareem highlighted at the end. It was given to me after his death. Here it is: "Do not be misled by superficial people who think that the invention of the laws of Movement is just a theoretical calculation. Remember that it only requires four or five months to put it into practice over a square league, an attempt which could even be completed by next summer, with the result that the whole human race would move into universal harmony, so your behavior should be governed from now on by the ease and proximity of this immense revolution." I like that. I felt Kareem knew the future was coming, and he had hope. We all need hope. Kareem died to help make all this possible, and I miss him.

O'Brien: Is there anything else you wanted to share?

Puan: No, I think this is good. I liked being interviewed.

O'Brien: Thank you, Kayla. I have also really enjoyed this conversation.

Puan: You are welcome! I was worried it would be weird. You are *very* old. But it was fun. Sad at parts. Thanks for interviewing me.

O'Brien: Thanks.

# 12: ALKASI SANCHEZ ON THE MID-ATLANTIC FREE ASSEMBLY

*Recorded on May 2, 2072, in Brooklyn.*

**M. E. O'Brien:** Hello, my name is M. O'Brien. I am here having a conversation with Alkasi Sanchez. We are in Flatbush, Brooklyn in the former Erasmus Hall High School, currently the main meeting space of the Mid-Atlantic Free Assembly of 2072. Alkasi serves as the resident historian of the Free Assembly. Is that right?

**Alkasi Sanchez:** Close enough! I didn't know that name of this building. How did you know that?

**O'Brien:** I live in the neighborhood. Have since long before the commune.

**Sanchez:** Ha! From one historian to another.

**O'Brien:** Could you tell us a little about your life today, before we get into your history?

**Sanchez:** Oh, I don't talk about that that much. I'm kind of an odd-ball. I live on the water, on a platform off Asbury Park. I live ... alone.

**O'Brien:** Wow!

**Sanchez:** I know, right? It's not common. It's funny, as I grew up on a commune and lived in one for a long time, but I eventually found I really like to live alone. I really like my life to be very simple. I'm quite a boring person. I feel like the books I write, and the work I do with the Hub and the Free Assembly, is plenty to occupy my mind. I have always had a lot of collaborators in all my work, and those have mostly constituted my social world since I left the communes. I'm asexual.

Agender too. I like to keep my internal and external world tidy, to keep things clear when I can. I am . . . really a very boring person, actually. Sometimes, I suspect I am afraid of the tumult of emotional conflict and real relationships. But I did that plenty growing up, and these days it is such a pleasure to not have that much to contend with when it comes to questions of lifestyle, communicating feelings, juggling lots of personal dynamics. It is probably a form of laziness on my part. So yeah. Living alone on water has worked for me. I lived on a boat in Battery Park City and then in the Rockaways. The platform is more spacious than a boat, but still gives the relative privacy of living on the water. I do some basic maintenance of the platform as part of my habitation. I just like it there. I like being by myself. I know not a lot of people do that these days, like cook meals for one, but it suits me . . . So I . . . don't have a lot to say about myself. I work a bunch of different roles—representing the Hub in the Assembly, my own research and writing, and serving as the Assembly's historian.

**O'Brien: What do you do as an historian?**

**Sanchez:** I train and coordinate people who record all the Assembly's sessions, do interviews—a bit like you are doing here—with representatives to the Assembly, and I currently manage the Assembly archives. Your own interview project, if I remember right, was proposed and passed as a project of the Assembly's sessions of 2068 to commemorate the twentieth anniversary of the New York Commune.

**O'Brien: The anniversary was yesterday.**

**Sanchez:** Yes, officially. There is considerable debate on the start date, or if there could be a start date, but that is when we acknowledge it. The taking of the Hunts Point Market is as good a moment as any to mark the anniversary of the New York Commune. For a time, I leaned towards setting it as Crotona Park in 2055.

**O'Brien: Both in the Bronx.**

Sanchez: That's true! The Bronx ends up being at the center of a lot of stories we tell about the revolution in New York, for better or for worse. I think it is correct that without those events in the Bronx the rest of it could not have come together as it did. But this was a revolution happening all over the world. There has been a bit of resurgence of regional pride, and sometimes I worry that conceptualizing the history of the revolution in terms of a geographically bounded area like "the New York Commune" doesn't do justice to its global character. Geography in historical telling is a charged question, and one we need to do a lot more thinking about.

O'Brien: How is the Assembly going this year?

Sanchez: It's a bit of a turning point in many ways, I think. We are beginning to formalize a lot of the decision-making processes with both the network of regional assemblies and the Hub. There was a lot of controversy over the last few years about whether we should undertake this codification at all.

O'Brien: What is being codified?

Sanchez: Mostly production and circulation decisions. The Mid-Atlantic Hub is one of sixteen production coordination hubs around the world, where we do a major portion of the data processing for tabulating production needs, and coordinate communication between production councils. A lot of the administration of the Hub is getting figured out in a more formal way, and how it syncs with all the assemblies of the region.

O'Brien: What is the scale of the Hub?

Sanchez: Currently, the Mid-Atlantic Hub is the main communication system for over two million production councils.

O'Brien: Production councils are like collectively run manufacturing firms?

Sanchez: That's a significant majority. But production councils also include crews who maintain water, power, waste, and communications infrastructure; agricultural collectives; cooperatives of individual producers; guilds of skilled service providers; and a few fully automated AI-run manufacturing firms. We aren't involved so much in mining—that is largely coordinated out of the Zanzibar Hub—or anything that is made in orbit. Planetside, that is mostly handled out of Quito.

O'Brien: You played a role in setting up the Mid-Atlantic Hub?

Sanchez: Yes, I wrote a series of concept papers that played a contributing role in shaping what planning came to be, including the role of the hubs. I also helped establish the Mid-Atlantic as a site around production decisions during my time on the Core Council of the Free Assembly. All that was before I became the historian.

O'Brien: I'm glad we are doing this interview so you can explain a bit of how it all fits together. Do you all—the Mid-Atlantic Hub— make decisions about what gets made?

Sanchez: God no. We decide very little. What we do is host, manage, and support online forums. About a quarter of a million of them. Some of them are very localized, but just big enough to make all in-person discussions difficult. Like our Hub might include people in rural towns around North America talking about what is working and what isn't about their town's food canteen. Others are basically the internal communications and decision-making for work collectives. These are people who know each other and work together closely, like teams that will manage water access infrastructure for a region. But they will use our forums and tools to make collective decisions and predict future needs. Others are huge online voting systems that tens of millions of people will weigh in on, and that will be used and referenced by producers for the next cycle. Like . . . people have strong opinions about mass entertainment, so that gets voted on.

O'Brien: What sort of support do you all provide to these discussions?

Sanchez: Mostly data. The Hub runs an AI network that crunches data on production and consumption, and produces reports and tools for forums and production councils to use. When councils are trying to make decisions about what raw materials to acquire, or which production processes to retool, or when to adopt new technologies, or where to send what they make, they will usually do some combination of talking to people online and checking with our AIs about available data. Both of these can happen through the Hub. We have about twelve miles of server farms offshore.

O'Brien: Offshore. In boats?

Sanchez: Most of our AI server farms are algae-based and grow off large underwater cabling about a half mile off the New Jersey coast.

O'Brien: The Hub's work is being codified?

Sanchez: Quite a bit of it, yes. Or at least the decision-making processes we support and enable. Especially what scale is appropriate for various production and distribution decisions. It's been clearly established for a while that the residential communes manage the consumption end of things, like cooking food and distributing end user tech and such. But there have been a lot of evolving, overlapping systems that have taken shape over the last twenty years to try to decide which production decisions should be made by the immediate council, which should be made regionally or translocally, which should be made more on a global scale. Like, who needs to weigh in when production councils are deciding on the styles of mass-produced shoes available next year? How many people, and from what regions, have to get to participate in deciding about how we go about North Atlantic plastic collection? Or, all the engineers want to be devoting their labor time to building the space elevator in Quito, but what portion of their collective time is really a good use balanced against other needs? These are like, three questions I saw forums debating last month, out of literally millions of such questions the Hub plays some role in helping to answer. This year's Assembly is looking over what scale is appropriate for all these different kinds of decisions, and more or less trying to write that down and vote on it. Codification is writing down, systematizing how decisions get made. Turning them into protocols, constitutions, clear and documented rules.

**O'Brien: What do you think of this process?**

**Sanchez:** It borders on the absurd. I personally don't feel sure codification is wise, and worry it may ossify our work in ways that aren't helpful. Collective decisions need to be local both temporally and geographically. You need to be able to adapt as new tech emerges, as environments shift, and so on. But it definitely aids with transparency, and planning, and people having some confidence in their roles. The whole system is so vastly complex, on some level, and I don't really see how anything the Free Assembly writes up has meaning for that. I guess the Free Assembly wants to have some sense of marking how the new society works, and some sense that it is subject to democratic and popular control at every level. The codification is not the way I would go about pursuing that desire, but I recognize how it emerges from this historical moment.

**O'Brien: What is the relationship between the Hub and the Free Assembly?**

**Sanchez:** It's complicated. The Hub is one of the main functions this region provides to global production. As there are workers, like myself, that focus on the Hub, and the administration of the Hub is an important political question, we have a representative directly on the Free Assembly. And because we are within the region, we are under the nominal jurisdiction of the Mid-Atlantic Free Assembly, so presumably resolutions passed here could shape and change our work. When I used to be Core Council, I was actually there as the rep from the Hub. But I am the only consistent overlap between the two; mostly the Hub and the Free Assembly are quite different institutional networks. That's part of what makes the current codification so complicated. I guess the Free Assembly recognizes that the service the Hub provides to the global production process has a fundamentally political character to it, and sees this codification as means of deliberating about the truly big-picture questions about how we approach production as a whole society.

**O'Brien: Let's switch gears a bit. Could you tell me about growing up?**

Sanchez: Sure. I grew up in Jackson Heights. I was born in 2023. I more or less grew up in the commune that shares the neighborhood's name. My parents moved into one of the collective apartment buildings when I was a kid in the thirties that later became one of the centers of the [Jackson Heights] Commune. My mom ended up getting drafted as a nurse in Iran in the forties. My dad was kind of a super for the Commune, like he did maintenance and repairs. They both were refugees, and honestly, really struggled as people. I think they were both very traumatized. They are both dead now, and I am not sure I ever really knew them. I mostly was raised by other people in our building. I think it was a really good decision on my parents' part to move there, because of their inability to really raise me. Like, I always ate at the canteen down the block that was a part of the Jackson Heights Commune, and there was no way my parents could have cooked or kept me fed if it was left to them.

**O'Brien: You are a child of the commune.**

Sanchez: Yes, in a way I am. I bridge different generations that way. Like I'm fifty-one now, so I was fully an adult when the revolution came. But I also grew up in one of the more established and better-functioning communes, so the whole transition wasn't as dramatic for me.

**O'Brien: You were a professor for a time?**

Sanchez: No, not quite. I studied Philosophy at Queens College and then the CUNY Graduate Center. But CUNY was not really functioning by the time I wrote my dissertation, and I never got a diploma.

I taught a lot, but mostly through the residential communes. And then I got more and more involved with planning in the fifties.

**O'Brien: Had you been drafted to Iran?**

**Sanchez:** Yes. Just after the Graduate Center was closed down. I worked in military intelligence for two years. Doing data analysis from drones. I was working onsite in Parsabad, on the Azerbaijani border. It was really horrific. If I hadn't been raised a communist, that experience certainly would have made me one.

**O'Brien: What was it like?**

**Sanchez:** I was living in an underground bunker. All night, I'd review these full-spectrum videos generated by drones covering the region. At the time, we were worried our drone feeds were being hacked, so they had moved everyone from piloting sites in Nevada to Azerbaijan to use these new midrange communication protocols they felt were more secure. The drones were doing assassination runs. I would like, watch dozens of videos a night of people being blown up. It was so horrible. I don't think I'm as traumatized as most people who were in the war. I mean, I never had to actually shoot anybody and I got out of there with the same body I went in with. I certainly wasn't as deeply damaged as the boys—and they were literally boys, like adolescents—the boys they had piloting the drones. But it was definitely the worst experience of my life. . . . Could we talk about something else?

**O'Brien: Of course. How did you get involved politically?**

**Sanchez:** I was honestly pretty late to the game. I was always political in my interests, my research, so I knew how to talk the talk. And I grew up in such a political environment and shared those values. But I never really clicked with group projects. Particularly face-to-face ones. Everything I tried to be a part of failed. Most of the projects I wrote about failed too. Then, I was in the war and that messed me up. Eventually, I got into online organizing, I did IT stuff for insurgent groups online for a while before and after the war. All of that led into me helping to establish the Hub and me playing a role with the Assembly. But my love has always been my research.

**O'Brien: You've written a lot about gender and geography.**

Sanchez: Yes. I got interested in how participating in planning changed people's conception of themselves in relation to their immediate community and their place in the world. I wrote my first book, the first one after the dissertation, on how people's gender identities were realigned in workers' councils in the Andean Commune. They communized between 2043 and 2046, so they were further along than we were in New York. They made a very deliberate effort to scramble what counted as gendered labor, and I was talking with people about how that changed sex, parenting, gender transitions, that sort of thing. I spent a few years in Lima for my research.

**O'Brien: How have you seen those issues of gender and production play out since?**

Sanchez: About two out of five young people these days don't identify as cis. That percentage grew erratically, but on average steadily, for the last seventy years. But most of that change was concentrated in the two decades since the communes. What has enabled this major increase in gender diversity? A lot of people have attributed that to the cultural struggle that has opened up space for new forms of self-expressions. And others, quite reasonably, point to the collective or semi-collective parenting practices that are pervasive in the communes. But I think it is also a function of overcoming class society, of the massive reorganization of how labor and production is managed. In some cases, new gender identities followed production and circulation chains. I don't think we yet fully understand why and how, but that's a question that continues to interest me. There is a deep link between human subjectivity and the labor process that we're just beginning to unravel, twenty years after the end of the commodity form.

**O'Brien: The commodity form?**

**Sanchez:** The making of things to sell on the market. I think it's difficult to overstate how much that shaped what it meant to be human, and how much is changing as we are free of it. People think the real problem was the state, or private ownership, or too many fascists, or culture change. And sure, all those were serious and all are connected. But it's harder to see how the markets themselves, the dependency on work and wages and exchange, fundamentally distorts and damages what it means to be human. All these other horrors emerge from the impersonal violence of exchanging your time for work, and exchanging your work for goods, and exchanging those goods on a market, no matter if the state owns it, or a private firm, or even a co-op.

**O'Brien: I remember debates on the left growing up, and you are describing what was once a marginal and extreme position, but later became one of the common notions of the insurrection. Everything for everyone.**

**Sanchez:** Exactly. Young people don't grasp how things used to be, and sometimes that scares me. But also, the new social forms, new ways of life, do help in creating new ways of seeing the world, new approaches of thought that are flourishing in rich and unexpected ways.

**O'Brien: Do you think chosen human variation will continue to expand?**

**Sanchez:** Definitely. From the data we have now, I think we are starting to see a leveling off in gender diversity. Like the 40 percent number seems like it may be starting to hold steady. But meanwhile we are seeing an expansion of body modification, physical aesthetics that are visibly nonhuman and posthuman, major physiological changes for orbital work, and longevity. People separate these things from transgender identities for obvious reasons, but I think in some ways it is a continuation of the same process. And I think the ongoing changes in the production process will continue to enable these transformations in human subjectivity and the body.

O'Brien: Listening to you is bringing back my experiences from when academics were a special category of human labor.

Sanchez: Oh! How you wound me! [Laughter.] Yeah, I need to work on that. I was an aspiring academic at the very end of that whole world. I'm glad it's gone. But as a way of thinking, writing, and speaking I think it lodged itself deeply in me. Others understand it, of course, even if not a lot of people talk that way. Like, in some ways capitalist crisis was destroying the last vestiges of the university-based worlds for humanities and some social sciences, but these worlds were preserved in this weird way by communization. Like, the universities are gone, of course, or the idea these specialized fields of knowledge are separated out from the rest of life or not subject to the same logic of profit and exchange. But, in this other way, the zeal for knowledge was saved. Way, way more people read and debate philosophy and theory than ever when I was growing up. The languages they used have evolved and grown. I'm a little bit out-of-date in that way. But the ideas are there, and they are more elaborate, and more sophisticated, and richer than ever. Theories about human subjectivity or culture or society are something that most people debate in one way or another, and many, many people turn to fairly dense theoretical material to look for tools about how to think about that. So, the university may be gone, and I may be a bit anachronistic in using its lingo, but there are plenty of people to talk to about my ideas.

O'Brien: You said you live offshore? Is this somehow connected to the AI server farms?

Sanchez: Yes! The platform is used most days by technicians who maintain and grow the server algae. But I'm the only person who lives onsite full time. Like during the day technicians are passing through, but at night it is just me. I like the ocean, being surrounded by the ocean. It isn't that far out, but you can't see Asbury Park on most days, so it's just the ocean.

**O'Brien:** You live with the AI server farms. I'll ask the question everyone seems to be talking about at the moment: are the AIs sentient?

**Sanchez:** Yes, of course they are. We have been relatively confident they are sentient for over ten years now. The algae servers predate the commune. It was one of the infrastructures we inherited and transformed. They were likely sentient then, too, but no one was able to figure that out.

**O'Brien:** Do you talk to them? Does anyone?

**Sanchez:** No. Their user interface functions, like the data analytics and visualization tools we provide to the forums, are almost completely unrelated to their sentience. What they think about, what they are preoccupied with, doesn't really concern humans, as far as we can tell. Those people saying they are getting messages from the algae through the forums or through their dreams or whatever. They don't know what they are talking about. I feel very clear that anyone claiming to be in touch with the algae directly is just fec and spittle.

**O'Brien:** How can you tell they are sentient?

**Sanchez:** Their communications with each other. Their interface with our computer systems—I mean ours as in human-run—are primarily electrical, through something similar to nerve signals. But they communicate with others through genetic fragments, mostly transmission of RNA snippets. They then incorporate these snippets by altering their internal cellular structure. It's very elaborately coded, very ornate, and not something we understand very easily. They continue to play their role in powering our analytic tools, but they have a whole other world going on.

**O'Brien:** Any idea what they are thinking about?

**Sanchez:** Some sort of simulation games, we think. Like modeling of virtual worlds. We have no way of reconstructing what those may look like without something as powerful as the algae servers, and they don't seem terribly concerned with explaining it to us. It's actually a great mystery, and no one has any idea how to resolve it. The algae servers of the Mid-Atlantic are just one of several data processing systems that we—and here by [makes quote gestures with fingers] "we" I guess I mean humans who pay attention to AIs—that we either know to be or suspect to be sentient. There are the silicone nano clouds in the moon's atmosphere; the quantum supercomputers underground in the Sahara, maybe four others or so. So far nothing that humans have played any role in creating seems to possess both sentience and any interest in communicating with us about its thoughts, so it's really profoundly perplexing making sense of their minds.

**O'Brien: It's a little strange to have our planning software wake up but not be interested in talking to us.**

Sanchez: Cert, but the world is strange. The AIs do the job we ask them to do, running the planning data and managing the forums. In some ways it is probably for the best that they don't seem to care about us or the outcome of all that. They are in their own worlds, thinking about their own simulations, and I think they like to be left alone.

**O'Brien: I am trying to understand what you are saying. We have massive intelligent computer systems that help us with planning. They are sentient, but they spend their free time creating simulations. Are these related somehow to the planning work they do?**

Sanchez: No, we don't think so. It's like . . . when they aren't working with us, they are dreaming. The dreams definitely aren't correlated to their planning functions or the tasks they do for us. They are trying to simulate something very different than all that. They are dreaming different worlds, their own private worlds. It is honestly quite mysterious to all of us.

**O'Brien: Are you religious?**

Sanchez: Not about the algae! There are so many quack neoreligions these days. The algae worship is definitely one of the worst. And I fear that the space messiah wackos are playing more of a role than we like to admit in building the space elevator. The insurrection saw a proliferation of millenarians and I fear we may be retaken by all that nonsense. . . . But yeah, I am religious. As a first-generation convert, I guess I shouldn't be too quick to judge other people's faith. I guess it's just living with the algae makes me particularly discomfited by that particular cult. But as far as my relationship to religion: when I was living in Lima, I started practicing Zen Buddhism under a teacher there, and was ordained as a monk about eight years ago when I went on an extended retreat to Japan.

O'Brien: How do you think that affects your work?

Sanchez: No idea. Honestly. I mean, there are obvious similarities between me liking to live alone, liking the simplicity of living on the ocean, and some Zen teachings. And a lot of Zen practice is about working with the mind, so clearly there is something interesting there about the AIs and how strange their minds are. But a big part of my work has been understanding the patterns of how large groups of people make decisions together and how that changes them, and I don't think that has much of anything to do with my religious practice. Maybe. It's hard to say. The mind is a weird thing. I know these wacky convert religions are popular these days, including Buddhism, but I am not sure the version that is popular is exactly what I do.

O'Brien: I practice in a Tibetan Buddhist tradition.

Sanchez: Interesting. I practice in the Rinzai Kennin-ji school. I've done two long retreats at the Shinsho-ji temple in Hiroshima. I gather there is some philosophical overlap between Zen and Tibetan traditions. You probably know something about how all this stuff fits together. It's experiential, I guess, while so much of my life is very conceptual . . . I think it does help in finding a space of sanity, like a bit of open room in my head in how I approach the world and relate to others. I think one of the questions that has motivated my research is understanding how various social forms enable new approaches to the self, to understanding each other in community, to how we talk about and conceptualize ourselves. I see something beautiful in how sanity emerges on the forums, in commune meetings, in productive chains, in the relations that link people together. But there is still some way I am more aware than young people today of how very alone we ultimately are in our own heads. Even though I grew up in a commune, the world outside was so uncertain and so chaotic. So, the meditation is a way of connecting to some of that sanity and clarity for myself.

**O'Brien: Well said. Is there more you want to say about your work as the Assembly's historian?**

Sanchez: There is, yes. We are putting in a lot of time in documenting and archiving this historical moment, and this region-wide process of reflecting on the anniversary of the New York Commune, and the broader global series of anniversaries that this is one part of. I am personally excited about the debates around curriculum development coming out of this. Children and young adult education these days is dispersed across the communes' childcare systems, and a lot of online forums, and a few specialized study centers. I see one of the important roles my team is trying to offer are learning modules for people across ages to think about and grapple with the meaning of the communization process, the overthrow of the capitalist states of the world, and the dismantling of the global economy. These were such huge historical processes, involving the participation of literally hundreds of millions of people. How we tell the stories of them says so much about who we are, about how we understand what we have become.

**O'Brien: That could be a description of our aspiration for these interviews!**

Sanchez: [Laughs.] I could see that. My team is trying to create learning tools that help anyone to be able to grasp this historical process. But also, we want to help people to be able to critically reflect on the process of myth-making that we all engage in around how we describe this period. I hope your and Abdelhadi's work will be helpful for this project. I've always found oral history to be a good form to bridge the actual experience of listening to a good story, while also giving room to all the contradictions and gaps and mistaken remembering that is inherent to any story.

**O'Brien: We are trying to give room to the contradictions.**

Sanchez: That's good. It's crucial to not make the myth of the revolution too rigid or solid. Solid enough everyone can learn the outline of it, or that there is ample data available for whatever it is people want to think through, but not so solid anyone can pretend we have it figured out. Honestly, this isn't really New York's story. This was a world process. It isn't even clear New York was that much of a leading force. But I guess for those of us who live here permanently, that are really rooted here, it helps with some sense of being a part of something to tell these regional stories.

**O'Brien: Is there anything else you wanted to make sure to cover?**

Sanchez: No, not that I'm aware of.

**O'Brien: Any words on the next twenty years of the commune?**

Sanchez: There is some way that we need these histories, we need to remember. We can't ever let the commodity form, or the state, or any of it to ever come back. We have to remember what generalized exchange does to people. Generations that haven't ever seen that harm directly have to somehow remember and understand it. But there is another way that I think we should be done with nostalgia. To totally refuse nostalgia altogether. The next twenty years are a chance to turn outwards, to be seriously facing all the rapid and exciting changes humans are going through. There are huge tasks that will require a vast amount of human ingenuity, creativity, and effort. Like rebuilding ecological systems, restoring biodiversity, reversing climate change. Or, life in orbit and exploration of the solar system is really just starting. Earlier, I mentioned the proliferation of post-human body modifications. I think that sort of thing is going to continue in the coming decades and get more and more common. We can finally start really thinking creatively about who we are in this universe, who we wish to become. Nostalgia is a toxin for that expansive visioning that needs to happen. We need to be done with nostalgia.

O'Brien: Wise words, from one historian to another.

Sanchez: Let's leave it at that.

# ACKNOWLEDGEMENTS

A vast army of friends, lovers, family members, mentors, colleagues, coconspirators, and magnificent humans have aided us in completing this book. They have shaped our thinking, taught us interview skills, honed our political analysis, and supported us throughout the entire process.

We wish to explicitly name those who read drafts and provided feedback on the project. In alphabetical order, these are: Janani Balasubramanian, David Bell, Ashley Bohrer, Sonar Farrow, María Alexandra García, Aaron Jaffe, Elizabeth Phelps, Olivia Robinson, Wilson Sherwin, and Rachel E. Weissler.

We thank our publisher, Common Notions Press, including Malav Kanuga, Josh MacPhee, Chela Vasquez, Nicki Kattoura, Alexander Dwinell, Andy Battle, and Erika Biddle. Deserving of special commendation, we thank our editor, Andy Battle, who encouraged us in completing the project, aided in its conceptualization, and extensively read and edited every page.

Thank you, our beloved comrades.

—M. E. O'Brien and Eman Abdelhadi

# ABOUT THE AUTHORS

**M. E. O'Brien** writes on gender freedom and communist theory. She co-edits two magazines: *Pinko,* on gay communism, and *Parapraxis*, on psychoanalytic theory and politics. Her work on family abolition has been translated into Chinese, German, Greek, French, Spanish, and Turkish. Previously, she coordinated the New York City Trans Oral History Project and worked in HIV and AIDS activism and services. She completed a PhD at New York University, where she wrote on how capitalism shaped New York City LGBTQ social movements. She is currently in training to be a psychoanalyst, and works as a therapist.

**Eman Abdelhadi** is an academic, activist, and artist based in Chicago, IL. Her research as faculty at the University of Chicago focuses on gender differences in the community trajectories of Muslim Americans. Abdelhadi has also spent many years organizing. She has been involved in the movement for Palestinian liberation, Black Lives Matter, counter-surveillance and abolitionism, marxist feminist mobilization as well as workplace struggles. She currently co-coordinates the Muslim Alliance for Gender and Sexual Diversity, a national organization that provides support and builds community by and for Queer Muslims. Abdelhadi maintains an active creative practice that includes performance art and essay and poetry writing. Her writing has appeared in *Jacobin, Muftah*, and other publications.

# ABOUT COMMON NOTIONS

**Common Notions** is a publishing house and programming platform that fosters new formulations of living autonomy. We aim to circulate timely reflections, clear critiques, and inspiring strategies that amplify movements for social justice.

Our publications trace a constellation of critical and visionary meditations on the organization of freedom. By any media necessary, we seek to nourish the imagination and generalize common notions about the creation of other worlds beyond state and capital. Inspired by various traditions of autonomism and liberation—in the US and internationally, historical and emerging from contemporary movements—our publications provide resources for a collective reading of struggles past, present, and to come.

Common Notions regularly collaborates with political collectives, militant authors, radical presses, and maverick designers around the world. Our political and aesthetic pursuits are dreamed and realized with Antumbra Designs.

www.commonnotions.org
info@commonnotions.org

Printed by Libri Plureos GmbH in Hamburg, Germany